Stay Back!

Stay Back! Trilogy Book 1

Lynn Stewart

UP WIND SYSTEMS, LLC

CAMBRIDGE, MARYLAND

Lynn Stewart/Up Wind Systems, LLC
Cambridge, Maryland

Publisher's Note: This is a work of fiction. Names, characters, places, and incidents are a product of the author's imagination. Locales and public names are sometimes used for atmospheric purposes. Any resemblance to actual people, living or dead, or to businesses, companies, events, institutions, or locales is completely coincidental.

Book Layout © 2017 BookDesignTemplates.com
Cover Design by Books Covered

Stay Back!/ Lynn Stewart. -- 1st ed.
ISBN-13: 978-0-9998905-0-9

For Sweet Petunia

PART ONE

Three Years Earlier

THERE WERE TWO THINGS on her mind that day: how to walk through the doors of Saint Vincent's unseen and how to remain unrecognized once inside. She had stuffed her long red hair under one of her husband's old baseball caps, scaly with age, but there was little she could do to hide the rest. At nearly six feet tall, her long narrow face covered in freckles, she usually stood out in a crowd. Anyone who might happen to catch a glimpse of her would be sure to notice her lanky frame, her averted eyes, her head always cocked a little to the left, as if listening to something in the distance.

She had decided to walk the mile and a half to the church rather than risk her husband or anyone else spotting her car in the parking lot. She wasn't sure what believable excuse she could give as to why she was at a Catholic church at nine o'clock on a Thursday morning. Other than weddings and funerals she refused to have anything to do with churches, let alone a Catholic one. No one in her circle had recently died nor was anyone getting married. There was no logical reason for her to be anywhere near a church.

She was thankful for the biting April wind, its gusts unseasonably cold according to the weatherman. It justified her attempt at a disguise: a long purple coat and scarf wrapped around her neck and pulled up over her chin. She walked briskly along the sidewalk, warily watching the sparse traffic out of the corner of her eye, scanning for her husband's patrol car. She knew that his beat was far away from this church, this street where she felt so exposed. She knew there was no way her husband would see her walking down this street, that he had no reason to be anywhere near St. Vincent's. But she hurried anyway.

The church stood tall in the distance, seeming to summon her, a disapproving parent. Its formal arches now hands on hips, now stern frowns. The cinder block lodged in her gut echoed the heavy retaining wall she passed along the sidewalk, its side scrawled with colorful, hastily spray-painted vulgarities. Accusations she felt written on her skin. Reminding her of what she has become. Unfaithful. Worse, adulteress. Or is the weight in her stomach more fear than anything else? Fear of being recognized? Fear of the angry parent and the punishment? Fear that all this will somehow get back to her husband?

She skirted around the sparsely occupied parking lot, taking one last glance around to be sure of her anonymity. She pulled her hat further down over her face and turned toward the heavy front door, bargaining with herself. If the door opened, she would go in, face the crossroads before her. If it were locked, she would consider it a sign. A sign that she had one more day to gather her thoughts and figure out what to do. One more day to figure things out without deciding anything, changing anything.

It was locked! Happiness gushed upwards through her body. She pushed a little harder, to prove it to herself, her gift of one more day. Sadness. On this second, harder push the door moved. Opened a crack. She panicked and turned, stumbling down the steps. Then reality hit and she stopped. Forced herself to dart back up the steps and into the vestibule. She found herself standing in dim emptiness, overcome with the scent of stargazer lilies and suddenly very hot. She took off the coat and unwound the scarf, confident that the faded baseball cap alone would disguise her sufficiently. She didn't know anyone who went to church here and the place seemed empty.

She wasn't raised a Catholic. She only knew of the confessional process through movies. Never detailed, always vague. The muted colors, the curtain, the screen. The fearful sinner weighed down with shame walking in, that same person buoyant and birdlike walking out. Aiming herself toward the double doors of the sanctuary, she slid one foot an inch or two in front of her. Then the other. Again, and again. Against the polished marble floor her Nikes made pathetic slow squeaks, faint cries like a mouse being squashed over and over. Squeak. Squeak. Cringing in the quiet, she passed walls cluttered with bulletins and flyers, photos of smiling couples and families. She paused in front of one section and scanned their faces. Missionaries in the field. Catholic charity workers. Brazil, Egypt, South Africa, China. Good people. Their faces and flags began to blur.

"Can I help you?" A voice from the left startled her as she pushed through the double doors.

A young man in jeans and green hooded sweatshirt stood in front of her. She glanced at him just long enough to dismiss him as an intern or some sort of technical equipment guy, someone who worked behind the scenes or some other such thing.

"I am here for confession." The words tumbled out of her mouth, her cheeks betraying her discomfort as she turned and scanned for the curtained alcove, the priest in his white collar.

The behind-the-scenes kid looked at his watch and then at her.

"Well, generally confession is offered on Saturday afternoons and evenings or the day before Holy Days."

"Oh." Her countenance deflated. "Sorry to bother you."

She took a step backwards toward the door, but the kid darted around ahead of her, reaching for the door handle to either open it for her or hold it closed.

"Don't go. I will be right back." Smiling, he strode through a side door and within seconds he was back, a black robe draped over his arm.

"I am Andy, Father Andy," he said, extending his hand and she shook it, giving it a business-like shake, two associates sealing a deal. She nodded without saying anything and then followed him back through the side door, only half listening to his babbling explanation that confession can, of course, be performed at any time of the day or night.

***

Halfway home from St. Vincent's the wind had gained momentum. Blowing from behind it seemed to push her farther and farther away from the church, buffeting her along. As if she didn't belong, as if she shouldn't have gone there. As if the whole confession had been some sort of mistake. A bad dream. A nightmare. She practically flew all the way down the street, the wind taunting her, pulling at her hat like a naughty schoolboy.

After she was safely back home, unrecognized, the components of her disguise put neatly away, she calmly made herself a cup of tea. She stood, mug in hand, staring out the front door. Fits of rain were beginning to shoot diagonally out of the racing clouds. As the clouds darkened she stepped out, sat down on the steps, tilted her face to the sky and let the rain fall. Daggers of cold struck her face, mingling with her warm tears. If only she could turn back the clock to the time before Phil had kissed her. If only she hadn't kissed him back. If only she could keep pretending that she hadn't gone too far, hadn't done anything wrong. She didn't need a priest to tell her that was impossible.

When the rain finally stopped, so had her tears. She dumped out her cold tea and went in to call Phil, her choice finally made.

***

He was funny, that Father Andy. A real comedian. If she had met him at a coffee shop or at a book store, she might have actually liked him. Might have enjoyed talking to him. But not at the church, in his dark robe, looking so young when she wanted him to be old and wise. If only she hadn't met him in the vestibule. If only she could have entered the confessional ignorant of his friendly, college-kid eyes and helpful expression. Her confession might have seemed more mysterious, more powerful. Less tawdry and small.

She wanted to be able to justify her strange feelings for Phil, what the radio psychologists might have labeled an emotional affair. Her feelings for Phil made no sense, if you could even call them feelings. She loved her husband. Very much. She had never been unfaithful to him, not even in her head. She almost wished she could tell Father Andy that her husband was mean or neglectful or that their marriage had become some sort of battleground. But all that would have been a lie.

She wasn't miserable in her marriage. Most of the time she was quite happy. They had achieved equilibrium and comfort – a good marriage. Not that a bad marriage justifies an affair, even an emotional one. But they give grounds, excuses.

Sitting in the small cubicle, looking though the darkened screen and imagining Father Andy's earnest face, she couldn't give him any excuses. She could only describe the bare facts of her marriage, her feelings, her uncertainties.

"Tell your friend that he's made a mistake, misread the signs, misread your intentions. Tell him you need to end the friendship. Tell him that what happened will never happen again. But, please, don't tell your husband." His words offered instantaneous relief but she couldn't believe he was serious.

"Don't tell my husband?"

"Don't tell your husband." His words were even firmer as he repeated them.

"But that doesn't make sense. Shouldn't I be honest with my husband? The man is also my husband's friend. They're partners on the street. My husband's nickname on the force is Hawk. He senses things. He sees and senses things in the distance. You know, like a hawk. How can I not tell him?"

Father Andy's voice was soft now. "Tell me, what good would come of you telling him? As far as him being your husband's friend, well, that complication isn't yours to worry about. Trust me, he's probably clueless about all this. Hawks don't detect everything. They're birds."

She laughed at this. Many people don't give birds the credit they're due – they are smarter than they seem. She thought about what it might mean to tell her husband. She knew him well enough to know that he might not forgive her. He certainly would not forgive Phil, ending years of friendship, causing fractures and divisions on the force. He might even leave her. Pack up his things and never come back. Maybe he would find Phil, argue with him, come to blows and injure another officer. Ruin his career. So maybe Father Andy was right.

"Okay, I get what you are saying. Sort of."

"I am not convinced," he replied, wise at least to her uncertainty.

"It's just that, well, it's just that I might have agreed with you two days ago. We were just friends. Really. Okay, so maybe we flirted a little. His wife was sick, we'd known each other for years. We were good friends, all four of us. Everything felt more intense, more real recently. It was something unacknowledged between us. Something that I could have kept to myself forever. If only he didn't kiss me. If only I didn't kiss him back."

She wanted nothing more than a do-over at that point. She wanted to rewind the movie of the past several months. To walk backward, away from the confessional, back home, to get into bed for a long reverse sleep. To keep walking and dreaming backwards.

December

MARINA BUTTERFIELD HATED interruptions. Especially when she was focused on something, as she was now. Especially when that something was something that she had been avoiding, not because it was something particularly difficult or unpleasant, or mundane, but simply because focusing was something she was chronically bad at. Abysmally bad. She put down her paint brush just as she was about to give the blackbird she was painting her signature swirl of color – on this particular canvas it was something of a cross between aqua and chartreuse.

Her husband, John, was in the basement tinkering with a vacuum that only partially worked. Why they couldn't just run out for a new one didn't make sense. Actually, it did make sense. John was a tinkerer. A fixer of things. And he was determined to fix this old, worthless vacuum. Her arbitrary deadline was noon tomorrow. If it wasn't fixed she was buying a new one.

"Leslie called." Marina was halfway down the basement stairs, wiping her hands on her artist's apron when she heard the familiar grunts and groans amid the smooth voices of the announcers. Football at its finest. The vacuum was untouched other than the fact that it was laying on John's workbench.

"Mel again?" John looked up from the TV. He held out his nearly full beer bottle and gave it to her. Then he reached into the mini fridge that doubled as an end table and got himself a fresh one.

"Yeah. He's agitated. She doesn't want to leave him alone. And she needs to run over to her mother's nursing home for something. Apparently, her mother is wheeling herself into other people's rooms again. Leslie is afraid they're going to kick her mother out." She looked at the TV. "How are your guys doing."

"Winning, of course."

They clinked bottles and each took a long, slow sip.

"Why isn't Mel in a nursing home? He should be. He's much worse off than Leslie's mother. I don't know what she's trying to prove keeping him at home like this."

"I don't know John. If something like that happened to you, I would want to take care of you."

"If I threw myself in front of a train, I'd have been successful."

Marina shook her head and started back up the stairs. "Don't forget about the vacuum."

"Yeah, yeah."

**

The sounds of the late afternoon football game were deafening as Marina descended into the basement. She had only been across the street at Leslie's for a little over an hour, but it felt like a little over a year. Mel had been sleeping in his specially outfitted recliner – the one he spent most of his time in, the one he insisted that he would die in, the one he chose repeatedly instead of the specially outfitted wheelchair that would give him some degree of independence. He claimed he didn't want independence. If he wanted independence he wouldn't have tried to kill himself, he ranted again and again. He was still going to do it, he assured anyone who would listen. Marina knew that Leslie mostly ignored him and persevered through the endless cycles of the minutia that go into caring for a quadriplegic who didn't want care, who only wanted the pain of living, whatever that pain had entailed before. Before he tried to extinguish it.

John didn't notice Marina from his perch on his stool, engrossed fixing the vacuum. Coming up behind him she coiled her long ponytail, wringing it like a dishtowel to let the rain water trickle onto the top of his head. His dark hair was so thick that he didn't notice until it finally rolled down his neck. He jumped a little and turned toward her, then rolled his eyes and grinned.

"Hey, trying to work here." He put down the tools he had been holding. "How's Mr. Congeniality?"

"John!" She hated that he was so judgmental of their neighbor. Even so, something in his tone made her laugh. "I'm heading up to finish what I was working on before Leslie called." She stepped around him to stand between him and the football game. "It's pouring out, by the way."

**

Marina picked up her pallet and tapped her finger on paint that she knew would be dried up and unusable. The chartreuse and aqua had bled into each other, creating an almost vein like look, almost like a navigational chart, almost, almost like the one that long ago hung in her parents' bedroom, the one that her father stuck pins in – ports and places he'd someday sail to. Of course, someday never came. The sailboat he had bought for salvage and would someday fix up now sits in a boatyard in Jersey City. Someday. Someday. Someday she and John would restore it and make it seaworthy again. Who was she kidding? John wasn't a sailor. He didn't even like boats. Hated them. Yep, hated them with a passion. Someday. Ha. Someday. He told her someday they'd fix the boat. But she knew he said those things just to appease her. It was easier that way. He says someday and she shuts up. Just like she said someday to his wanting children. Someday came and went for children. Then it was a child. Just one. But she always said someday. Someday. Just to appease him. Because it was easier that way. She said someday and he shut up. She'd never been shy about not wanting kids. Still, telling him someday was easier than arguing. She was in her mid-forties now and abhorred the thought of having a kid. Yeah, it was still physically and technically possible. But she didn't want to be one of those elderly mothers at the playground. Didn't want to explain that no, she's not the Grandma. Didn't want her kid to be embarrassed or ask why she was so old and decrepit when all his or her friends' mothers were so young and nimble. Mostly though, she just didn't want a kid. Never had wanted a kid, never will want a kid. The topic never came up anymore. And when John converted the one spare bedroom into an art studio for her a few years ago, well, she thinks that was his way of waving a white flag.

She peeled the hardened blob of acrylic paint and placed it on the windowsill beside her canvas. It was a pretty blob. Something she could imagine dangling from a silver chain around her neck. She would keep it and consider it. Christmas was just a few weeks away. John probably had the right kind of drill bit to make a small hole. That's it! Not a pendent. An ornament for the tree. Perfect.

She studied the blackbird she'd been painting before Leslie called and decided it would be a Christmas blackbird and would get a fuchsia and lime green swirl. She perched him on a holly branch lightly dusted with white paint to look like snow. She stepped back from the canvas, moved back in closer, and stepped back again. Then she regarded it from the other side of the room. Finally, she walked out the door and entered the room again, pretending to see the painting for the first time. She stood in the doorway for a long time. She crossed her arms and tilted her head. Yes. She was happy. This painting would be perfect in Urban Birds. She'd sold many of her bird paintings there over the years. She'd drop it off in the morning and see if Sadie had room for a series of them, which she could crank out over the next few days.

Hawk

I HATE BOATS. The first time I set foot on one was my senior year of high school. My best friend Toby got me invited up to the Finger Lakes with his family and of course the whole weekend revolved around their pontoon boat. Looked like an oversized raft to me. All the old ladies – Toby's mother and her sisters – sat on this thing in plastic lawn chairs, wearing their old lady bathing suits as if any minute they would abandon all reason and dive into the dark green water. They sat there sipping whatever it was that old ladies in those days sipped, cackling the way old ladies cackled about who knows what, reminding me of my mother's Tuesday night bridge club. The kind of laughter that made my father disappear down to the Elks Lodge when mom played hostess.

The menfolk that weekend consisted of Toby's father and uncle, and of course Toby and myself, if you wanted to call us men. The men had their own laughter, a chuckle usually given at one another's expense. Toby and I weren't old enough to legally drink, but they let us each have one beer. Which would have been a memorable weekend in and of itself, if only I hadn't been too seasick to drink it.

Toby laughed at me that night as we lay in our bunks in the cabin. I had spent the day sitting on one of the built-in benches, as far away from the cackling hens as possible, my chin resting on the rail, my face lifted to the breeze, and my stomach trying to force its way up. I never even opened the beer. The lake was as smooth as glass, Toby said. How can anyone get seasick floating on glass?

It was worse the next day. The old ladies stayed ashore while the men tied a huge inner tube to the stern, taking turns driving the boat fast, the tube crashing and banging on the 'glass' as it followed. I felt better in the tube than on the boat, but once back aboard nothing made my stomach stop heaving. Toby's family thought it was the funniest thing on the lake in a long time. The minute we got to shore I ran to the nearest tree and fertilized it with the nice lunch the cackling hens had packed for us and I swore off boats forever.

Until last year. Marina received a letter from a lawyer regarding her father's boat. Her dad's been dead now for years but apparently, the bloke who'd kept it in his boatyard hadn't kept track of who owned or paid for what vessel. He'd finally caught up with the estate and announced he wanted the boat gone. More accurately, he wanted the beat-up tangle of teak and fiberglass gone. What was I supposed to say? It was her dead dad's boat.

Okay, so all she wanted me to do was go to Long Island and pick up this boat. Unfortunately for me I had just got a new Chevy truck. The lawyer said it was parked on its trailer, ready and waiting. Marina painted the whole thing as an adventure - driving up to New York, staying in a bed and breakfast, driving back, and leaving it in a boatyard somewhere near us in Jersey. I didn't think to ask why we just couldn't sell it in New York.

The kicker came on the way back home, after a nice weekend together, when she mentioned how fixing the boat would represent closure for her. Closure with her father. She didn't add, but I knew she was thinking about them, that it would also be closure with her mother, dead a year before her dad, and even the sister who died so many years earlier. Lizzie, for whom the boat was christened.

For some reason, she's been badgering me about this boat lately. She wants to start working on it this spring, or, right after New Year's, weather permitting, of course. And of course, I'm praying for a winter full of blizzards.

Of course, we both know which of us will be doing the actual work and which of us will be helping. I was in school to be an engineer before I left to join the police force and have always been good at tinkering, good with tools. I like to fix things, always have. Give me a bathroom to rip out, a wine cellar to construct, sure. But spend my precious weekends fixing a boat? I hate boats.

But I love my wife. So, I mostly keep my mouth shut and do what makes her happy. I will buy some books on boat repair (if they don't magically appear under the Christmas tree) and I will teach myself to work with fiberglass. The very thought of all this makes me want to gag. Seems like everything to do with boats makes me want to puke. Agreeing to do this was a mistake. I realize that now. I hate everything to do with boats. Of course, the problem is, I love my wife.

CHAPTER 4

December

MARINA LET THE OVERSTUFFED gingham chair in the corner of her studio swallow her. The mostly mauve thing screams eighties, but it was the first piece of real furniture she'd bought for herself after college. She refuses to get rid of it. Someday, maybe, she will have it reupholstered. Someday, maybe. There's that elusive word again. *Someday.* She regarded her painting and took in the still lingering smell of the chicken pot pie they'd had for dinner. She yawned and felt her eyelids grow heavy. The stairs up to their bedroom creaked. She was happy John was going up to bed, leaving the silly vacuum to be fixed another day. She would buy a new one tomorrow.

She yawned again. And then she was dreaming. Dreaming of snow, wildly falling, then hitting her angrily, snowballs flying at her with the force of a fourth-grade bully. Then Sadie, the owner of Urban Birds, throwing snowballs, perversely angered at her arrogance in thinking her paintings were any good, then Mel chasing her around a football field with his turbo-charged wheel-chair, and then finally her sister Dale taunting her, blaming her for all of the world's problems.

The snowballs morphed into bubbles. Hundreds of thousands of bubbles, falling down, yet coming up, and her chest tightened. In a half-sleep stupor, she became aware of herself trying to take a deep breath, but nothing happened and the bubbles were all around her and she realized that she is at the bottom of a champagne flute, filled to overflowing with pinkish, yellowish dry champagne and she smiled and tried to swim like a dog with dolphin fins, but her body was leaden. She turned into a dog and barked with hundreds of other barking dogs that were now in the champagne with her. She was drowning. Until she wasn't.

She rubbed her eyes and realized that Leslie's two dogs were barking wildly. She must have just let them out. What time is it, anyway? Later than she thought. She turned off the light in her studio and padded up the stairs to her bedroom, expecting to see John in bed, but the bed was neatly made, untouched since this morning. She knew he was still in the basement but doubted he was still working on the vacuum. It was well past two. She could see John in her mind's eye, sitting on the couch in front of what was probably now an infomercial.

Leaving the peace and quiet of the bedroom behind, she headed back downstairs. The basement smelled musty. Water flows toward the house during a rainstorm, seeping in a little bit at a time, making the basement smell like an antique store, not an altogether unpleasant smell.

She picked up three empty beer bottles and tossed them in the recycle bin, causing a crash that she knew would not wake John. She sat down next to him and put her head on his shoulder. She couldn't decide how far to push him to wake up. The last thing he needed was to be stiff and sore tomorrow from sleeping on the couch. But John in a post-couch stupor is never very pleasant.

She nudged him a bit, pushing on his chest.

"Come on, let's go up."

"In a minute." John mumbled. "Still watching." Snore, snore, snore.

"No, not in a minute. Let's go up now." She shook him again.

"In a minute!"

It wasn't always like this. Marina tried to remember when it started, but like a lobster in a pot, it happened so gradually and so subtly that it was barely noticeable. The nights in front of the bedroom TV, falling asleep propped up against a stack of pillows, the volume long muted, but the flickering light from the info-mercial-of-the-day keeping her awake, but not daring to touch the remote – an act that turned her quiet husband into a different and not so pleasant person. Gradually, oh so gradually John started to spend more and more time in the basement unwinding.

She left him there and headed back upstairs, stopping in the kitchen for some water. She gulped what she could and poured the last of it into the parched basin of an orchid, sitting pathetically above the kitchen sink, its fatigued yellow tongue begging for moisture. She turned off the lights and checked the front door.

* * *

Marina stopped at the top of the stairs, confused by the light under the closed door to the master bathroom. She was certain the door had been open before. In fact, she rarely closes it. John had renovated it a few years earlier, a little bit of luxury in the old house. He had knocked down a wall, exposing a tiny walkthrough bedroom that he not so playfully mused would have made a great playroom for a kid. The playroom is now their cozy bathroom that they decorated the way a bathroom might have looked a century ago when the house was built – with modern touches, of course, a separate toilet, and orange walls. Marina loves orange and often thinks about painting her kitchen some shade of tangerine; but an orange bathroom is as far as John is willing to go. An east facing window next to the tub with enough trees provides just enough privacy to warrant the lack of window dressings. Six orchids, much happier than the bedraggled one in the kitchen, sit on three shelves in the window and provide a floral curtain, screening the goings on in the vibrant bathroom from the outside world.

She pulled a robe from the closet and walked toward the closed bathroom door, peeling off her clothes along the way – jeans, turtleneck, white t-shirt, socks, bra, pink and orange striped panties, leaving them in little piles like stepping stones. She heard something that sounded like it was coming from behind the bathroom door. *It must be squirrels.* There had been four of them living in the attic. John trapped and moved them to a small wooded park about a mile away. They needed to figure out how the squirrels were getting in and deal with it. Soon. John was on tap to hang Christmas lights this weekend. She will have him look at the roof then.

She opened the bathroom door and that's when she saw him. A man. Tall and thin, light brown hair almost faded to grey, face hidden by a baseball cap and a thick unkempt beard, dark green jacket wet with rain. She stood frozen, paralyzed. She couldn't breathe, she couldn't move. She didn't remember that she was naked.

"Nice to see you again." The man spoke in a husky, barely audible voice. The sound of it jolted Marina back into the present moment. She tried to scream for John, turning to run. But she couldn't breathe, couldn't see, couldn't utter a sound. She tripped over the pile of clothes on the floor. She fell to her knees. She scrambled to get up, but the man was right there, close behind her now. She froze.

"I've missed you," the man said. He was closer to her now. "I've missed you so much." He put his arm around her as if to hug her.

Finally, finally, she found her voice and started to scream. She flailed. She screamed more. The man didn't flinch. His hold on her was gentle yet too tight to get away. She screamed and screamed and screamed.

"Stop it Marina. You know he won't hear you."

"What do you want." She bit his forearm, near his wrist – the only place she could reach. She knew who it was now. The man who had her in a death grip on the carpet was Phil. Phil Riley. He was thinner than she remembered, almost unrecognizable behind the beard. But he was her husband's former partner and, once upon a time, a man she kissed.

"What the fuck! Ouch! What the hell are you doing. I've missed you. I just want to talk."

"There's nothing to talk about." She bit him again. "Get. Off. Me."

"Dammit!" He loosened his grip on her just long enough for her to leap to her feet. He struck her in the back of her legs with his foot and she fell down again, hard. He stepped over her, slamming her only exit closed, before turning to kick her again. He pushed her onto her stomach and sat on the small of her back.

She struggled against him, still calling out for John. But then she felt something cold and metal against her bare back, moving now to stroke the back of her neck, and she froze. She knew it was a gun.

"Give it up Marina. He'll never hear you."

"What have you done to my husband?"

"Nothing. Nothing. I'm pretty sure he's asleep in the basement. Isn't, that right? Just like in the old days. Don't you remember crying that night? Crying to Pam? Asking for advice? *He always falls asleep on the couch*, you said. *He doesn't mean to*, you said. *But he does it anyway*, you said." Phil was quiet for a moment. "You asked my wife for advice. Then you asked me to talk to John. Well, I never did. I never did talk to him."

"Why are you here?" Marina was sobbing now. "Why? What do you want from me?"

"Pam died." He took a deep breath and let go of her then.

Marina sat up and collected herself enough to mutter that she was sorry. She brought her knees up to her chin and wrapped her arms around them. She was suddenly freezing.

"Yeah. She died a few weeks ago. Wanted to be cremated. She was very specific in her request to be sprinkled here. We're having a service. That's what I came here to tell you. She'd be happy if you and John came."

Something in her snapped. She balled her right hand into a fist and threw it at his chin. His reaction was textbook. Just how a cop would react. He cuffed her.

***

"Please don't hurt me," she begged.

He slowly moved the gun barrel down her back, over her cuffed wrists, thrusting it between her legs, shocking her again to silence.

"I just want to talk to you." His voice cracked a little, almost whining. "I miss you."

"Please," Marina tried to sound calm, "Please Phil, we can talk, just don't hurt me."

"Oh, I won't hurt you," his voice changed again, harsher now. Different from the Phil she used to know.

He moved the hand with the gun back up toward her head and she began to thrash and scream again. He tried to pin her ankles with his empty hand, but she was bucking so hard her legs broke free. He let the gun drop to the floor and moved back. He was now sitting on her ankles, immobilizing her. Leaning down he rubbed his bushy beard on the back of her neck.

Marina, still writhing under him, bit her own tongue hard enough to draw blood. The feel of the beard made her skin crawl. He'd gone through a mustache phase a decade ago, when he and Pam were regulars around the dinner table and the grill. He used to come over and shoot hoops with John. If they stayed long enough pizza would be ordered and movies would be watched. The recollection made her wretch, mouth open against the carpet. She screamed again.

"Get. Off. Me." Marina grunted and coughed these three words over and over until he hit her on the back of the head and told her to shut up. Through her tears, she saw a small white feather under the bed. So very stupid she is, taking great care to make sure she is aware of her surroundings. How could she have been so oblivious to the closed bathroom door? Why did she second-guess herself? How could she have been so clueless that someone was hiding in her house? Of all people, she should know better. She's a police officer's wife. They have gone over personal safety hundreds of times. John even made her take the women's self-defense class taught by the department. She sobbed with shame as Phil moved his hands over her body.

Now he was fumbling with his belt buckle, the buzz of a hastily opened zipper. She lifted her throbbing head and a hoarse groan escaped her mouth. Phil shoved her head back down to the floor.

"Please don't do this," she pleaded. "John is downstairs. Please. Please don't do this." She screamed again, though by now her throat was raw, the scream pitiful and small.

"Shut up!" He grabbed her thick red hair again, wrapping it around his hand, and jerked her head up so hard she thought he might break her neck. Her back was painfully arched, his mouth near her ear, the smell of beer and hot dogs wafting over her face.

"I want you to be quiet. John's not here. He's not coming. He can't hear a thing above the TV. And if he does come up here I am going to have to kill him. You don't want that, do you?" He pulled her hair tighter to the side, twisting her face till she could see him over her shoulder, her torso shaking with the strain. His eyes held hers, his hat lost somewhere in the struggle, his face visible in the light of the bedside table.

He slammed her face back down and reached under her, pulling her bottom up into the air, holding her up and pounding into her. Her cuffed arms were useless; her face ground down into the carpet, her body filled with pain.

It was over in a few seconds. Phil relaxed his grip, dropping her down as he collapsed against her back. Then he grabbed the gun and unlocked the cuffs. He dragged her up off the floor and pushed her toward the bed, the gun pressing against her back as she limped along, a wounded prisoner, too shocked now to cry. He shoved her down onto the comforter. She stared numbly at the wall, as he kicked his legs the rest of the way out of his jeans and boxers.

"I am so tired." He took off his jacket and shirt, tossing them to the floor with his pants, and plopped down next to her limp form, the gun still cradled between them. "I miss you Marina." He reached over, cupped her chin and gently turned her head away from the wall, forcing her to look at him. He inched his face closer so that their noses were almost touching. She tried to jerk her head away, to twist it back toward the wall where she couldn't see him, where she could pretend this wasn't happening. But his grip tightened and she couldn't move, the fight gone out of her.

"I really do miss you." His eyes were tender, though unfocused, as if he'd just made love to her. Marina started to feel the faint stirrings of panic, fuzzy through the pain. "You know, I miss what we used to have. The four of us, really. It was never the same, after, you know. I wish things could have been different. But you know, I get it. I got it then, I get it now." His voice was softer than it was before. "I took a chance and I let myself in. I wanted to surprise John in the basement. But he was asleep. Go figure! John. Asleep in the basement." He started laughing then. Loud, hard, deep, belly laughs. She prayed for John to come through the door.

Phil's head drooped toward his neck and a disjointed snore wrestled its way out of his nose and mouth. He was falling asleep. Marina didn't move. Phil continued to snore. She needed to stay still, to not wake him, to let him drift deep enough to give her a chance. Slowly, inch by inch she began to slide away, to slide out from under his arm. It took almost twenty minutes to make it to the edge of the bed, to lever herself up a heartbeat at a time, to stand up on shaky legs.

Phil bolted upright. He leapt for her, his arm snaking out around her abdomen, and dragged her back toward the bed.

"Oh no, I can't let you leave me again," he said, and she knew then that he would kill her, that she would not see John again, that she would die this night.

It came back to her then, the class she took, the pointers John gave her. Like a remembered dance step her elbow came up and struck back toward Phil's face, connecting with his nose, the surprise releasing her from his grip. She turned toward him now, fear and anger flooding her wounded body, aiming a knee at his exposed groin. He doubled over in agony and she punched his face with all her strength, grabbing his shoulder and kicking for his knees. Trying to flee now she turned back toward the door but he grabbed her from behind again, swinging her away from her escape. She kicked backward, the back of her heel grazing his bruised scrotum. He yelped and leaned forward but this time did not lose his grip, bending her in front of him. Clawing at his arm, she tried to regain her balance and desperately swung her right elbow up and back with all her strength. She struck him. Hard. His grip fell away so abruptly that she almost stumbled as he collapsed to the floor.

She turned around to see Phil lying on his back, tugging at his neck, gasping for breath. A tiny bubble of blood slid up out of his mouth as he struggled to speak. His eyes were wide, fearful, and desperate. Without words he pleaded for help, his face that of a hostage facing down the swinging machete.

Marina stared down at him. She leaned closer. She could see what he needed, see how to open the airway, how to breathe for him until paramedics arrive. There was still time. The phone was on the nightstand, less than a foot away. She could dial those three magic numbers. She could act quickly to buy him enough time. The station is not far, they could be here faster than she could put her clothes back on.

She looked at the phone. Then back down at Phil, clawing at his own throat, eyes glued to her face in panic, the fog of his struggle filling the room. She straightened up and carefully stepped over his body. Without looking back, she was out the door, flying down the stairs, around the corner, through the kitchen, and into the basement.

Hawk

SOMETHING ABOUT THE VACUUM. Fixing the vacuum. The next thing I remember is the game. I didn't really need that last beer. We'd had wine with dinner. She said something about just buying a new vacuum.

But I wanted to fix her vacuum for her. She loved that vacuum. And I knew she'd need the vacuum soon, with Christmas in a few weeks. Nothing makes sense. Everything is fuzzy. I barely acknowledged her when she said she was going over to Leslie's. We had dinner at some point. And wine. Did she go to Leslie's before dinner? Or after? It was still early. She wanted to paint. I wanted to fix that vacuum.

When Marina came down looking for me well into the night, I was watching some mindless movie. A stupid movie. I guess I fell asleep. What movie was I watching? I don't even remember. That's how stupid I feel. I don't even remember the movie that I fell asleep in front of.

Next thing I know my naked, bloody wife is pounding on my chest, shaking the crap out of me, shaking and crying. I thought I was dreaming.

Then it all clarified. This was no dream. I grabbed my piece, which was on the couch beside me. I grabbed my radio. I called the station. I called 911. I ran through the house. Then I saw him. Phil Riley, naked and dead on the floor of my bedroom. Within minutes the guys were here and Marina was gone and the rest is a blur and a fog.

How the hell did Riley get into my house? He must have still had the key from when we patrolled together. I never thought to change the locks. Something like this never occurred to me. God. I can't think straight. I keep thinking I will wake up on the couch in the basement, the stupid movie still on. I want to wake up from this nightmare and find it was just that – a nightmare.

CHAPTER 6

December

IT WAS THE ELBOW: hard, sharp, deadly. Thrown into Phil Riley's throat with enough force to shatter his windpipe and kill him. The preliminary report from the coroner's office was detailed in the medical chart. The attending physician read it aloud, using his finger as a guide.

"You are one very lucky lady. I am going to have to get my wife to take one of those self-defense training classes." He gave a little cough, clearing his throat after this uncertain complement, and set his chart down on the swivel tray next to Marina's bed.

He looked at her right hand, which was bandaged and elevated above her head. She broke her index finger at some point during the fight, fractured and dislocated some of the smaller hand bones, though she had no memory of hitting him with her hands or feeling any pain. She stared at it as he unwrapped the bandage, disturbed, as if the hand did not belong to her. She had welts and bruises all over, especially her face, arms and legs. The hand that did not belong to her was scheduled for surgery later in the afternoon.

John stood in the doorway, talking to two other men in a low voice. Both were cops, though only one, John's friend Nester, was in uniform. Nester was still on duty and was one of the first of dozens of cops on the scene after John began frantically shouting into the phone.

Marina closed her eyes. The throbbing throughout her body was incessant. She heard a woman's voice yelling out in the hall, Leslie demanding to see her. Then Leslie rushed through the doorway, John and the cops parting like the Red Sea.

"What's going on? Marina! What happened?" Just before she reached the bed, John caught her, firmly grasping her by the arm, stopping her forward momentum toward the hospital bed. "My God! The van came to get Mel and there was all this commotion. My God! What happened?" Her eyes were huge, bulging marbles, rimmed with the redness of recent tears.

"It's ok, she's ok," John gripped her arm, his calm police voice attempting to minimize and limit the hysteria.

"No, she's not! Look at her!" Leslie's voice rose an octave. She broke away from his grip and his professionalism and lunged for the bed.

"It's a long story." Marina gave her a weak smile and closed her eyes.

Leslie grappled with a visitor's chair, pulling it close to the edge of the bed, taking Marina's undamaged hand in her own, and listened as John attempted an explanation. At least, of the part he understood. Marina did not watch her friend's face. She kept her eyes closed, feeling only Leslie's shock through the tremble and tightening grip of her hands. Marina was certain that the commotion Leslie saw this morning brought back, in vivid color, the details of Mel's accident. No, it wasn't an accident, even though that is what Leslie tells people. Mel's suicide attempt. The field by the tracks where they'd found him, well, Marina is certain that's what her house looked like this morning.

The doctor's return broke into the small silence that had settled over the room. The surgery would go ahead as scheduled. Someone would be there soon to prepare her. *Has she eaten anything? Don't eat anything now.* As if food was even on her mind. The doctor puttered around with her charts, collected signatures from John, and nodded apologetically on his way out.

* * *

Fatigue flooded her body as she floated in the delicate twilight between sleep and awake. Old songs faintly flow through her head, tinny and far away, like songs from the Great Depression, the ones her father always listened to. Her thoughts were pale and washed out, matching the black and white images cycling through her head. She floated above them, feeling nothing. But for hours now she has felt nothing. Washed out like an empty beach.

But she should be feeling something. Shouldn't she? Good, bad or indifferent, but something. She should feel something because she was raped last night. Violently. And she broke her hand fighting. And she killed someone. She killed Phil Riley. So now the feelings came, surging through her, a black tsunami of pain and despair. Phil had been a friend. Someone she had trusted. Someone her untrusting husband had entrusted with free reign and access into their home. Someone who, at one time, was like family. Someone she once kissed.

She opened her eyes and saw Leslie sitting beside the bed, her arms resting on her thighs, her face staring off into the distance at nothing and at everything. Then she saw Phil again – bright images of him in the doorway. But he wasn't there, not in this doorway. That was last night. Then he was behind her, pinning her down, and then, dead.

She woke up again, slowly, lost in blankness. And then the wave crashed down again, flooding her with the knowledge of where she was and why. She sat up, the room spinning. Color drained from her cheeks.

"Marina, what's wrong?" Her room seemed crowded now. John, Leslie, Nester, and another cop were standing next to the bed. John took Leslie's abandoned chair, pulling it close to the bed, and sat down. He took her good hand and kissed it.

Marina shook her head, a wordless signal that after two decades of marriage conveyed a disinterest in talking. John massaged his temples with his other hand and ran his fingers through his dark hair. She could see the silvery sheen of sweat on his forehead and a deep furrow between his brows that seemed new. She took a deep breath.

"John, I feel like I am going to be sick."

He turned to Nester and the other cop, "Not now guys." He nodded his head toward the door and the unknown cop left.

Nester paused, told Marina to hang in there. He touched the top of her head.

"Thanks Ness," John answered.

"They want to ask you more questions," he explained, gently squeezing her hand. "They'll probably want to come back later. Or maybe tomorrow. We'll see."

Marina moved her hand away and turned her head so she wasn't looking at him. After a moment, she turned back slowly.

"John."

He gave her a ghost of a smile, a smile similar to the smile he wears whenever they argue or passionately disagree or even, in rare instances, fight. It was a smile not of accord or defeat, but of resolve. A smile that did not concede to her point, but rather said that while he may think he's right, while he may think his argument is superior, that above all he loves her. That whatever they were arguing about, no matter who was right or wrong, none of it mattered because it was nothing in the larger scheme of things.

John smiled this smile now. But it didn't comfort her. It was a harbinger of arguments to come. After the hospital, after the other officers ask their questions, after everything is cleaned up and put back together again, he will begin. Gently at first, of course. He will begin his Monday morning quarterbacking. He will want to know the chain of events. She would have to reiterate them over and over and over. Marina knew him, knew this is what would happen.

Nester and the other officer have already talked to her once. She knew that there would be other cops and detectives to talk to in the next few days. She knew the routine. And John would likely sit with her in these sessions. Still she knew it would not be enough. He would want to go over it himself, his methodical police mind processing this thing that has happened. And eventually he would begin to point out things she could have, should have done differently. As if she couldn't see that for herself. Marina felt herself growing weary thinking about it.

"I'll be right back," John said, standing and gesturing toward the door. "Nester is trying to get out of here and I think he wants to chat with me a little more." He kissed her lightly on her parched lips.

"John, I love you." Her eyes filled, the panic starting up again. He sat back down and hugged her lightly, careful to not disturb the IV line or hurt her ribs or any of her other tender spots. "Please don't leave."

"I'm not going anywhere. I'll be right over there."

Leslie came back over to the bed and looked at John. "I'll sit with her."

He nodded gratefully and stepped to the doorway.

Marina's emotions began to ebb, the slack water she now recognized as the calm preceding the next crashing wave. She tried to focus on her friend, to anchor herself to only this moment. In a strange twist of compassion, she thought about the past year of Leslie's life. Leslie hadn't even known Mel was depressed. Hadn't known. How is that possible? How is it possible for a person to harbor such quiet desperation that jumping in front of a train seemed a better alternative to talking to someone. Talking to his wife. Marina feared that she was soon to be engulfed in such a quiet desperation. She could feel the outer edges of it. Soon enough the edges would fill in and cover her in a thick layer of soot.

Leslie sat with her elbows on her knees. Her wispy bangs hung below her eyes. It was a new haircut, one that Marina didn't care for yesterday. Today though, it looked different, better.

"I really like your hair that way. You look beautiful."

"What?" Leslie, startled by the incongruous complement, ran her fingers through her hair. As it fell it caught the light; caught the light like Marina's little sister Lizzie's used to do. Lizzie's was just as feathery and fine, although a little bit blonder than Leslie's.

Marina closed her eyes, tried to picture Lizzie, tried desperately to remember the thirteen-year-old whirl of bliss and mischief.

But the only image she was able to recall was her mother's quiet desperation as she slid to the floor, the wall phone's receiver dangling by its tangled cord. She knew her mother would have given anything to have gotten Lizzie back alive, even as a quadriplegic like Mel, or worse. What could be worse for a mother than the death of her child?

Shaking her head of these thoughts, Marina opened her eyes to see John return from his quiet hallway conference. A nurse entered the room to roll Marina into surgery. John flashed that smile again.

CHAPTER 7

Hawk

THEY JUST WHEELED my wife off to surgery and I feel like any moment the gush of tears will come. It's building up inside my gut, ready to boil over. My innocent, good, pure wife. None of this makes any sense to me right now. Why her? Why now? Shit, I don't even know what time it is. My watch is still on the end table in the basement, right where I took it off when I sat down after dinner to watch that stupid movie. I don't know where the clock is in this room. Where is the damn clock? Don't cry. Just hold it together Hawk. Just hold it together.

I should call someone. Who the hell should I call? My mother? Ha! She never liked Marina. Said I should have chosen her sister. Marina is dull; my mother would say when we were dating. But her sister. Dale has gumption; my mother would say.

Nester and I talked last night of course, at length. He came back to the house for me, after riding in the ambulance with Marina. It should have been me in the ambulance, but he said it was important for a cop to go. Well, dammit, I am a cop! Through all the fog and hullabaloo, I remember looking at him with one of my unmistakable looks. Nester knew this look and acknowledged that he knows I'm a cop – a damned good cop – but also the victim's husband. And last night that's the one and only thing I was – the victim's husband. I guess I was also the intruder's friend. The unwelcome, now dead intruder who had once been a good friend. Even when Riley and Pam moved across the country we were in touch regularly. He called me just a few weeks ago to tell me that Pammy had been moved into hospice. I wanted to visit, but Phil said no. That Pammy was having a hard time accepting things, was loopy from morphine most of the time, and it would be better if Marina and I didn't come. But what about you, I said. I'll bet you could use a beer with an old buddy. A Bud with a bud. He said no. Not now. Maybe later. But not now. What the hell happened? Why did he do this? What was he thinking? FUCK! I feel like I'm going to explode.

Nester praised Marina right and left all morning. She did all the right things, he said over and over. He said that all the things she learned in the self-defense class were applied in a textbook sort of way. I haven't really thought about it much yet – too much commotion and confusion and plain old worry. But when things settle down I need to examine what she did, recreate the scenario, get my mind around this thing. Around the idea of Riley dead on the floor, my wife screaming at me, covered in blood.

My wife. She is so good. Such a good heart. Just the other day she was walking the perimeter the yard, scoping out a place for some new Christmas decorations. Loose tendrils from her long red hair escaping the confines of her hat, the one I gave her for her birthday last year. FUCK!

CHAPTER 8

December

SPICED STARS. By the way these women were going on and on about Spiced Stars, you'd think this was an orgy and not a whole-hearted attempt by your husband to get your mind off your woes and put you in the Christmas spirit by forcing – forcing! – a cookie exchange on you. Only he didn't force. He didn't need to. Marina simply didn't have the fight in her to refuse. John had enlisted the help of their neighbor Leslie, who quietly told Marina that she'd tried to talk John out of it. She told him she thought it was a terrible idea. Funny that Leslie could be more perceptive and insightful than John, who pretty much knew her better than anyone else in the world.

Another ooohhh, another aaahhh. Most of the women standing around Marina's kitchen and dining room were neighbors and a few officer's wives from John's department.

Maple Walnut Cookies. Chia Tea Eggnog Cookies. Chocolate Ginger Meringues. Peppermint Pinwheel Cookies. Orange

Walnut Butter Scotties. Toffee Chocolate Chip Shortbread. Chocolate Covered Marshmallow Cookies. Chocolate Blackout Cookies. Chocolate Nut Rugelach. Black and White Sesame Seed Bars. Coconut Lime Snowballs. Oh, and let's not forget the coveted Spiced Stars. Marina was on the couch, quietly sipping a glass of chardonnay, while the women crowded the dining room table filling their tins with all the fancy cookies that would look beautiful on a coffee table or kitchen counter until it's time to plate them as part of the Christmas Eve dessert spread where everyone would instead go for the Yule log cake or brownies or peppermint-stick ice cream, leaving the gorgeous and aromatic cookies to harden and eventually be boxed away to come out next year as a fancy centerpiece or even Christmas tree ornaments. These cookies would not be eaten. Except maybe the Spiced Stars. Those would certainly make the prettiest ornaments.

"Whatever happened to plain old Toll House cookies?" Leslie sat down beside her, her own glass of chardonnay, refilled to the brim, splashing a little as she settled into the too soft cushion. She balanced a plate of cookies on her knees.

"That pretty much sums up my thoughts about all this." Marina picked a Chocolate Ginger Meringue off Leslie's plate and took a bite. "Not bad. But really? Who has time for all this?" She set the partially eaten cookie on a napkin. "I'm sorry. I'm being a sourpuss. This is the last thing I need." She gestured with her hand toward the cacophony emanating from the dining room and kitchen. "I think John's heart was in the right place with this, but a cookie exchange? Really? I never hosted or even attended one in twenty years of marriage. Where did he even come up with this?"

"I'm sorry." Leslie took a rather large sip of her wine. "I may have mentioned it as an idea, but then quickly rescinded it when he started to get serious about it. I never expected that it would turn into this."

Marina laughed. And laughed. And laughed. She doubled over she was laughing so hard. Then Leslie started. John walked through the family room and paused in front of the couch. Marina looked up at him and in a fraction of a second caught a glimpse of his classic I'm pleased with myself look. She figured that to him, the laughing meant she was having a good time. Quite the opposite. But in this moment, the absurdity of his attempt at distraction was the funniest thing that Marina could remember. She rarely smiled these days. So, John, satisfied with his thrusting a cookie exchange upon her, and, perhaps, a bit glad to see her merriment, bent down and held her. When he loosened his arms, and proceeded to his original destination of the fridge, she said to Leslie that this was akin to arranging a golf outing with the boys for Mel. The minute she said the words, she worried that she offended Leslie. But no, Leslie wasn't one to be easily offended. The crescendo of their combined laughter at that moment gave some healthy competition to the orgasmic moans of more than a dozen women admiring all those ridiculous cookies.

The days following the party were a parade of visitors baring flowers, genuine get well wishes – well-meant but entirely without regard for the fact that she may never recover, may never be the person she was before, well, before. Before the rape? Or before the one and only kiss, three years earlier, that set the tiny pebbles in motion – pebbles on the shoreline which over time became a mosaic that changed every time a wave crashed onto the beach. Mostly though, these visitors brought food. Lasagnas, casseroles of every variety, bagged salads, baguettes, brownies, you name it. She couldn't stand it. She wanted to scream. She wanted to hide. During these very strange days, John finally called his mother and left a message to call back. He did not expect to hear from her. Marina's sister Dale offered to come up from DC. Marina just wasn't sure. Dale would certainly be more of a hindrance than a help. Leslie, though, was a constant presence. She came over in the morning after the van picked up Mel (depending on the day it was physical therapy, occupational therapy, or psychiatric therapy), and just kind of parked herself in the house with no expectation of idle chit-chat, deep conversation, or even close proximity. She cleaned and made lunch and decanted uneaten or surplus food into freezer bags which she neatly labeled. She sorted the mail that quickly began to accumulate in the sunroom. She even brought over several two-serving portions of her famous lasagna for the freezer, one of John's favorites.

Most importantly, though, Leslie served as a buffer to greet the visitors, thank them, invite them in for an obligatory cup of something or to share some leftover cookies from the exchange. What a gift, the skill to entertain strangers in the home of your friend in the aftermath of her rape.

***

Throughout Marina's childhood her mother rarely entertained, if ever. Oh sure, there were the dinner parties. As the wife of sociology professor and department chair at Columbia, her mother often had to throw dinner parties for her husband's colleagues, and she did, grudgingly. Her mother had been an artist too, but unlike Marina, her mother had been Bohemian and colorful and eccentric, and try as she might to blend in and appear academic during those dinner parties, she clearly was not. The other members of Columbia's distinguished faculty and their wives would sit around the antique glass dining room table and would boast about their departments, or the latest research, or who was attending what conference, while Mother mostly sat silent, wearing a faraway look.

Even as a small child, Marina had been keenly aware of her mother's discomfort. She remembered being five years old, in her pajamas, being shooed upstairs just as the first guests arrived. Dale was crying in her room – loud, pathetic, wailing sobs, punctuated by high-pitched whimpers. She remembered a lady with a green hat and a man with a funny red beard standing in the doorway, Daddy taking their coats. When she came through the door, the lady was carrying a large white box, tied with blue, pink and yellow ribbons. Marina was desperate to know what was inside the box, what kinds of goodies they brought this time. Usually guests brought candy, mostly the yucky kind with gooey stuff inside or worse, nuts. But sometimes there was a gem – a solid milk chocolate nugget of one shape or another.

The lady followed Mother to the kitchen and Marina floated down the stairs, unseen, unheard. She sat on the floor that separated the dining room from the kitchen. She knew from previous dinner parties that everyone would stand around in the kitchen before falling into chairs around the dining room table for a meal Mother spent the whole day preparing. She remembered her mother's laugh – not her normal laugh, like when Daddy snuck up behind her and tickled her, or when Aunt Dottie and Uncle Pete were visiting. Mother's laugh was different when Daddy's work colleagues came. Less musical. Almost like Mother wasn't really laughing but just pretending to laugh.

Marina remembered looking at the white box, knowing she would probably get in trouble, but giving in to its beckoning to be opened. As carefully as she could, she loosened the ribbon, lifted a corner, and stuck her hand in to grab a chocolate. A thin layer of tissue paper gave way to something soft underneath that didn't feel at all like chocolates. Careful not to rip or crease the box she lifted the lid a little bit higher, grabbed a handful of tissue paper and whatever was beneath it and pulled it part of the way out. A blanket? With pink and blue and yellow birds, all over it. And musical notes and ABC's. It had a strip of white silk around the perimeter. Boring. She stuffed it back into the box and ran upstairs, grateful she didn't get caught and highly annoyed that there were no chocolates.

"A quilt?" Later, Mother's voice was a loud whisper, carried all the way upstairs from the kitchen through the heating ducts. Marina jumped out of bed and put her ear against the vent next to her bookshelf.

"Didn't you tell them I lost the baby?" Mother was yelling now. Baby? Marina looked around the room. Dale was sleeping in her big-girl bed, plus Dale wasn't really a baby anymore. She went to preschool and she talked. Babies don't talk. What baby? There was no baby in the house. How could Mother lose a baby? Maybe one of Daddy's other guests brought a baby and Mother lost it.

"What do you want me to say, Barb? I'll take the damn quilt back to them Monday."

"No, forget it." Mother's voice was softer now. "Ed, I hate these dinner parties. They're your colleagues, your friends. Please don't ask me to host another one."

"There goes my tenure." Marina understood none of these words. All she was concerned about was the baby. What about the baby? Shouldn't they be looking for the baby and not sitting in the kitchen yelling? "I'll tell you what, I'll give the damn department my notice and we can move back to Jersey and I'll go back to teaching at the community college." Daddy's voice was harsh, mean.

"Don't be ridiculous, Ed. You know I'm just not an entertainer. You knew that about me when you married me. I'm not your mother."

"Thank God you're not my mother." Mother laughed then, but it was her pretend laugh. The next day Marina told Dale about the lost baby and they looked all over the house, hoping to find it and make Mother happy.

***

Marina's favorite place in the house these days, was her chair by the window in the bedroom she shared with John; the same room they have always shared in this house, but it was very different now. She had stood frozen at the threshold on her first night home from the hospital. Paralyzed. John had been behind her on the stairs and didn't understand why she wouldn't go in, and then, in an instant he did understand and just stood with her and held her and let her sob.

They had a guest room with two twin beds and a foldout in the basement. He told her either place would be fine, that they didn't have to go back into their bedroom. Ever. They slept in the guest room that night. The next morning, John and Nester went out and came home with a new queen mattress and put its defiled predecessor out for the trash collectors to take. John emerged from the shed later that day with two gallons of banana colored paint, left over from when he had painted the living room.

"I'd like to paint the walls for you. Make it look less like the room it was before."

She looked at him and couldn't keep the tears from rolling down her cheeks. He was a good man and she knew that he would not rest until everything that could possibly remind her of the attack was erased. She pressed her thumb and forefinger to her eyes and wiped her cheeks with the back of her hand.

"You like these?" He held up the two cans of paint to show her. She looked at the yellow dot on the top of each can, considering it as she rubbed her fingers over each.

"Irises. I want it to be the color of irises."

"Purple?" He raised his eyebrows. "Are you sure?"

"Yes. Take Leslie with you. She'll know what to get."

They came back several hours later with the new paint. They had also stopped to get new bedding and some throw rugs to complement the new walls. Leslie made all the choices, confident that it was a good thing Marina was aware of her environment and not falling down a dark, ugly sinkhole.

The next couple of days were like watching an episode of This Old House. The room was transformed. The accents Leslie had selected were a pale yellow, like the moon on a hazy night. The room turned out lovely. The bed now stood against the opposite wall, leaving the wall with the window empty. The window became room's focal point and the perfect place for Marina's worn, old reading chair. Books were stacked so high next to the chair that she could rest a cup of tea on it as if it were a table. A few of the books were ones that Marina had picked out to read during the holidays. She doubted she would get to them now, as her focus was nonexistent. All she seemed able to do was sit in the old chair and stare out the window, looking down at the street in front of the house, yet seeing nothing.

A dark blue Suburban pulled up and stopped in front of the mailbox. The passenger door opened and skinny, blonde, pre-teen boy got out. He leaned back into the car and emerged again with a mound of something on a paper plate, covered with aluminum foil. Marina didn't recognize the boy, nor did she recognize his mother when she finally got out, carrying a paper shopping bag with a French baguette sticking out between the handles. Marina braced herself for the doorbell. Today was rare in that she was alone in the house. It was a few days before Christmas and Leslie was home with Mel, who's schedule was mostly disrupted during major holidays. John was at the grocery store, which, now that she thought about it, seemed completely unnecessary, with the feast that was about to arrive on their doorstep. He'd offered to take her out to lunch, but she wanted nothing of it. She assured him she would go downstairs and fix herself a bowl of soup later. She lied.

Here it comes – the doorbell, and several knocks on the glass panes that flank the door. It was up to Marina to go downstairs and answer. She had to take this one herself and she simply didn't feel she could do it. The few times over the past few weeks, when she did come down to greet the bearers of food, there had been other people in the house to hide behind. She was disgusted with herself for this behavior but simply could not find the desire or the will to break the cycle. And the thought of having to make polite conversation now with this woman and her son – who probably took great care in selecting the contents of the shopping bag and baked a plate of cookies or brownies or some other treat – nauseated her.

A several second pause of blissful silence before the doorbell and the knocking started again. And again. And again. She got up from her chair and moved away from the window to avoid being seen. One more ring. Two more knocks. Silence. She waited to hear the car doors slam and the engine rev up before sinking back into her chair, feeling socially reprehensible.

She waited a respectful amount of time before going downstairs and opening the front door. Sure enough, she found the bag and the paper plate with a note attached to say they would be by next week on the same day with another meal. She folded up the note and put it in her pocket to show John later. He would know who they are. She would also tell him to get in touch with his buddies and tell them enough with the food. Enough.

***

Marina was about to close the door when a blur of shiny movement tugged at her heart. It was Mel, alone and in his electronic, chin-powered wheelchair, cruising up the driveway. Thank God, he didn't have a plate, casserole, or grocery bag on his lap. She opened the door wider and saw Leslie standing in her own front door, shrugging her shoulders. Marina signaled that it was okay. There wasn't an easy way for Mel's wheelchair to navigate the paving stones that led from the driveway to the porch, so she opened the garage where John was gracious enough to build a little ramp for him into the kitchen. Marina was waiting for him as the garage door went up.

"It's fine, it's fine. I don't need to come in. I'm just here for a minute." It was either a blessing or a curse that Mel's incident didn't leave him permanently brain damaged. Marina didn't think she could live trapped in her own body like that. In some ways, though, she was trapped in her own body – the body that her rapist defiled, redefined, and essentially stole from her. She had taken to referring to Phil as her rapist, because the Phil she had known would never have done this to her, or to anyone.

"No, please, come in. It's freezing out here. I could make tea. I have one of those things, you know, Leslie gave me one. You'll just need to remind me how to put it together." She would have never imagined such a thing existed, allowing someone like Mel to drink beverages – any kind of beverages (she had seen him down a few beers with this device).

"Nah. I'm not staying." He looked hard at her, his vitriol at his fate emanating from his pores. "Listen. I came over to tell you Merry Christmas. We're leaving for Iowa tomorrow to see her Dad."

"Does she need me to look in on her mother in the nursing home? You can give them my number."

"Nah. No. Nothing like that." His face softened. "It doesn't seem like it, but I am getting better. Not all this," he tilted his chin toward his frail body, "but in my head. I'm on new meds and I'm starting to feel better. A ton of head stuff to work out. A ton. I still have days I want to do myself in. But not like before. Now I'm just furious with myself that I didn't get help sooner. Way sooner."

"Leslie mentioned that the other day. About your meds. I'm so glad."

"What I'm trying to say is that if you need someone to talk or to vent to, just let Leslie know. She'll bring me over, or you can come over, or I can just come over, or whatever."

Marina took a deep breath and swallowed her own despair that threatened to flood her eyes and choke her. "What I went through – am going through is nothing, nothing like what you went through."

He cut her off. "Shush." And with that he turned the chair around and disappeared down the driveway just as quickly has he had appeared. She saw that Leslie was waiting for him in the doorway across the street. Marina caught her eye and mouthed *Merry Christmas.*

CHAPTER 9

January

"DID YOU MAKE AN APPOINTMENT to see Zina?" John called from the kitchen. Marina had promised herself that after the holidays she would tackle the pile of paper that she had been ignoring since the rape. She had also promised John that she would talk to her therapist. She was sitting at the table in the sunroom and was working her way through the piles. She had heard the garage door open, signifying John's return, but she didn't get up to greet him. It all seemed like too much effort. But rather than have a shouting conversation with two rooms between them, she left her piles and joined him in the kitchen. She rummaged through the grocery bags he had brought home with him, pulling out items and handing them to him to put away. She found a pint of coffee ice cream – normally her favorite – but wasn't interested. Not even a little.

"I'll call her tomorrow." She avoided looking at him. They were all encouraging her to talk to someone – John, the police, her sister Dale, even Mel. Everyone. Except for Leslie. Leslie was the only person not pressuring her to get help.

The last time she talked to Zina was three years ago, after she'd gone to confession, after her chat with Father Andy.

Over the course of several months, that discussion had led to the topic of Lizzie and the responsibility Marina felt, still quite acutely, in her death. Zina was quick to minimize Marina's role, negated her part in Lizzie's death, and after several additional attempts, Marina gradually let the sessions grow fewer and farther between until they dwindled down to nothing.

Right now, Marina simply didn't want to talk to anyone. If anything, she just wanted to forget. It's been just over a month since the rape – of course she's edgy. Of course, she's upset. Of course, she's cranky. Of course, she's quiet. Of course, her body still aches. Of course, she has no appetite. Of course, she can't sleep.

"Come on, sweetheart, please. I'm begging you. Look at you." John waved his arm toward her. "When you're not upstairs you're walking around this house like a zombie. You're wasting away."

"Actually, I was sorting my way through the piles just before you came in." She motioned toward the sunroom. "Look, John," she paused to take a deep breath. "This is going to take time. I'm not ready to talk about this. I'm really not." She turned away from him and made her way back toward the sunroom. He followed her. She wished he wouldn't do that. He has been following her around the house like this since she was released from the hospital, driving her crazy. All she wants is to be left alone. She will be grateful when his family leave ends and he goes back to work.

She shuffled over to the window and looked at the bird feeders. She lifted her broken hand up to her face and studied it, wondering what it will be like to paint once the cast comes off. The surgeon told her that she might have trouble because she won't be able to bring her fore and middle fingers all the way down to her thumb, as you would need to do to hold a pen, pencil, or paintbrush. Physical therapy might help, but he told her it would take a long time to heal.

John came up to the window and stood beside her, but said nothing. Birds, bunches of them, whizzed by, flying from here to the feeder and there to the feeder and back again. So many sparrows. She'd once read that a ridiculously small number of sparrows survive winter. She wondered if she would survive this one.

"I'm just worried about you, that's all." He inched a little closer and put his arm around her shoulder. She let him – something she had a bit of trouble doing lately. Most of the time she doesn't want to be touched. By anyone. He pulled her in a little bit closer.

Hawk

WHY WON'T SHE TALK to someone? She seems to be shutting everyone out, including me. The department gave me family leave to be with Marina and help her through this. But she won't let me help her. I am getting more and more frustrated at the whole thing, so much so that I can't even think about it without wanting to hit someone. I want to be there for her, but she really doesn't want to talk to me, so what's the point? I think she would truly benefit from seeing her old therapist, Zina. But she won't budge.

I keep waiting for the bomb to detonate, the clock to tick down to zero. I am tiptoeing over land mines, desperately trying to avoid the explosion I am sure will come when she finally confronts me over the fact that I wasn't there for her that night. I am amazed that she hasn't uttered a word about that yet. Every morning I wake up wondering if today is going to be the day.

I wasn't there. I try to convince myself that being asleep in the basement had zero impact on the outcome of that night. When I'm lying in bed at night, wide awake, I play the scene – the scene I missed, the scene I can only imagine – in my head. Over and over again. I do this to prove to my police-tainted brain that no matter how I slice and dice the situation, the fact that I was in the basement means nothing.

How did Riley get in the house? When did he get in the house? How long was he in the house waiting? Did he come in while she was across the street babysitting our asshole neighbor? If I had come up to bed with Marina, would Riley have snuck away to strike again another time? He could have come in at any point during that day or night, hid in some obscure place – he knows all the nooks and crannies of our ancient house. And he knew me well enough to know that once in the basement, particularly with a couple of beers and a stupid movie. Well, he just knew.

This is the thing that I most often get stuck on. That he knew my patterns so well, because he knew me so well. Damn, I even gave him a key to our house. Were we that close? What the hell was I thinking?

Mostly though, I imagine him slinking here later in the evening, after a few beers at the corner bar, seeing the light through the basement window, peering in, seeing me working the vacuum, waiting until he watched me gravitate toward the couch, knowing it would be a matter of minutes before I was out like a light. Funny how I can sleep so deeply that a bomb could go off around me and I'd barely stir. The bastard knew this about me.

I wonder now if he saw Marina go across the street. I wonder what would have stopped him from grabbing her and dragging her into the bushes and doing it right there by the side of the house? Scratch that scenario. Riley knew better than to expose himself like that. But I remember the old Phil. Once he had it in his mind to do something, he stopped at nothing until it was done.

I console myself with this thought: even if I had gone up to bed with her, he would have just come back another day. He was sick, he was insane. And that's the part that's so fucking hard to grasp. So fucking hard to understand. We talked regularly. Pammy was dying. I'm pretty good at noticing when something is even a hair off kilter. Nothing in the last few months or weeks raised my hackles. Maybe he just snapped after Pammy died. Maybe he was trying to win an Oscar holding it together taking care of her. Listen to me! I'm defending him now. No! I feel no compassion for the asshole. None! So, if not that night, then he would have struck some other night. There is nothing I could have done to prevent this. But I still think Marina is going to explode over it at some point. Because she is going to see it differently. She was always harping on me about falling asleep down there. Always. I didn't see what the big deal was. Until now.

February

MARINA KNEW WHAT A PANIC ATTACK felt like. She used to get them frequently during her early twenties. The first one happened on a trip to San Francisco with her younger sister Dale. It was the first time they travelled together as adults. They had planned the trip for months and on the first day, they had a blast taking long walks up and down the hilly neighborhood streets in search of some hole-in-the-wall, local restaurant to have dinner.

About three days into the trip, on an incredibly sunny, crisp fall morning, Marina struck out on her own to explore, hoping to find a souvenir or two. It had been invigorating, up the hills, down the hills. After an hour or so, she sat down on a bench in a grassy area at the top of one of the steeper hills. She could see the Golden Gate Bridge in the distance. All the way at the bottom of the hill, she saw a small dot, getting bigger and bigger. It was a trolley heading up the tracks. She remembered wondering if it ever stalled halfway up the hill and if it did, would it roll backward or was there some mechanism that prevented that? She knew it was a silly question; one she wouldn't have dared articulate to Dale for fear of incessant teasing. She supposed there had to be good brakes, powerful enough to stop it in its tracks and hold it there until help arrived.

She sat on the bench, eating chunks of a bagel she had bought from a bakery halfway up the hill, amazed at the beauty of everything around her. She watched the trolley make its way all the way up and then start its slow journey back down.

After a while she got up and headed a few steps toward the beginning of the descent. Without warning she imagined tripping on a raised tree root or getting the toe of her sneaker caught in a crack in the sidewalk. In her mind, she could see herself tumbling down the hill, the weight of her frame causing increasing momentum and inflicting injuries. Perhaps she would even roll into the street and onto the tracks and get run over by the trolley. And then her sister would have to deal with the aftermath. And what if all this tumbling and then getting hit by the trolley killed her? She couldn't let herself die and leave Dale alone with the guilt of yet another sister's demise. Not that Dale would have been guilty – she wouldn't have been, not in the least. But the thought of it sent Marina into a whirlpool of panic. Suddenly dizzy and hot, her heart pounding, she couldn't breathe. She practically ran back to the bench. She didn't know how she was going to make it back down the hill and the many more blocks to the hotel. In her fear, she berated herself for leaving the area around the hotel, the familiar blocks she had already explored with Dale.

An older woman with a little dog walked by the bench. The woman paused at a tree just beyond. Marina felt like grabbing hold of her and screaming for help. Instead, she forced herself to stand up and walk around the bench several times, forcing deep breaths up from her diaphragm, as her high school choir-director used to instruct. She made her way toward the woman and then continued to the trolley stop. When the trolley came, Marina got on.

The incident on the hill scared her. And that wasn't the last time. It happened again on the airplane on the flight home. Just as the flight attendant closed the cabin door. When they reached cruising altitude she had regained control. Aside from squeezing Dale's hand during the worst of it, she never shared her fear with her; Dale never knew anything was wrong.

The next attack happened a month or so later at the hardware store, in the seasonal aisle. Stopping at the store had been a spur of the moment decision on a Sunday afternoon. She was by herself, looking at artificial Christmas trees of all things, as if her tiny apartment needed a fake six-foot Douglas Fir. The hardware store held no impending danger, no hill, no impending air disaster. Yet she still ran out of there with no tree, and sat sobbing in the parking lot behind the wheel of her car. A panic attack with no conceivable trigger. She began to think she was losing her mind.

Over the next few years these incidents happened with sporadic regularity. Sporadic in the sense that she never really knew what would trigger an episode but regular in that they happened several times a week. And then, one day, the panic attacks stopped. As suddenly and unexpectedly as when they started. One afternoon, about ten years ago, in the car with John driving past the new Home Depot where that hardware store had once been, she realized it had been a very long time since she'd had a panic attack.

She never shared any of this with John. Over the years, she'd imagined telling John about it, tried to picture such a conversation with her practical, logical husband. The tough cop. The kind of guy who embodies the cliché *mind over matter*. He has always been her rock. Her stability. Her happy, restful place. But somehow, she could never quite begin the conversation. So, she never did. Marina supposed there are some things in every marriage that for inexplicable reasons can never be shared. For her, this was one of them.

***

Walking down Main Street with John, Marina avoided thinking about their destination and focused instead on the rain. It has rained for nearly two weeks, a steady pelting rain that Noah would have recognized. But after seemingly endless days of gray, the rain looked like it was finally beginning to settle down; its stinging darts changing into drops as soft as flower petals, the air full of mist. The late winter air was cool, on the warmer side for February, and not terribly unpleasant. Except in one regard: the misty rain was exactly as it was two months ago, the night she was raped. If only it were ten degrees colder. They would still be digging out from under multiple feet of snow. And they wouldn't be walking down Main Street.

Working their way toward the business district in the mist, Marina's chest felt tight and her heart began to pound. She'd been feeling dizzy for the past few weeks, but now she felt that at any moment she could suffocate. She held onto John's arm, listening to the sound of his voice as he filled the quiet between them with this and that, not hearing a word he said, doing everything within her core to keep moving – one foot, then the other, left-right-left-right-left, forcing herself to keep breathing. Breathing is good. Breathing is so very good. She managed to get a hefty helping of air into her lungs and began to feel the panic ebb a little. She kept taking deep breaths as they walked, and now, in no time at all, they were standing in front of a two-story red brick building with the sign, *Janet Rosen, Attorney at Law*, hanging beside the well-worn door.

John opened the door for her and they walked up a narrow staircase to Suite 202. Marina's heart rate seemed to have stabilized. The office was surprising, one wall painted bright red behind two huge velvety chairs more suited to the corner of a coffee shop than a law office. One was purple with oversized arms. The other was cobalt blue, equally big and cushy but with wooden arms. Between the two chairs was a table composed of a simple piece of glass supported by a stack of antique law books.

"Wow." John shook his head as he looked around before sinking into the purple chair. He leaned back, stretching his long legs out in front of him, affecting a relaxed pose.

"This is quite something." Marina paused, looking around. "Do you think she did this herself or did she hire a decorator?"

"No idea," John answered. "What would you call this?"

"Vivid. Striking. Incongruent." Marina absently answered as she focused her attention on the far wall.

Painted in bright yellow, it was covered with close-cropped, framed photos of amusement park rides. Roller coasters, Ferris wheels, merry-go-rounds, a log flume, bumper cars. So many pictures. They framed the lime-green couch that took up the rest of the waiting area, flanked by a square white end table. Marina sat down on the couch and knocked the table with the knuckles on her good hand. She picked up one of the magazines, surprised to find it an ordinary *Golf Digest*, and put it back down.

"This doesn't seem like the type of place that should have *Golf Digest*."

John rolled his eyes and they both laughed a little. He got up out of the chair and joined her on the couch. He put his arm around her and gave a gentle squeeze, the kind of squeeze that conveyed *don't worry*. Then, restless, he got up and stood in front of the wall, examining the amusement park photos for several minutes before sitting back down again.

"How many times have we walked past this building?" John pondered aloud.

"I don't know, a million?"

"Would you ever have guessed that in this building was a criminal lawyer with a reception room that looks like this?" He put his arm back around her and she leaned her head on his shoulder. Criminal lawyer. Criminal. Outlaw. Felon. Crook. Malefactor. Marina looked at her hands. Rubbed her elbow. She killed a man; of course, a criminal lawyer wants to talk to her.

The palpitations started up again and she quickly got up and paced back and forth on the parquet floor. The pattern reminded her of her grandmother's apartment in Queens. Her grandmother had a beige carpet with a raised swirly pattern. Every few feet or so, one of the swirls looked exactly like the letter *S*. When Marina was in kindergarten it was her favorite letter and she remembered her five-year-old self squealing and twirling around on her toes every time she found an *S* in the carpet.

The sound of footsteps startled her and caused John to jump up from the couch. A tall skinny woman in her late fifties with short brown hair appeared from an inner hallway. She wore wire-rimmed glasses above a small upturned nose, a blue and white floral jacket over a plain white camisole. Her matching skirt looked loose on her and hung at mid-calf. And on her feet, a pair of flat, blue gemstone jeweled flip-flops. Coming close to Marina she extended her hand. Marina took it.

"You must be Marina."

"Yes, hello." Rosen's handshake was almost weightless, like a tulip in the first stages of wilting – not what Marina would have expected of a criminal lawyer.

"John." Rosen nodded at John and he nodded back. "Nice to see you again." They had met a few years before, when she had defended Nester after he shot two suspects who had charged at him with guns drawn during a drug raid. Janet Rosen is an expert in justifiable homicide and came highly recommended. She turned on her heel and motioned with her head for Marina and John to follow.

"Can I offer you a coffee?" she said over her shoulder as they filed into the small hallway leading to three separate doors. The closest of the three doors was open, revealing an empty desk and several dead plants in the window. The walls were stark and white, the office obviously vacant. They walked past a broom closet that had been turned into a concession stand, complete with a microwave, small counter, sink, coffee, tea, and snacks. John accepted a coffee, but Marina declined. Finally, they were at the door to Janet Rosen's office, another plain white room with a tidy desk flanked by two black leather chairs. Having been in vividly bright Oz for the past few minutes, Marina felt like she just woke up in Kansas.

Rosen sat down behind her desk and motioned for Marina and John to sit. She picked up a folder and one by one, pulled out clippings of newspaper articles, reading aloud the headlines and various snippets: *Former Cop Rapes Partner's Wife. Wife of Cop Raped, Assailant Killed During Struggle. Local Artist Raped – Kills Assailant.* She read similar words from several more of the articles and then pushed the folder across the desk toward Marina.

"I've already seen these," she said and pushed the folder back. In the days after the attack, Marina had read every article, pouring over them for a mention of the slightest suggestion that she could have intervened after incapacitating Phil. She knows she could have saved him. She didn't have to walk away and let him die.

"Marina, my goal is to keep you out of court." Rosen opened another folder and pulled out the police report, medical examiner's report, written statements from the doctors who treated Marina in the ER, as well as a statement from the Sexual Assault Nurse Examiner. "It's all right here." She put the papers back into the folder and closed it, giving it a firm pat.

"So, what are you saying?" John looked hesitantly at Rosen, then at Marina, and back at Rosen.

"What I'm saying is that I have enough evidence here in front of me to take to the District Attorney. I am sure that when he reviews the facts he will agree that this is a clear case of self-defense." She looked directly at Marina, who noticed that Rosen's eyes are the exact same mousy brown as her hair.

Marina blinked, and tears began to stream down her face. Without missing a beat, and as though she had done this hundreds of times before, Rosen handed her a tissue.

"But I could have done something," Marina said between sobs, her head hanging and shoulders heaving.

"What do you mean?" John turned in his chair to look at her, startled. He put his hand on the back of her head and stroked her hair.

"I could have done something," she repeated, blowing her nose.

"What could you have done?" Rosen asked, pulling more tissues out of the box and handing them to her.

"Something, anything." Her voice faded.

"Sweetheart, don't say that." With a gentle finger, John lifted her chin and looked at her. "You fought back." Marina could see that the top left corner of his mouth was twitching – something it does when he is upset but trying to convey a state of equanimity. She wondered how many times his mouth twitched like that when he was dealing with some of the miscreants he's had to arrest over the years.

"I could have checked his pulse. I could have called 911. Once he went down, he wasn't a threat anymore. I just left him there."

"You didn't know," John said, his mouth still twitching. "You threw the elbow and he went down. That's all that mattered. You didn't know. He could have been faking. He could have gotten back up. You didn't know." He massaged his temples and pushed both hands through his hair.

"Let's review the chain of events," Rosen said. She opened one of the folders and pulled out a piece of paper. "Let's see. He was hiding in your bathroom. He had a gun. He overpowered you. He raped you. He held you hostage in your bedroom. He started to doze off." She swallowed, making the prominent Adam's apple on her skinny neck slowly rise and fall. "Am I on track so far?"

Marina nodded, tissue crumbling in her hand.

"When he relaxed, you saw that as an opportunity to escape, am I right about that?"

Marina nodded.

"The movement roused him, and he came after you, grabbing you from behind."

Marina nodded.

"Your instincts kicked in and you fought him, using the techniques you learned in the self-defense class."

"And some things I've taught her over the years," John added. Marina nodded.

"You fought until he was on the ground. You left the scene. He died. This is a classic case of personal self-defense."

"She's right, Marina," John said.

Marina nodded. She was aware of Rosen and John talking, her voice calm, John's increasingly adamant, but she couldn't quite grab onto the words. John was talking about instincts but Marina interrupted, shaking her head.

"No, no, no. You weren't there. This is basic stuff. I could have opened his airway. I should have known better then to let him lay there and die."

"What he did was inexcusable Marina," John said between clenched teeth.

"I know that! But did he deserve to die over it? He could have just gone to prison." At least if he had gone to prison she could have gotten to the bottom of why he did this to her. He would be alive and slowly, over time, the reasons would have revealed themselves.

"It's not that simple." John's voice was quiet now, barely a whisper.

Rosen reached across the desk for Marina's hand and said: "Would you have deserved to die?" This created a fresh round of tears. Rosen reached for yet another tissue and then thought better of it, handing her the whole box instead.

***

Back outside it was no longer misting. The sun poked over the trees behind the bakery. Marina was glad to be outside, glad to be away from Janet Rosen and her loud waiting room. Loud. That's the word Marina had been searching for. No, it was worse than that. Janet Rosen's waiting room was screaming. A high-pitched, blood-curdling scream. Which is what she wanted to do sitting in her office, which, strangely enough, had a calming effect. She wondered if there is some psychology to all that – a loud room connected to a soft room. She decided it's not important enough to think about and instead, thought about Rosen asking, *would you have deserved to die?* She turned to John then, who was walking beside her but not holding her hand or putting his arm around her this time. She opened her mouth to speak, but no words come out.

"What was that? In there." John broke the silence and motioned toward the two-story brick building they had just left.

"I don't know." She stopped walking and looked at him. "I honestly don't know."

"I don't understand you." He shook his head. "I mean, why would you even think like that?"

"Have you ever killed someone?"

"You know I haven't."

"Is there anything more to say then?"

"Look, Rosen said you have nothing to worry about. The meeting with the DA is just a formality – I've been telling you that all along."

"Is having a criminal lawyer's representation just a formality too?"

John took a deep breath. "You didn't kill him on purpose. Self-defense negates the criminality of your actions."

Marina considered this for a moment. She didn't feel like a criminal. She felt worse than that. Not because she killed a man in self-defense. And not because the man she killed in self-defense was a man she knew. She felt worse than a criminal because he was still alive and she left him lying there, and while he was lying there he died. Would she have left a bloody, injured dog lying in the street? Probably not. She would scoop up a bloody dog and run it down the street to the vet.

She thought she would be feeling very different if the elbow strike had killed Phil instantly. Then she would have had an easier time agreeing with some of the things John said. When Phil hit the floor, her *get the hell out of here* response paused just long enough for her to bend over his body. His pleading eyes begged her not to leave. She left him there to die.

"John, you're right. I'm sorry." She tucked her arm in his arm and they continued walking home. They turned left on Pine. On the small, gradual down slope of the street she clung tighter to John, lest she fall and tumble all the way down to the bottom. Her heart rate shot up again. She took a deep breath and reminded herself that this is Maplewood, New Jersey, not San Francisco. That she is not going to fall, and if she does, John would catch her before she hits the ground. She took another deep breath, but the air didn't go in. The spaces between her heartbeats got smaller and she felt like she would pass out. She looked at the sky. Three crows and a seagull were circling high above the dumpster in the alley between the bakery and the vet. John didn't catch her the night she was attacked. She was falling and he didn't catch her. The one time she needed him to rescue her he was oblivious, content and happy with his beer and remote beside him.

CHAPTER 12

Hawk

THE SKY YOU WERE BORN UNDER. Why the hell am I thinking about that right now? The sun is suddenly brighter, compared to this morning's mist and black rain clouds. Well, not black exactly but quite dark. According to my mother, the day of my birth was a robin's egg blue sky – a brilliant light blue with tiny dots for clouds. When I was a kid she sometimes referred to the sky I was born under. Rarely did we see one, but when we did, she always made a big deal about it. The day I brought Marina home to meet her, my mother made a big deal about the sky that day being the same sky I was born under. All throughout dinner, the conversation was punctuated with comments about my sky and the fact that today's sky was the same sky. She said it was a good omen. A few years later Marina and I were married under a completely different kind of sky. A few years was enough for my mother to somehow decide Marina wasn't good enough for me. Our wedding sky was a stormy sky. My mother talked about that one for years. Not a good omen, she said. You should have dated and married her sister, she said.

Marina doesn't know what kind of sky she was born under. There are no living relatives to remember it or to tell her about it. If I had to guess, I would say that Marina was born under a mild and temperate sky, nothing flashy about it – just an ordinary sky. The kind of sky that you don't think twice about when you walk out your front door. It's just there. Just as it should be. Just as you would expect.

Her sister, Dale, on the other hand, I would have to guess was born under a blustering, howling and wild sky. A squall that instead of leaving a path of fallen limbs and branches in its wake, leaves a trail of broken-hearted, lovesick masochists. They come back again and again for more of the same. I wonder how she's doing. We haven't seen her in a while, maybe a year or so ago when Marina and I went down to DC for a cop's funeral. Dale had time to meet us for dinner the second night, but that was that. And as always, we had a great time with her, even given the somber reason for us being there in the first place.

I should call her and insist that she come up for a few days. I called her from the hospital when Marina was having the surgery on her hand and she, of course, was horrified and, of course ranted and raved and said all the right things. She said everything except, I'll hop in the car right now and be there. Nope. Nothing like that. But, what did I expect? That she would drop everything and walk into such a volatile situation? Dumb of me.

You'd think enough time has gone by. It would do Marina a lot of good to have her sister around for a few days.

I'll talk to Marina about it later. I have mentioned it to her several times, but she keeps blowing me off. Or maybe I'll just call Dale and tell her to come. Why do I need Marina's consent? Dale is my family too. I have the right to invite her down. Don't I?

The sky right now is similar to the sky I was born under, but not a perfect match. It is sunny, and the sky is indeed robin's egg blue, but there are no clouds. Not one. None. They all blew out of here on the wings of the wind that blew the storm away. I would prefer a different sky right now. The mood is dark between Marina and me. A darkish sky with smoky clouds would be more apropos. The bright sun-shiny day that it has turned out to be is like a slap in the face – a mockery of what is happening in our lives. It is incongruous with the growing tension between us.

CHAPTER 13

Three Years Earlier

IT WAS THE FOUR OF THEM - Marina, John, Phil, and Pam - playing cards in Phil's man cave, drinking wine and carrying on like they did so many times before. Only this time Pam was drinking a tall glass of what looked like a Bloody Mary. John had watched Phil pour it and looked askance at the cocktail. Pam was barely finished with her first glass when Phil jumped up from the table, leaving his cards visible for the world to see, and poured her another. Marina and John looked at each other, and as if waiting for this cue, this opener, Phil started talking. It wasn't until after Phil's speech that they learned it was only a V8.

"And that's that," Phil said after rambling for several minutes about the pebble under the skin that Pam had found in the shower, which was just the tip of a larger tumor. "Her surgery is next week."

"Just say it, Phil." Pam finally spoke. "You can say it." She laughed and then shook her head, her long blonde hair framing her face and making her blue eyes pop. "I'm getting my boob cut off. Maybe both, we'll see." She combed her hair with her fingers. It was thick and wavy and naturally blonde, like something out of a salon commercial, and Pam was never shy about her pride in it. She took a fistful of it and held it while the rest of them just stared. "This is what's going to kill me. Losing this." She released her grip and let it fall back down and when it did, it fell over her face and covered her eyes.

"Wow," was all Marina and John could say, almost in unison. The four of them had been together quite a few times in the past several weeks, for dinner or drinks, and of course John and Phil had been together at work – every shift. And all this had been happening in the background. John sat stunned, looking at his partner in disbelief.

"V8," Phil said, not answering the question in John's eyes. "*Prevention* magazine. Something in the V8 is supposed to help." He handed Pam her drink, turning toward her and away from his partner. "I don't know. It made sense when I read it. And it can't hurt."

John turned toward Pam and started to say something, then stopped. Marina got up and stood by the French doors that led out to the patio under the deck. John had helped Phil build that deck a few years before. Endless trips to 84 Lumber and hot summer afternoons, working side by side, the celebration cookout when they finally finished. Phil himself had finished the patio underneath last fall. He hadn't asked for help.

Marina watched her husband's expression in the reflection of the glass doors. She could see the same strain on his face as she felt on hers. Why did Phil and Pam not tell them earlier? She opened the door and went out and through the glass on the other side, watched John get up from the card table and wander over to the pool table, the card game on hiatus. Phil followed and queued up the balls. Pam joined them, putting her arm around Phil. Marina watched them through the glass, their unmoving mouths belying their silence, Phil's especially. Why wouldn't Phil have said something? Privacy? Could it be they just wanted privacy? No fussing from people, no sad looks, no pity? Nope. Marina wrote that one off almost as soon as it popped into her head. Why would they be private about this? How many personal stories of every ilk had she and John listened to over the years? How many intimate details of their daughter's struggles had Pam shared with Marina? Too many to count. Too many details given, too little mystery spared. The silence surrounding the cancer made even less sense. It was clear that had it not been for John's quizzical look at the glass of V8, Phil and Pam might have stayed silent yet.

***

Marina stood outside in the darkness. The air was thin and dry. And cold. The contrast between Phil's overheated house and the crisp April stillness was shocking. Like splashing into an icy pool on a hot summer's day. She wandered to the edge of the patio, out from under the deck to look up at the sky. Phil and Pam lived on the ninth fairway of a golf course and beyond the manicured greens were dense woods. It was a new moon, but the darkness was punctuated by what seemed like a million stars.

Unusual to see so many stars in North Jersey, especially in subdivisions like this. Too many houses, too many lights.

She heard the door open and shut behind her but she didn't turn. She knew John would be worried about her silence, knew he too would be taken aback by this news. But the voice she heard in the darkness wasn't John's.

"Are you ok?" Phil asked, suddenly behind her. He put his hand on her shoulder reassuringly, offering her a glass of wine with the other.

"I'd rather have a V8," she replied, accepting the drink. It was a poor attempt to make light of a heavy situation and Marina immediately regretted it. "Sorry. I just don't get why you guys kept this from us. It's not like this is the first time we've seen you in a while."

Phil grimaced in the dark. "I know John's pissed."

"Can you blame him?"

"No. And yes." Phil sighed. Then he tapped Marina's shoulder and pointed to the woods beyond the golf course. "Do you know the developer can never build houses back there?" Marina didn't respond. "It's some sort of nature preserve or something. The only nature I've ever seen back there are squirrels and sparrows. But it's not like I spend a lot of time there. I think I wandered around there once. Maybe twice."

Sipping her wine, Marina mentally attacked the litany of reasons Phil and Pam might have had for their failure to mention the cancer. With all their history as a foursome, with John's history with Phil on the force, it just didn't make sense. Unless Pam and Phil didn't feel the same, didn't feel the same connection.

Maybe it was an accident that the information was suddenly spilled. If John hadn't made that curious expression when Phil was pouring Pam's drink, would the subject have even come up?

Marina suddenly felt left out, like an outsider, like a vessel full of holes, unsound. Her reaction was unjustified, she knew. It was not her fault that while the four of them fit together well, and John and Phil had had a more than satisfactory working history together, she and Pam had never really fit together, never grown particularly close as girlfriends. They were friends by default. They liked each other well enough but would never have selected each other from the friend bin. They just never connected that way.

"Did you see that?" Phil suddenly pointed at the sky, a flash of something, maybe a shooting star?

Yes, she did see it. She was pretty sure it was a shooting star, but since she had never officially seen one before she wasn't sure. They stood silently watching the sky and in due time, another flash, and this time Marina was certain. It was indeed a shooting star.

"This is a first for me," Marina shook herself out of her self-absorption, smiling up at the dark sky.

"Wow. You've never seen a meteor. Poor deprived thing you are." Phil's voice was playful now, his blue eyes crinkling with laughter. Marina had to remind herself of the gravity of his and Pam's current situation. Standing in the cold looking at the stars was a diversion, an escape. In a minute, they would be back in the house playing pool and pretending nothing was wrong.

"I'm glad I got to share your first time," teased Phil, flashing a warm smile she could see by the starlight. His smile still on his face, his voice became serious, "Look Marina, we aren't all like John. Some of us need to feel our way toward things; some of us don't have all the answers right way. Pammy and I just needed time to work through the diagnosis, before we told anyone."

He gave her shoulder a gentle squeeze, turned and walked back toward the house. Marina watched him hesitate at the French doors, almost as if he were having second thoughts about going in. For a flash of time, like the shooting star, Marina willed him to turn around, walk back out to the middle of the yard and stand beside her again. The light and action inside the house enveloped him as he stood at the foot of the door in a sort of purgatory. Marina was struck by how much older he looked from behind. His baggy jeans and slightly bowed legs made his gait a bit craggy, like an old man. She was surprised she never noticed this before. From the front his arms were sinewy and tight, but from behind the excess skin at his elbows was yellowish and rumpled like dirty sheets on an unmade bed. It also hit her at this moment that although she had known him for years, she really didn't know him at all.

Marina ran toward the doors, spilling a little bit of her wine. She got there just as Phil was stepping inside. He held the door open and she walked in behind him, licking the buttery-fruity-oaky bouquet off her wrist. John was back at the table reshuffling the cards. Pam emerged from the back of the room and plopped a copy of *Prevention* magazine down in front of her. She mumbled something about the V8 article as the cards were soaring through the air and landing in exactly the right spot all the while Marina's peripheral vision was glued to Phil.

***

A week later, the day of Pam's surgery, Marina found herself sitting in a comfy chair at *Barnes and Noble*, right across the street from the hospital. The weather was perhaps the reason the coveted chair was available. Although the store seemed crowded it really wasn't, as most sane people were outside, enjoying the unseasonably warm April day. She went to the bookstore hoping to sit quietly and jot down ideas for her next series of paintings. Anything to keep her mind off Phil and V8 juice and shooting stars. Anything to remind her that his eyes were no bluer, standing under the stars, than they had been two minutes earlier when he'd had his arm around his wife.

Marina looked at her watch. Pam should be out of surgery by now. She and John planned to drop in on Phil that night, bringing a casserole and friendly concern. She considered sending John over there alone, but John would want to know why.

Eleanor Rigby, was piping through the store when she saw him. Phil. He had two books and a box of Godiva chocolates under his arm. She lifted her sketchbook up a bit, covering her face and appearing to be in deep concentration – at least that's what she hoped her appearance suggested. Peering over the top edge of her pad, she watched him get swallowed in the cookbook section. She felt safe enough now to put the pad back in her lap and resume her sketches. She moved her pencil in circles, one eye on the paper, the other eye on the wall of language books that separated her and the culinary tomes. She mindlessly traced the same circle over and over, like a figure skater practicing the perfect loop. This was no use. She just needed to get out of there. She stuffed the sketchbook into her satchel and stood up, practically bumping into Phil as he stood directly in front of her – eyeball to eyeball – smiling with his discovery of her hiding spot. His eyes really were bluer than she realized.

"Well, the deed is done." Phil announced, looking at her intently, as though the week between the moment on the patio and this moment in the bookstore had passed in heartbeat.

"How's she doing?" Marina tried to focus on Pam.

"Kind of in la-la land, groggy. They took both breasts, and her lymph nodes. We probably won't know the extent of things for a week, ten days or so. She wanted chocolate." His eyes glanced at the gold wrapped box in his hand.

Marina was glad for a convenient topic. Like instant oatmeal or a frozen microwavable dinner when you're too tired to cook and too hungry to not eat. She didn't have to think about anything, just plop it in or add hot water and viola, a meal. Not that Pam should suffer for the benefit of Marina's conversational ease, but after her encounter with Phil under the stars the other night, well, the viola-a-conversation-topic-without-much-work, is welcome. "I'm sending John over with a chicken pot pie tonight." She decided then and there that she would, indeed, send John by himself.

Phil looked around and dropped the books and chocolates down on a small table pushed up against the wall. "Do you want something to drink? I suddenly feel like I need something."

"Well, it's really time for me to go." She hesitated, looking at her watch. She had nowhere to go, nothing that needed her attention at home that couldn't wait.

"Oh, okay then." Phil's smile faded a little, and he turned to recollect his wares.

"Wait." Marina looked at her watch again. "It's okay. I can stay for a few minutes. But shouldn't you get back to the hospital?"

"Tea, right? Something herbal and fruity?" He ignored her question.

Marina laughed nervously, surprised that he paid that much attention. She smiled and nodded, then thought better of it and let her upturned lips drop a bit. She put her satchel down and held out her hands to take Phil's books, then sat back down and watched Phil make his way to the Starbucks on the other side of the store. She thumbed through one of the two books, *Beating Cancer with Nutrition*, and skimmed the first few pages with eyes that might as well have been looking at an abstract painting. She set Phil's things on the floor beside her and sat straight up in the chair, crossing one leg over the other, attempting to look elegant. She smoothed her hair and ran her tongue along her teeth, hoping there were no rogue pieces of this morning's bagel caught there. She uncrossed her legs and slouched a bit, thinking it would be better if she looked more relaxed, less stiff. That didn't feel natural, so she leaned into the chair's oversized arm, letting her own arm dangle over the edge a bit for a more cool and aloof look.

She really felt like she had something stuck between her two bottom front teeth. She quickly scanned the store for Phil and in the comfort of his absence, pulled a small mirror out of her purse. Sure enough, a mound of soggy bread was wedged in her trouble spot. She tore a small corner of paper from her sketchpad and folded it until it was stiff enough to wedge between her teeth. She dug out the offender and was about to examine it when she saw Phil approaching, looking a lot less troubled than she thought he should, given the fact that his wife was lying in a hospital bed after major surgery, fate unknown. Sigh.

"Raspberry green tea. Iced." He handed her the drink.

"It's a pretty color," was all she could think to say. She held the drink up to the light where it shimmered lavender and gold. Phil had two frappe-type drinks, one loaded and overflowing with whipped cream, the other one bald. He sipped the bald one and Marina suddenly realized he was probably taking the loaded one to Pam.

"Pam likes whipped cream?"

"She's been known to shoot it straight into her mouth from the can." Phil picked up the nutrition book. "This one's claim to fame is that cancer cells eat sugar and you can starve them by not eating sugar." He put it back down. "I figure we'll clean up her diet when she comes home. I think the doctor said three days, at least."

"I know you said it will be a week or so before they really know, but did the surgeon say anything, you know, can't they tell just by looking?"

"No, not really. I mean, I think they can tell but they don't want to give people false hope. I'm just guessing." He looked at his hands.

"Well, lots of women beat breast cancer. Every day they do. It's not a death sentence. Not necessarily."

"I don't know what I'd do." He looked up at Marina.

"Don't think about it right now. Help her get through this part of it, you know, losing her breasts and everything."

"When I met Pammy, I won. Big. But I don't think it happens twice, does it?" His eyes held hers, as if an answer to this question was important.

Marina was certain she'd stayed too long. She should have bolted out of there the minute he disappeared into the cookbooks. She should have declined Phil's offer for a drink. Because despite his words about Pam, something changed between them and she wished she knew what.

Over the years, they'd had many brief moments standing around, conversing like they did that night in Phil's backyard. Under the stars too. Tilting back longnecks or sipping wine. So why was this different? It wasn't, really. But at the same time, it was. Marina was at a loss to understand why or what. She willed the whole thing away, mentally whacked it with a fly swatter. To no avail.

CHAPTER 14

March

THE HOUSE ON LONG ISLAND was rickety. At least that's what Marina thought when her father took the girls to see it, a week after he and her mother had bought it. *You could start your freshman year in a new high school,* he said. This suited Marina just fine. Dale, however, was hysterical. Marina and her other sister, Lizzie, scrambled out of the car onto the overgrown front lawn but Dale refused to get out of the car and screamed that nobody cared about her. All in one breath: *How could you do this to me, it took the first twelve years of my life to make friends and it will take the next twelve to make new ones, and by then I'll be OLD! I'll just roll up the windows and die in this car!* Of course, none of this was true. Dale made friends easily. Their father ignored her wails. Up the stone path they walked.

Several blocks from the water, the house was set back on a square lot anchored with two older trees and a small garden. Lizzie was still young enough to appreciate a yard and to hope for dogs or pet rabbits and such to go with it. It needed work and it came with, of all things, an old, hurricane damaged sailboat. It was in the backyard on boat stands and after looking at it for about two seconds Marina turned back toward the house and told her father that she couldn't wait to move in.

The boat quickly became a lawn ornament that the whole family grew blind to. It was as permanent a fixture as the other houses on their street. Dale hid in it and smoked cigarettes and snuck boys in it. Lizzie found kittens under it one spring. No one else in the family had any use for it. At least not until about a year before Lizzie was killed.

One day their father decided it would be a fun project to fix up the boat. A family flotilla he called it. He began working on it most weekends, learning what he needed to learn along the way, often enlisting the help of neighbors and sometimes a colleague who knew a little bit about fixing boats. He frequently came to the dinner table smelling of fiberglass and epoxy, full of talk about the adventures they would have as a family, ignoring the teenage sighs and eye-rolls directed his way. Even now, the smell of fiberglass brings Marina back to that happy anticipation, that time where the future only promised good things. Family laughter, a time of security, confidence in the world. Who knew if the adventures of the Long Island Sound would have ever lived up to their father's imaginings? As it turned out, life didn't deliver on its promises. But Marina remembered those years, those dinners, as happy ones, and at least they had that much.

***

Marina stood in the sunroom, steadying herself on the edge of a stone plant stand in the corner, as she tried to water her neglected plants. The dizziness was back. After last month's meeting with the district attorney, she'd been hoping the dizziness would stop, chalking it up to stress and anxiety. The meeting had, in fact, been a mere formality. Marina would not be charged. With anything. She thought she heard the DA mutter something like *the bastard got what he deserved.*

But instead of feeling better, this dizziness and fatigue remained. She stood at the window, waiting until the feeling dissipated a bit. There were no birds at the feeders, the yard unusually still. Waiting in vain, she let herself fall into one of two Adirondack chairs flanking the floor-to-ceiling window, her head swirled as it lay against the cheerful cushions.

Since the attack, Marina has been unable to bring herself to keep up with the bird feeders, a joy she once relished. John picked up the slack, sort of. Most days her body felt leaden. But it was more than that. The days were sunny and the color palette beyond the window was all happy, bright, and rainbow-like – harbingers of spring – an animated scene in a Disney film – everyone and everything around her abuzz with the promise of new life, picnics and spring revelry. Marina couldn't bear the sweetness of it all. Neighbors, shedding their winter skins, were outside gardening, smiling, talking over fences. But she wanted no part of it, couldn't bring herself to step out into its aliveness.

She looked up at the sky – not a cloud in sight – and willed a storm. One with clouds, lots of them. Dark ones. Thick and impervious. Unrelenting. The kind that, in their eeriness, make children cry and adults pout because their perfect picnic might end up a soggy mess.

"Hi." John appeared in the doorway to the sunroom. His work jeans were so faded, and the dirt was ground so tightly into the knees that it has become part of the fabric. He had been in Jersey City, at the boatyard, finishing up the fiberglass work on *Lizzie*. He walked over to where she was sitting and bent down to kiss her.

"You smell good," she said, taking in the caustic scent of fiberglass resin, and attempted a genuine smile.

"How are you doing?" When he left the house this morning she had still been asleep, and he didn't get to ask her the question he asks her, it seems, ten thousand times an hour.

"Eh." She shrugged her shoulders. She was feeling better. Most of the physical wounds that had been a direct result of the attack had healed. The cast had just last week come off her hand. Like the orthopedic surgeon had predicted, she can barely hold a pen or a fork or spoon with her right hand, but she can hold a small watering can, as she discovered a little while ago. She starts physical therapy next week, but in the meantime, considered teaching herself to write and possibly sketch with her left hand. But there are other things she thinks are physical manifestations of her raw emotional state, like the dizziness, fatigue, and cloud musings. And of course, this phase of being a recluse.

"What does *eh* mean?" He raised his eyebrow and looked at her with the harshness of an interrogating cop fishing some key bit of information from a guilty sixteen-year-old. It infuriated

Marina when he did this. She clenched her teeth and breathed in heavily through her nose, held it for a second or two, then let the air slowly hiss back out through her teeth.

"It means I feel lousy. No better or worse than yesterday. Just plain lousy."

"But what, exactly, does that mean?" He raised both arms and let them drop with a hard slap to the side of his legs. He looked completely exasperated by her lack of communication.

"I basically feel like I've been hit by a bus."

"It's been two months, Marina. You should be feeling better by now. I'm calling the doctor." He started walking away and then turned back to face her. "Why are you acting like this. Why are you being so difficult?"

"Difficult? Difficult! I think I have a right to be difficult, John." She felt the sting of salt in her eyes. She put her head in her hands, and then hung the whole package between her knees. "I'm not deliberately trying to be difficult." Her muffled voice softened. She looked up. "I just think it's going to take time, that's all. Look, I'll call the doctor. Hand me the phone."

He walked over to the phone, lifted it off the receiver, and then pausing, gently placed it back down. He went to Marina and extended his hand. She took it and stood up. He pulled her toward him and wrapped his arms around her. The poisonous sun coming in through the window felt like it was coming in through a magnifying glass, making the back of her neck feel hot. She buried her face in John's chest, breathing in the fiberglass chemicals, trying to calm her mind.

She inhaled the smells of boat and the soft flesh of John's chest, which she felt through his sweat-damp tee shirt. She felt a long-forgotten stirring in her belly that radiated south – the first time her body has reacted in a womanly fashion since...well...in a long time.

It had been over three months since they'd last made love. Aside from the one-time John had pneumonia, this was the longest they have ever abstained. She didn't know how John felt about it – he has been oh so careful to not approach her. She suspected he simply wanted to give her time and space. It was a topic that hadn't dared been broached, by either of them. Suddenly she felt shy. Throughout their marriage, they have never shied away from the tough topics that other couples often do. Even sex. They have always been able to openly and freely talk about sex. But not now. The word is simply not uttered. It is stepped around like a pile of manure in the living room.

The other night they were watching *Top Gun* – John's favorite movie – and he casually changed the channel to check the basketball score just before Tom Cruise and Kelly McGillis made love. Marina realized right away that John did this only to be sensitive to what he believes would conjure memories of the attack and push Marina further into her current dark state of mind.

John had nudged her to contact Victim's Services early on. More than nudged; practically demanded. Lacking the energy to disagree or argue with him, she did. The counselor was kind, with the voice of a younger woman, and full of helpful information, things to expect. The counselor had warned her that it could be years before a rape victim could watch a sex scene in a movie – even after they have resumed normal relations with their partners. Watching other people engaging often triggered painful memories of the event. Marina was certain John knew this, since the police department works closely with Victim's Services. She was certain he was projecting this theory on her – that she would go through the same things other rape victims go through, and react the same way to external stimuli the same way other rape victims react.

She was not prepared to argue with John about this. He can only be who he is, a cop with years of experience in violent crime. But even before she left the hospital Marina felt repelled by the clichés. No one can know except herself. She will get through this. She will move on. She will forget, even if only for an hour, but she will put it behind her.

She lifted her head from John's chest and looked at him. He returned her glance with inverted eyebrows, like a sullen caricature of himself. She kissed him on the lips, very gently, and then, more urgently until finally her tongue made a tentative acquaintance with his. He accepted the visitor in his mouth and they kissed like that for several minutes, standing in the sunroom, pressing their bodies together like they used to do when they were dating. They would lean against his car for long, long minutes kissing like that, finding it terribly difficult to say goodnight.

Finally, he pulled back a little bit. Out of breath, he said, "Really?" Marina nodded and pulled at his arm, her previous dizziness forgotten. They walked like this, she in front, he in back, through the house and up the two staircases to their purple bedroom high above the rest of the world.

"Are you sure about this?" He stood in front of her, taking off his shoes.

"Yes."

They undressed each other and fell onto the bed. But from that point forward, nothing worked. John couldn't sustain his end of things despite Marina's efforts. Nothing worked.

They held each other for a while and dozed, and when they woke an hour later, he was ready, but Marina's cavern had gone dark and dry and unused and she half expected a flock of bats to fly out. The wave of desire that had overwhelmed her downstairs was gone. She rested her head in the crook of his arm and, not wanting to disappoint him, stroked his chest, moving down to the hairs on his belly. But he was flaccid once again and there was no point continuing. He put his arm around her and they lay like that for a very long time, not talking, just breathing.

"I'm sorry," he finally said.

"No, don't, there's nothing to be sorry about." She sighed. "I think I may have jumped the gun a little. Maybe I'm not ready."

"Me too," he replied, rubbing her shoulder absently. She wondered what he meant by this. No, she knows. Her attacker might as well have been in the room with them. Painting the room and rearranging the furniture helped. A lot. But Phil's presence in the room loomed – three in the bed instead of two.

**

Marina stood at the kitchen counter and stared into space. She was famished. Her appetite for food seemed to be reviving. It didn't happen often lately, but tonight she felt completely empty in her gut – like she could eat anything and everything. She opened the freezer and looked for something to reheat, perhaps some dish someone brought over during the cavalcade a few months ago. Didn't Leslie leave some lasagna? Leslie made the best lasagna. Marina sensed John behind her and turned her head. He stood there in shorts and an undershirt. His hair was messed up, like he had just rolled out of bed, which he had. She stood up to face him and reached around the back of her head to tie her hair in a loose knot at the base of her neck. He kissed her, and, seconds later her hair came loose – something she knew John had always found particularly attractive and sexy.

"What's for dinner?" he asked.

Marina's head was in the freezer again and she didn't answer right away. She pulled several packages out and laid them on the floor beside her.

"Here it is!" She handed him the Ziploc containing two perfect, generous pieces of lasagna.

"Ah, Leslie's lasagna," he said with a grin. "How about I make a salad?"

"That would be great." She reached out and touched his arm. "Thank you."

They rummaged around the kitchen, John pulling lettuce, peppers, a shallot, and a lemon out of the fridge. Marina transferred the lasagna to a dish and stuck it in the microwave to thaw. She stood against the counter waiting for the lasagna, arms crossed across her chest. John selected two wine glasses hanging under the cupboards and set them on the counter next to Marina.

"I'll be right back," he said over his shoulder. She heard him on the basement stairs, and when he returned he was cradling a cold bottle of chardonnay. He had built the wine closet last year as a sort of joint present for their twentieth anniversary. They had both always wanted one and he derived great pleasure from building it. He opened the wine and poured a little bit in each glass. They swirled it around, as if they knew what they are doing, and laughed. The ritual of the wine tasting always cracked them up. They had no idea why they liked certain wines – they just knew what they liked and what they didn't. He filled their glasses and raised his to hers and they lightly touched one to the other.

"I told you everything would work out okay," he said, referring to the meeting with the district attorney.

"I'll admit – I was worried." Taking a deep breath Marina continued, "Look, John, I'm really sorry about what happened upstairs a little while ago. I'm sorry things didn't, you know, work properly."

"Me too. I'm sorry too. Let's not talk about it, okay?"

"But I kind of want to," she said, somewhat hurt that he wasn't eager to try and get to the bottom of it.

"I'm not sure there's anything to talk about," he said. "I'll admit that I was surprised you were interested. It took me a while to get used to the idea myself."

"And then when you did...I couldn't." Her face reddened. She felt like she would cry.

"Ah, forget about it, it's okay. We'll do better the next time." He got a cutting board and knife and started chopping his veggies. Marina didn't look at him. She lifted her wine glass to her lips and let the cold, silkiness bathe the tip of her tongue. She took her glass and the newspaper and went into the sunroom. It was still light outside and she decided to try sitting on the patio for a little bit. The sliding glass door opened and she turned to see John coming down the patio steps with his wine and a bowl of potato chips.

"There you are," he said. "it's actually nice out! Warmer than I thought." He sat down beside her and placed the bowl in front of her. She looked at it and realized that the voracious hunger that had gotten her out of bed after the failed lovemaking attempt had all but disappeared. John picked up the newspaper, flipped through several pages, and then put it back down.

"Wow, look over there." Marina pointed to the corner of the yard where ordinarily she would plant tomatoes, pumpkins, zucchini, and peppers. Next to it, on a smaller patch of dirt was her herb garden. It was getting close to the time when the gardens needed to be prepped for the spring planting season. It had been a relatively warm winter and weeds were beginning to sprout. "I guess I need to get busy on these. I'm not sure I'm up to it. Maybe we can skip it this year." Until now, she had not thought about her garden.

"I saw the beginnings of a few plants at Home Depot the other day. I'll get you some tomorrow."

"Oh, don't bother. I'm not up for it this year. I'm really not."

"You won't have to do a thing. I'll take care of them."

"John, please," she tried to keep her tone level, "I don't want a garden this year." She got up and went back into the house, which now smelled of garlic and basil and all the wonderfully mingled smells of Leslie's lasagna. A bowl of salad sat on the counter, dressing not yet applied, wooden tossing utensils standing by. The table was set, complete with a wooden board with half a loaf of some sort of rustic bread John must have found in the freezer. Just like him to think of everything. She opened the microwave oven and the steam and aroma suddenly overwhelmed her, and not in a good way. She felt bile rising in the back of her throat and turned to the sink with surprise, gripping the cool stainless steel. For a moment, she felt sure she was going to vomit, but the feeling subsided. Taking a few breaths, she forced herself to relax. John was just trying to take care of her. She went back outside.

"Thank you for getting dinner ready," she said, returning to her chair, feeling suddenly and unexpectedly tender toward him. How could she feel truculence for him one minute and utter tenderness toward him the next? She really didn't want to talk to her therapist about the rape, but she was beginning to wonder if she should. She was having trouble articulating this thing toward John that has been welling up inside of her since the attack. It is not quite hostility, not quite anger, but something she feels now and then toward John that she is afraid will burst open and destroy their marriage.

The bird feeders were quiet this time of day. It was well into dusk with only a pair of cardinals looking for an evening snack. Marina watched as the male landed on the weathervane on top of the shed. He sat there for a few minutes and then made his way across the yard and onto the top crook of the shepherd's staff that holds his favorite birdseed. Cardinals are supposed to be ground feeders but this pair has adapted.

"Did I do something?" he asked, brows furrowed, trying to understand.

"No. I'm sorry I yelled at you. It would make me happy to have a garden this year." She needed him now to be tender too and regretted the tone in her voice over the garden. She moved her chair closer to his and put her arms around him. To her great relief, he returned the affection.

"I think everything should be just about ready," she said. "What do you say we go in and eat?"

John gave her a squeeze, got up, and together they went into the house. He refreshed their wine and tossed the salad. He then heaped the lasagna onto two plates and brought them over to the table. Marina followed him with the salad bowl.

"Have you heard from Dale lately?" he asked after they sat down.

Marina sighed, anger beginning to seep back into her. She ignored him and helped herself to some salad and tore off a piece of the bread. She took a taste of the lasagna and though it tasted great – a comforting classic that is always the same – she had no desire to eat it, or much of anything else on her plate. She pushed the salad around a little bit with her fork, speared a green pepper chunk, looked at it as she raised the fork, paused to look at it some more, and then reluctantly put it in her mouth. She did this several more times before John noticed.

"You're not eating very much."

"For some reason, I'm not very hungry anymore." Marina put her fork down and peeled the napkin from her lap, placing it on the table beside her plate.

"Come on, eat your dinner."

She rolled her eyes and they both laughed. Shaking her head in defeat, she unfolded the napkin and put it back on her lap. She ended up being able to force down half of the lasagna, most of the salad, and a bite of bread.

"Dale emailed me," she said, pushing her plate away for the final time. "She wants to come up for Easter. I'm just not sure I can deal with having her here." She expected this dusty topic of her sister to fall back to the floor and half float, half roll across the room like tumbleweed where it would settle under the wrought iron baker's rack in the back of the kitchen, where the vacuum couldn't reach. She would prefer it stay there until she had the gumption and strength to push the rack away from the wall and deal with it.

John's voice pulled her back to reality. "I think having Dale come down would be a great idea. We can cook one night, go to Peterson's the next, maybe even go to church, if you want. I can call Peterson's and make a reservation."

"No, John, I really don't think so."

"I think it would be good for you. You need to start getting out and doing things. And it would be something to help distract you until you can start painting again."

"Easier said than done."

"Well, we can keep it easy. It's just your sister. Let me call her for you, I'll do all the planning, get the groceries and whatnot."

Marina sighed, "No, don't call her. Not yet. At least, let me think about it some more."

He considered her statement for a moment. "Hey, why don't you come keep me company tomorrow when I'm working on the boat." He looked at her hopefully. "You don't have to do anything – just bring a book or a sketchpad or something."

"It's supposed to be cold tomorrow," she said, not at all enthusiastic about the forty-minute drive to the boatyard in Jersey City, or about reading a book or sketching. She was not enthusiastic about anything. But he seemed to be making an effort. She should too. Her tagging along might do them both some good.

"We'll go mid-afternoon. It's supposed to be sunny, so it will be warm enough." He paused. "But if it's too cold, you could sit in the car with the heater."

"Sure, I'll go with you," she said, mustering a smile. "It might be fun."

"Back to the Dale problem," she said.

"What problem? So, she'll come down for a few days," he shrugged. "We haven't seen her in a while. It will be fun."

"Fun for you, but strained for me."

"You two were close once." He was trying hard to be convincing and looked closely at her before continuing. "Maybe you can, you know, confide in her. Or something."

"That's the last thing I want to do." Her tenderness evaporated.

John watched her for a moment. "Can I ask you something? Totally unrelated."

He wore a look of caution; she knew that he was about to ask her something sensitive, on some topic that had the risk of hurting her feelings. She braced herself for a conversation about their failed lovemaking attempt, feeling relieved that they were going to talk about it, finally. It had been chipping away at her, in the background, all evening. She wasn't even sure why. It's not as if they have never had a sexual debacle. Of course, they have; lots of times over the years. Mostly it had been a matter of timing – one wanting it or needing it and the other not. Sometimes it was a matter of one of them not being sensitive to the other's stress level.

The classic had happened early in their marriage when John was working nights. Unable to sleep, and knowing that John would be walking through the door at around seven, she took a hot shower, dabbed White Linen on her neck and between her breasts and then, as an afterthought, in dots leading the way from her breastbone all the way down to her pubic bone. She put on a white teddy – one of several she received at her lingerie shower – and waited for him downstairs, stretched out on the couch like a Greek goddess. To keep warm while she waited, she wrapped herself in a blanket from their bed upstairs. She lay there waiting for him, pleased with her plan of seduction, and then finally, right on schedule, he walked through the door.

Surprised to see her on the couch, he bent over and kissed her forehead. She threw off the blanket, revealing a very beautiful but unexpected sight. He removed his gun holster, took off his shirt, and stood looking at her, still in his bulletproof vest. She got up and finished undressing him, and all looked promising, but in the end, he couldn't make it work. She felt foolish and insulted and unattractive. They went upstairs and she climbed into bed, the teddy in a crumbled ball on the floor. John took a shower and when he came back to bed, was all over her, until he realized that she was asleep, only she wasn't asleep, just pretending in a fit of pique.

They'd talked about it, off and on, all the next day, and finally, after multiple attempts at expressing himself, John was able to get out that it was hard for him to switch gears so quickly. That it would have worked better if she had been upstairs instead of on the couch. If he'd had some time to unwind and relax a bit, if only for a few minutes, he would have been thrilled with her seduction. It turned out to be one of those early lessons you learn – one you never forget. They often laugh about the white teddy incident.

"Ask away," she said, now more than ever eager to talk about what happened between them upstairs a little while ago. She wanted to know what was on his mind, why things didn't, at first anyway, work for him. Perhaps it was as simple as a timing issue. She did kind of surprise him when she expressed interest. It had to be a timing issue. He had just spent the morning working on the boat, he must have been tired. It was a white teddy incident. She took a deep breath and a smile of relief floated across her face.

John laid his hands flat on the table, "Why didn't you say it?"

"Say what?"

"Stay back." His face was stilled with the effort he was making at self-control. "Why didn't you say *stay back*?"

"I have no idea what you're talking about." She was confused. Did he think she didn't want him? She kissed him first.

Suddenly she understood. Her face reddened. He was not talking about what had happened between them in the bedroom. He was talking about the night of the rape.

"When you opened the bathroom door and saw Riley." Picking up his fork, he reached across the table toward her plate and cut himself a corner of her remaining lasagna, affecting calm she knew he couldn't possibly feel. "I wonder what would have happened if you got into your fighting stance, like we practiced, and told him to stay back."

She felt her face go hot and her heart start to pound.

"I'm sure he would have listened to me and gone on his merry way." She wanted so much for her voice to sound as calm as his. But it didn't and now she felt the tears. She wiped them away with her napkin.

"Probably not. But you may have been able to slow him down, fend him off long enough to get out of there without getting raped." His voice was quiet.

"He had a gun." Didn't John remember that important fact? The tears fell more rapidly now.

"I know he had a gun." His eyes softened. He got up and bent over her chair, wrapping his arms around her. She should hate him at this moment, but she didn't. She turned toward him and let him rub her back while she sobbed.

* * *

All relationships have their highs and lows, Marina knew this. She was never under any illusions, even early in their marriage. So yes, Marina and John certainly have had theirs, even before the attack. But until now their highs have always been miles high, their lows haven't been terribly low. Most of the time they talk easily to each other. But now she was beginning to wonder if they have really been talking all these years.

Does she really know John, at a deep level? Does he really know her? Sure, they sometimes speak without words. They are sensitive to each other's subtle nuances and minuscule changes in demeanor that would go unnoticed by anyone else. But she knew there were things in her own jumble of a soul that were too difficult and complicated to put into words and make someone else – anyone else – understand their depth and breadth. Like how completely and utterly responsible she felt for her little sister Lizzie's death, and, ultimately, by default, the deaths of her parents. And how, at the peak of a panic attack, she is afraid of what she might do. And how she will never forgive herself for letting Phil die, here in this room. No matter what he'd done to her, he didn't deserve death.

Marina is certain there are things John doesn't share, deep things, things that make him the way he is, needs that she is certain he is not even aware of himself. Like his need to escape to the basement to fix things after his most brutal of days as a cop. Everyone needs a happy place, she knows that. Her happy place has always been the sunroom.

She wonders why it bothers her so much that John's happy place is the basement? Is it because the basement seems so far away from the rest of the house? Is it because when he falls asleep down there she often wakes up in the bed alone at dawn? Or is it because when he falls asleep down there she might wake up to find a monster in the bathroom?

She wills sleep to come. She didn't want to think about this stuff. About two weeks after the attack she was napping away a Sunday afternoon, and when she woke it was to the din of a football game and John, perched on the edge of their bed, was engrossed in a game between two teams he didn't even care about. Didn't he remember?

She buried her head in the pillows and sobbed quietly, careful not to wake John, who was snoring softly beside her, the day's eggshell walking apparently not enough to keep him awake. Her tears went undetected by the very man who has always been able to smell crime hours before it happened. The very man whose police brethren dubbed him Hawk, in honor of his sixth sense, his eye for crime. But the hawk had certainly gone out of him lately.

Hawk

THE END OF THE DAY is a time I have always treasured. Even during periods of my career when the end of my day was the beginning of a normal person's day. There was a point in my life when the world was in bed, rolling over after hitting the snooze button on the alarm clock, or lazily willing their bodies to come to life, I'd only just be driving home in my police cruiser after a long, sometimes boring, sometimes exciting night on patrol.

I loved patrol assignments. On the streets. Especially at night. At night when darkness looms and crimes tend to happen. When the little old lady living alone in a brick rambler hears a noise and calls 911. Of course, we all know that most likely the little old lady heard a raccoon knocking over a trashcan or some other such thing. But we cops love it. Two or three cars will race to the scene, each cop wanting to be the first one there, the knight in shining armor on the white horse. Pounding on the door, the deep husky voice – Ma'am, it's the police! – and the little old lady so very grateful in her pink robe and fuzzy slippers, stepping off to the side of the small foyer to let the heroes in, watching in awe as we bob and weave our way around the tiny house, emerging a few minutes later to tell her that everything is okay, that it was almost certainly a raccoon. She sighs in great relief and apologies for the bother. Ma'am, it's no bother, this is what we do. And she offers us some fresh coffee and perhaps a stale cookie or two from her cookie jar, and we gladly accept.

At the end of such a day, the sun would be rising instead of setting. After a few years, I had become an expert on the dawn sky. Not in scientific terms, but in my own way, I began to see patterns in the various ways the sky looked in that half hour or so period before sunrise. Recurring themes. Recurring motifs.

These days, the end of the day for me coincides with what the world thinks of as the end of the day. A normal cycle, circadian rhythms as they were meant to be. And that should be ok. But my problem is after midnight. Because after midnight – especially as I lay in bed willing sleep, as I am now, still struggling after all these years to adjust to a normal schedule, my conversations with myself become accusatory.

Most people would describe me as a level headed, clear thinker. Even Marina thinks of me that way. But I can't stop beating myself up in the middle of the night. The more I try to sleep, the stronger my self-flagellation gets. The deepest dark of night is my critic's favorite domain. If I am unfortunate enough to be awake, as I mostly am these nights, my inner voice is one of accusations and taunts. Finger pointing and harsh words and all-encompassing blame. A magnifying lens over the story of my life to be sure I see every blemish, every imperfection.

April

MARINA SAT AT THE KITCHEN TABLE, slightly nauseous and absently thumbing through an art supply catalog that had just arrived that morning. She was waiting for Mel, and per Leslie's request, had sent John out yesterday to buy a bottle of scotch. The official start of the universal concept of happy hour was more than a half a day away, but, what the hell. If the guy wants to sip a scotch before noon, well, if anyone has the right to imbibe, at any time on any day, it's Mel. John had gone to the boat, leaving Marina alone in the house. Over the past few weeks, Mel had become somewhat of a regular visitor. The fact that he even wanted to be social in the first place was something of a marvel, one that Leslie refused to question or over analyze, and chose instead to latch onto the thread of hope provided by his new cocktail of medications. With or without the scotch, he was improving, and Leslie had confided that his countenance was different than she'd ever known it to be, even before the accident. In a word, Mel was becoming a different man before her eyes, and she liked this version of him better than the version she'd married.

The scotch sat in the middle of the table, flanked by two glasses. Marina didn't know much about scotch, didn't even much care for it, but figured she'd have some with Mel. Just a toast and a sip. In the past month alone, he had gained some movement in his hands and with the aid of arm braces and a lot of gumption, he was able to hold a small glass and lift it, albeit unsteadily, to his lips. He practiced his new skill as if it were an Olympic event and his goal was the gold.

The phone rang twice and stopped. That was Leslie's signal that he had left the house and was on his way across the street. Marina got up and opened the front door. He was wearing his orange Syracuse hoodie – the decade old one that was faded almost to white, the one with the missing hood strings and frayed arm cuffs – not one of the several new ones Leslie had bought him over the years. The thing looked like it could disintegrate into vapor at any moment. In his lap and leaning against his chest was some sort of potted plant. As he got closer, she realized it was a tomato plant, likely from his prized greenhouse, the one he'd neglected for the past few years and was only now showing interest in again.

"I hope you like *The Famous Grouse*. I take no responsibility for its purchase." Marina took the plant from him and directed him to the garage door, which was open and ready to receive him. She stepped aside and followed as he wheeled himself into the garage, up the little ramp, and through door into the kitchen. He stopped in front of the table and gave an approving nod. She put the tomato plant on the counter and helped settle his chair at the table.

"Did my husband put you up to this?" She pointed at the plant, with a mock-accusing look on her face.

"I don't recall."

"Well, it just so happens that we had a little conversation just last week. And it just so happens that it was about tomato plants and my lack of enthusiasm for growing them this year."

"I don't recall." He repeated, this time with a hint of laughter in his voice.

"It's beautiful. The tomatoes look almost ripe."

Mel nodded. "Give 'em a day or three. Then they'll be perfect. Just slice 'em and put a little salt and pepper. Olive oil. Balsamic vinegar if you must. Let me know how they are. The plant should survive in your sunroom until, maybe, Mother's Day. So, if you only decide to do one plant this year, well, I already did the hard work for you."

"Thanks." She felt gratitude and shame competing for a place in her heart. Gratitude for this dear neighbor – even if John had put him up to it – to be so thoughtful. Gratitude for the friendship that she and Leslie had developed over the past few years. And shame. So much shame. It had been three months since the rape and she felt no better inside, even though, outside, to all but the most astute observer, she seemed to be making tiny bits of progress.

***

"I saw the guy." Mel had slowly, oh so painfully slowly, finished a second glass of scotch. Marina was still nursing her first. "Yep. Saw him. I recognized him as the skinny cop that used to hang with your husband. And that party you guys had a few years ago. I think I talked to him for, like, a minute." They'd been sitting at the kitchen table for nearly two hours and talked about everything from botany to art, to Bill Clinton, to the upcoming Paralympic Winter Games in Nagano, Japan, to Leslie, to life to life l'chaim. This was the first mention of the elephant in the room.

"Where?" She took a larger sip of her scotch and let it sit in her mouth for a long second before swallowing it.

"At the door. Where else would I see him?"

"So, he came to the door?"

"Yep. It was in the afternoon. I don't know when, really, but sometime around lunch. Something like that. I saw him ring the doorbell. He knocked on the glass a few times."

"Then what?"

"He left."

"In a car?"

"Nope. He walked down the street, toward Main."

"You never saw him come back?"

"What do you think? I sit in a chair all day and look out the window?" He smiled. Marina wanted to laugh at this, but the visual of Phil at the door unnerved her. Where was she and what was she doing mid-afternoon? Was it before or after Leslie called? Was she even home? The damned doorbell had been broken for the better part of a year. A year! It was something she didn't often think about. Until after the rape. During the parade of visitors. John decided that they needed to be able to hear the doorbell. Oh, the irony. The tragic irony. The nausea that, surprisingly, had abated with the scotch, was back. She wanted to scream.

Hawk

WHEN I WAS A TODDLER, I TWITCHED. Not sure twitching is the scientific word for it – perhaps tic is better, although a tic, I think, implies involuntary movement and in my case, the movement was not involuntary. My mother called it a twitch. Or twitching, as in stop twitching, or today we're not going to twitch, or starting tomorrow no more twitching.

I remember very little from my early childhood, but for some reason I remember this forbidden activity – tilting my head to one side and then jerking it back in the other direction. Typically, I would do this motion one time, one quick back and forth shake to restore equilibrium. But when I was feeling particularly emotional, say, I had been sent to my room for time out, or if I was overtired or too hungry. If no one were looking, I'd sneak in a series of twitches. It made me feel powerful and in control. The three-year-old equivalent of an adrenaline rush. Yet I don't know how or why or when this started, and likewise, I don't know how or why or when it ended.

My twitch was both deliberate and compulsive. The need would come to me and I would do it. If the desire came to me but I knew I shouldn't do it, I did it anyway, because to not do it made me feel like the walls of whatever room I was in were going to come toward me and crush me, or, if I happened to be outside, I felt like I was going to be swept away by an invisible force.

I didn't twitch every day, but I did it enough so that for a while its cessation seemed to be the focus of my mother's existence. Every night, as she tucked me in, she wagged her finger in the air and ordered me to not twitch in bed. And of course, the minute the door closed, I twitched and twitched and twitched, sometimes giving myself a headache. And as predictable as the rooster on the farm next door, my mother opened the door at daybreak and wagged the finger in the air again. And, of course, I would twitch before my mother even left the room. Now her whole hand would descend upon my pajama-clad bottom. Hard. And it hurt. Not nearly enough to make it worth not twitching, however. To not twitch would be far more painful, not just in my head, but also in my whole body. In my heart and soul.

And this is precisely how I am feeling now, only it's not an urge to twitch, but an urge to call Dale and beg her to come down, despite Marina's protests. I can't seem to do or say anything right these days. Only moments ago, she collapsed into tears because I made yet another insensitive comment about how she handled the rape. After her sobs abated I puttered around the kitchen a bit so she could collect herself.

When I returned to the couch her eyes were dry and we launched into a discussion about the weather, the birds, anything safe. I think she is upset about our failed lovemaking attempts. I really should reassure her about that. It's my fault, I just can't seem to do it. It's still too soon, too raw for me. Another man was with my wife and I can't, for the life of me, stop thinking about that. And that has been killing any semblance of libido I frequently start with. I can't shake the image of Phil Riley rolling on the floor with my wife. I can feel my head pound whenever I let myself acknowledge the facts. I can't believe I am thinking like this, as if it had been an affair and not a brutal attack. This is decidedly not fair to Marina, but I can't help it. Thoughts and feelings can't be changed, can they? If this is how I feel, then this is how I feel. How can I change how I feel? Maybe time will help. I don't know.

I know he liked her. Riley liked my wife. When we worked at the same station he talked about her a lot. And when we were narcs together, he mentioned her at least once or twice during every shift. He used to look at her with a sort of sparkle in his eye. My hawk-sense told me all of this at the time. But I chose to ignore it.

And then it stopped. He stopped talking about her, stopped coming over, stopped calling. At the time, I told myself it was because he was totally wrapped up in his wife's cancer. And then they moved to Seattle, or Portland, or wherever it was they moved. To be near Pam's family. But now that I think about it, I wonder. Did something happen between Riley and my wife? Something that changed how they felt about each other? Could they have fooled around and then it went sour. No! What am I thinking? Not Marina. She would never have an affair. She is too good, too shy. She wears her emotions on the surface. I would have known. I'm certain of it. My hawk-sense told me nothing of the sort.

Damn, I wish none of this were happening. What I keep saying to her is insensitive. But I mean it. I don't think she handled things well enough that night. We teach our self-defense students to immediately get into a fighting stance and yell – deep and powerfully and from the gut. The whole point of that is a first line of defense, because the goal is no rape. She knows this. She attended the course. And she even trained to be a volunteer instructor. If nothing else, her fighting stance reaction should have been muscle memory.

Why the hell did she freeze like a deer in headlights? Her intuition should have told her that the bathroom door wasn't supposed to be shut. She should have never opened that door! What the hell was she thinking? She should have at that point, turned her pretty body around and come down the stairs to get me. I would have checked it out and would have found him and would probably have shot him.

But I should have let a lot more time go by before bringing this up. A few more months at least. Maybe even a year, if I could have held it in that long. I talked at length about this with Nester a few days ago. He thinks I'm being too hard on her. He thinks she's a hero. He wants to bring her to the self-defense class as a guest speaker sometime when she's ready to talk about it. I told him I think it's a bad idea. A very bad idea. We're all about preventing rape, not getting raped and fighting back after the fact. Nester might push for this, but I will see to it she doesn't make herself some sort of anecdote. I can usually talk Marina out of things and I will certainly see to it that I talk her out of this.

I wonder what Dale would think. My urge to call her is making me crazy. Marina doesn't want me to, but I think it would be good for her to have her sister around. It would be good for me too. I'd really like to see her. We need help blowing away the dark cloud that has been hovering over this house, this marriage, for the past few months.

I think I'll do it. I'll call. To not do so would cause a physical pain like the pain of trying not to twitch forty-eight years ago. And, like the twitching, I'm not sure why I feel physically pained at the thought of not calling her. Twitching hasn't crossed my mind in God knows how long. Decades, at least. I know I should respect Marina's wishes and not call her sister. But I also know that I must make that call. If I don't, the walls will close in on me and I won't be strong enough to stop them.

PART TWO

May

THERE SEEMS TO BE ONE in every group. One on every team. One in every family. It is the annoyingly loud, obnoxious, know-it-all who dominates every conversation, who relishes the sound of their own voice, who jumps at every opportunity to share their knowledge with anyone within earshot. Marina, Dale and Leslie tried to focus on their own conversation, to no avail.

The three women were sitting at a picnic table on the patio of Jasper's Java Shop, the weather surprisingly pleasant for mid-May. Marina sipped her iced green tea, surreptitiously glancing at the entertaining group. With what she hoped were casual glances, she assembled the cast of characters in her mind. The most vocal was a young man wearing a cycling outfit. She christened him Loud Mouth. The expensive bike leaning patiently against the adjoining patio fence must be his. A young woman sat next to him along with an older woman and an elderly man. She dubbed the elderly man Mute Man, as he was the only one of the bunch not talking at full volume, not talking at all. If she were here with John, they might amuse themselves making up stories about them.

"Let's just move," said an exasperated Leslie, looking around for a table as far away from the gabbing gaggle. She pointed to the far corner, to a table closer to the curb.

"It's too close to the street." Dale replied, frustrated.

Leslie sighed and sat back down. "I guess you're right."

Dale took a sip of her chocolate-banana smoothie. She licked around the whipped cream with her tongue before taking several more long, slow sips. "We would just be trading one kind of noise for another."

Marina nodded in agreement.

It was a bright morning in May, early enough in the morning to soak in the abundant sunshine without it being overly hot or humid. The kind of morning that begs you to be outside, that promotes wellbeing. For the first time since the attack, Marina felt good being outside in the sun, her earlier desire for inky clouds, if not completely gone, has abated for now. And for the first time since the attack, she was feeling a little bit hopeful. Her talks with Mel have been encouraging. He has been an unexpected source of inspiration. She has been thanking Leslie every chance she gets for her involvement in Mel's regular visits. Marina has even started painting again. Her hand is surprisingly more functional than it was a month ago and she has gratefully abandoned the notion of teaching herself to be left-handed. Because of the injury her grip on the paintbrush is lighter, leaving her with a more casual, fluid line in her bird paintings, making them look almost surreal. While she was unsettled by the change at first, Marina is finding she likes the effect. Gets lost in it, a relief from everything swirling around her these days.

She still tires easily and sometimes swoons a bit when she stands up too quickly. Marina acquiesced to John a few weeks ago and went in to see the doctor, who gave her a thorough check-up. As for the dizziness, her blood pressure is a bit on the low side, but the doctor seemed unconcerned. He noted that her appetite seems irregular, a result of stress and trauma, and told her to take it easy when she stands up, especially if she has been sitting for a while. When the doctor asked about sex, she just shrugged and looked at the floor and told him they are trying.

How could she have told him that making love has becoming an exercise in futility? She and John have tried again two or three times since the big debacle. He responds now, after a while, usually with a lot of work on Marina's part. But then, when he is finally inside of her, her mind is hither and yon, on everything but the pleasure that she doesn't feel. She feels nothing. In fact, she has not had the urge to make love again, not since that first time.

The doctor prescribed multivitamins, eight hours of sleep each night, and a visit to a psychiatrist. She takes the vitamins every morning with her toasted English muffin, and has no trouble anymore getting eight hours of sleep. Lately she has been sleeping more than that. As for the psychiatrist, she is just not ready to rehash it, relive it. She doubts she ever will be. On her own however, she has been trying to get out more. She has started taking walks with Leslie a few days a week, usually when the van comes to pick up Mel. And on cool weekend mornings, she has started to try jogging a little bit with John.

Marina's attention was drawn back to Dale and Leslie's conversation. Or at least their attempts at conversation.

"These people are driving me crazy," Leslie said, keeping her voice as low as possible, not that Loud Mouth and his clan would even be aware enough to be offended. They were in their own world indeed, seemingly oblivious to Marina's threesome and all the other people sitting at the coffee shop's coveted outdoor tables. "I'm telling you, we should move." She started to get up but the table she'd had her eye on earlier was taken. "Maybe we should move inside."

Dale laughed, "You mean you are aren't interested in hearing more about so-and-so's divorce and the grandson's upcoming wedding?" She was waving her arms in mock exaggeration. Marina and Leslie started laughing. Dale smiled and took another sip of her drink. Turning toward Marina, she dropped a bomb. "I heard from John's mom."

The laughter suddenly stopped, all attention from their too-loud neighbors withdrawn.

Marina opened her mouth to speak, but the words were stuck and never made it out.

"I got an email from her last week," Dale cut Marina's attempt off. "She and what's-his-name are thinking about getting married." Marina looked at her sister, frozen in a contorted state of shock and disbelief. John apparently didn't even know his mother was seeing someone.

"Married? How did John and I not know this?" Marina's voice trailed upward into almost a squeak.

"Don't make something out of nothing, Mar." Dale was the only person in the world who has ever called her Mar. "She wanted my opinion, that's all."

"When was she planning to tell her son? Why didn't she want his opinion or my opinion for that matter?" The second the words were out Marina realized how ridiculous she sounded. She knew John's mother hated her. And because of that John has had little to do with his mother over the years. And for some reason she had taken a shine to Dale. They'd been close for years.

Leslie excused herself to get a second cappuccino. All the times they have been to this coffee shop together, whether morning, afternoon, or night, Leslie drinks one and then gets a second. Marina asked her once why she doesn't just get the next size up, which would sort of be the equivalent. Leslie said she always gets two. It is a quirk. Certain things are better in two's. This was one of those things.

"When was she planning to tell John, Dale?" There was a tone in Marina's voice that she immediately regretted. "I'm sorry. I just thought she would want to catch up her son before catching up her daughter-in-law's sister."

"No offense, but you two don't exactly have a good relationship, if you know what I mean." Dale looked at her hands. She took a big, loud slurp of her drink. They sat without speaking, Dale looking at the sky, Marina watching a sparrow hop around under their table. She broke off a piece of her scone and tossed it to the ground. The bird pounced on it then flew away with his treasure to some undisclosed, secret location just as Leslie returned with her drink.

"Did the two of you talk about," Marina waved her hand up and down in front of her body, "you know, all this?"

"Yes."

"You know, John called her right after it happened, and she never called him back. The bitch."

"Am I interrupting something?" Leslie stood a slight distance away, seeming afraid to come closer.

"No, we were just sitting here relishing the sound of Loud Mouth's voice." Marina attempted a smile.

"Mar, stop this." Dale turned to Leslie. "We were having a sisterly argument, but don't worry, you didn't interrupt anything."

Marina was silent. She had tried to tell John that having Dale visit might not be the panacea he was hoping for. But when he said he had called her sister anyway, she found herself a tiny bit hopeful that the visit would do them both good. Maybe they could begin to rekindle something lost a long time ago. Maybe they could have more than a surface level conversation, something they haven't really done since their father died. But now that Dale is here, Marina felt naïve for hoping things would be different. She had arrived two nights ago, unapologetically late and full of the Nation's Capital vitality. For Marina, it was an inauspicious start to a week of attempting to renew sisterly bonds.

Dale had said to expect her around five. Marina and John had gone shopping to get the olive tapenade that Dale loved. They picked up several nice bottles of wine and together started making John's celebrated manicotti. Marina's appetite continued to wax and wane, but she kept it to herself, not wanting to dampen John's enthusiasm. The appointed hour came and went. As did the next hour and the hour after that. There was really no way to get in touch with her, and by seven thirty, they were worried. She sauntered in just past eight thirty, bearing gifts of bread, wine, and good cheer, as though she had never said she would be there by five, as though everything was according to plan. John was sucked into her vortex of merriment. Marina was unamused and sat through the meal with clenched teeth.

The dinner conversation dragged on, as it usually did with Dale and wine. Most of it was about her job, her guy, her life. It was the kind of conversation you might have with an acquaintance you occasionally see at a dinner party, not the sister you were close to for most of your childhood. Marina said very little as Dale loquaciously told stories about the other two partners at her law firm, and the thirty-two-year-old musician she had recently met. She seemed particularly flattered by the interest of a man ten years her junior. Dale was tall and pretty with black, curly hair, strikingly white skin, a galaxy of freckles – all of it converging to make her look significantly younger than forty-two. With a series of apologies, Marina excused herself after the dishes were cleared, leaving John and Dale to continue the evening alone.

Now the three women sat silently, awkwardly sipping their smoothies and coffees and tea and listening to the drama from the next table.

"Listen, I could leave," Leslie said. "Honey, I'll see you later." She got up from her chair and started to collect her bag.

"No Leslie, please don't." Marina reached for her arm and pulled her back down into the chair. "You and my sister stay." She started to get up, but immediately felt light-headed and sat back down. She put her head down on the tabletop.

"What's wrong?" Leslie and Dale said, almost in unison.

"I don't know." She lifted her head slowly. "I guess I'm feeling a bit woozy." They looked at her with concerned, pitiful faces.

Marina cringed to be the object of pity. "I'll be fine." Their faces didn't change. "Ladies. Truly, I'm okay. My stomach has been a little funny lately. And I stood up too fast. My doctor specifically told me to stand up slowly. I didn't listen, obviously. Or maybe I'm getting the flu."

Putting her head back down to avoid their expressions, Marina found her mind wandering. Flu. *Influence.* One *flew* over the cuckoo's nest. Crazy. Cuckoo. Loco. Her mind wanders too much these days. She can't seem to focus on anything except painting. But is that really a problem? Who decides what are normal thoughts, feelings, or behaviors? Marina shook her head, trying to clear it and sat up.

Leslie and Dale sat quietly and watched her, Leslie not touching her treasured second coffee, and Dale turning to stare occasionally at Loud Mouth and his clan. Marina found herself grateful for their loudness, grateful for the distraction they un-knowingly provided. They sat listening as Loud Mouth complained about his mother and her apparently unacceptable and highly offensive independence in planning her own funeral arrangements. Loud Mouth, all of twenty-five or twenty-eight at the most, knows better of course. The two women, who encour-aged his indignation, second him in every particular; Mute Man said nothing.

"Well, what do you say ladies?" Dale broke the impasse. "Let's get Mar back home. I brought a case I need to read through, so I figure I'll sit under a shady tree while she rests."

"You two go. I'm going to walk home. It will do me good." Ma-rina didn't really think it would do her good, she was just not willing to spend another minute with Dale, and, unfair as it seemed, Leslie either. She was simply unwilling to be the object of scrutiny.

Marina took her napkin and dabbed at the beads of sweat that have started forming around her hairline. She broke the remain-der of her scone into small pieces and scattered them on the pavement beneath the table. Almost immediately she had grate-ful recipients.

Funny, but the elderly man in Loud Mouth's clan – Mute Man – had a voice after all. He began giving biking directions to Loud Mouth, apparently in response to a planned destination. Mute Man surprised her with his alacrity. Marina turned to get a bet-ter look at him. He was taller and fitter than she'd realized, with a full head of gray hair. She couldn't see his face, and wondered now if he was older than she originally thought. To her surprise,

Mute Man claimed the expensive bike and with little fanfare rode away, leaving the rest of the clan seemingly unanchored for the moment, based on their uncharacteristic silence. At least for now.

Watching the biker pedal away, envious of his ease of escape, Marina started to rise, reaching for her bag at the same time. But then she found that the sun was spinning around the earth and the table was spinning and the birds under the table were spinning and the people were spinning, their voices muddled and slow. *It must be the flu after all*, she thought. And then...darkness.

***

Marina was five when her grandfather, Poppy-G, died. On the eve of his funeral, she felt restless. Three times she'd asked her mother why she couldn't go to the funeral, and three times Mother had answered that a funeral was no place for little girls. Marina thought about this, in a manner known only to five-year-olds, and then returned to Mother with a declaration of love for Poppy-G, and when that didn't work, she waged an all-out war, complete with tears, screeching, a roll on the floor, and several iterations of head banging. If Mother was frustrated, she didn't show it. She simply scooped her up, sat her on her lap, and told her yet again that a funeral is no place for a little girl.

"But," Mother said, "I will tell you a secret." This, of course, piqued Marina's interest. "If you look out the window tomorrow morning, you will see Poppy-G's soul going up, up, up, all the way to heaven."

Marina's decided then and there that this would be a fine alternative to attending the funeral. She didn't really understand the words she was hearing Mother and Daddy talking about: die, death, deceased. Funeral was a new word too. She didn't even really know what a funeral was, she just knew she wanted to go, because everyone else she loved was going. She did know about heaven and souls though, because she went to Sunday school. And when she imagined what it would be like to see Poppy-G's soul going up, up, up, she imagined him waving as he passed the window. Not knowing better, Marina was excited and jumped off her mother's lap. She twirled around the kitchen floor, her blue dress floating up around like a ballerina's, her long red braids flopping up and down. Marina never did see her grandfather's soul go up, up, up. All she could recall is the blue dress, the twirling, and the intense happiness she felt to have been let in on the secret.

Her sister Lizzie's was the first actual funeral Marina attended. The whole thing – Lizzie's funeral – was mostly a blur, the blur that started the day Mother lay in a crumbled heap on the floor, the phone dangling from its cord. She had never seen her mother like this. She seemed paralyzed in that moment. *Mom? Mommy? Mom!* Marina crouched down beside her, shaking her gently. *Mom? What happened? What HAPPENED?* This is how her father found them.

The camp had called him at work, after calling Mother. His eyes were red and crazed. He lifted Marina up and held her tight. She pushed herself away and studied him, wishing someone would tell her what was going on. Dale, oblivious, came sauntering in saying something about an important tennis match with a very cute guy. Stopping at the scene in the kitchen.

"Lizzie was killed this morning," her father said, his words no more than a whisper.

Killed? The first image that popped into Marina's head was a gangster shooting. But Lizzie had been in a forest somewhere, at a camp for children. Okay then, a car accident. Not a shooting. Had to be a car accident.

"How?" That's what Dale said. "How?"

"A tree fell on her." Those were the last words Marina remembers her father saying for a long time.

The casket was miniscule. At thirteen, Lizzie had not gone through her growth spurt yet and was tiny, unlike Marina or Dale had been at that age, already taller than average. The casket was the same size as the bench they'd had on their front porch – Lizzie would often lay down on it to read a book, her head at one end, feet at the other, with room to spare. Mother had wanted to get a pink casket, but couldn't find anyone who sold pink, and so she bought a white one and painted little pink flowers all over it. How she could paint flowers on her own daughter's casket is something that Marina will never understand. It was, perhaps, her mother's last official act – that and getting rid of the bench – before her insides gradually turned to mush, never to recover.

The funeral service was a blur of Marina and Dale looking at the floor, then later, looking at the ground, not able to look at each other, not able to look at their parents who did nothing but sob in that wretched, uncontrollable way that grieving people do, taking deep screechy breaths, pausing for a long second and starting all over again. It would be years before Marina could fully comprehend the depth of their pain. She had never seen her father cry before that day. Dale sobbed in a similar way back at the house that night after all the guests left.

Marina's own sobs started and ended the morning of the funeral, when she woke up before the sun and stood at her window and waited for hours. Waited to see Lizzie's soul going up, up, up. Waited and waited. By then, she was too old to believe that she could see a soul ascending. And yet, she held tightly to a glimmer of enchanted hope that she would see something. Anything. If not Lizzie herself nodding and whispering her forgiveness, then a bird or a butterfly or a pink flower petal floating by. Some sign that she forgave her big sisters. Some sign that she forgave Marina, specifically. She believed with her entire being that it had been her fault that Lizzie had been walking in the path of an angry tree branch that fell on an unsuspecting and innocent girl at camp. Marina barely shed a tear during the funeral or after, a fact unobserved by parents too consumed by their own grief to notice anything within the world around them.

Mother's funeral four years later – almost to the day – was as gut wrenching as Lizzie's, maybe worse. Daddy wouldn't let go of the casket when it was time to lower it into the ground and had to be pried off by three of his colleagues. But that didn't stop the hysterics as he practically threw himself into the hole. The same three colleagues held him back until the last mound of dirt was released. They stayed with him night and day until they believed he was no longer a risk to himself. Looking back, Marina realized that she and Dale were of little help during those days. They tried. They organized the logistics of his life, attempted to distract and entertain him, without much success. Marina truly felt that she had lost her mother four years before. This latest funeral just made it official.

When Daddy died, Marina and Dale decided not to have a funeral. The family was decidedly small, with the few remaining distant relatives being just too distant for them to want to share in the grief. Daddy's colleagues – the very ones who were so supportive when their mother had died, scattered like cockroaches fleeing a sudden flick of the light switch when Daddy had his breakdown. It was as if they had never known him. His cremated remains are in a wood box that for several years rotated between Marina and Dale like an exchange of custody. These days the box resides in Marina's living room and will someday be sprinkled into the Long Island Sound from the bow of *Lizzie*.

Lately, Marina found herself wondering about Phil's funeral. Would his daughter eventually have one for him? As far as she knows, there was never anything for Phil's wife, Pam, who had died just a few weeks before Phil snapped. Marina wondered now, if it had not been for the rape, if she had not killed him, would she and John have attended his funeral? If he had died of something else, a heart attack or falling off a ladder fixing the roof, something ordinary, would they have jumped on a plane and headed to the West Coast? Yes, probably. Yes. Even though the four of them had understandably drifted apart. John would have wanted to go. Phil had been his partner after all.

***

The attending doctor in the emergency room had been very kind. One minute Marina was at a coffee shop with Dale and Leslie, and the next minute she was in the back of an ambulance, Leslie hysterical and Dale yelling at her to be quiet. The doctor had ordered a battery of blood tests. John arrived, his face pale, panic in his eyes. He had calmed down once he saw Marina, sitting up and drinking juice.

"Mrs. Butterfield. Mr. Butterfield. I have some difficult news." He handed Marina the test results, the fact of her pregnancy described in no uncertain terms by hormones and chemical markers. He mumbled that he remembered Marina and John from the night she was brought in as a rape victim. He said he was sorry, his face somber as he put in Marina's shaking hand a card with the phone number of a nearby abortion clinic. John's face was streaked with tears.

***

Marina shivered, a thin, paper gown cloaking her against the blowing air conditioner and serving as the last remaining cloak around her rapidly dwindling dignity. It was only two days since her ambulance ride and visit to the emergency room, yet it felt like a lifetime. She was sitting on an exam table in a small women's health center across town. John sat in the only chair as the young man in the white coat explained the procedure. Was he even a real doctor? Marina couldn't be sure.

"Can I keep the remains?"

John made a sudden choking sound as the man in the white coat looked uncertainly between the two of them. She turned to see an unfamiliar expression on John's face, one of sheer disbelief. It was an expression of complete incomprehension, a total rejection of Marina's question.

The man in the white coat sort of nodded and then resumed his professional demeanor, telling her to relax and he would be back in a few minutes to get things started. Marina wondered if he knew the circumstances, did he know who she is, who John is? Perhaps to him they are just a middle-aged couple that doesn't want a baby. Marina tried to imagine what, to the man in the white coat, she and John must look like: a forty-something year old woman and her husband, sitting in an abortion clinic, seeking a termination at almost sixteen weeks, expressions of relief and guilt and weariness on their faces. But now John's teeth were clenched so tight that there was a visible bulge under each cheek. He was looking straight ahead, not at her, not at the wall, but far beyond it.

Marina swung her legs over the edge of the table and stepped down onto the cold floor. She turned to look at John steadily for a moment, then untied her gown and disappeared behind a flimsy curtain separating the tiny changing area from the rest of the room. Her clothes were neatly hanging from a hook on the wall and she began dressing. She was stepping into her panties when John jerked the curtain back and stood watching her, confusion and disbelief all over his face.

"Do you mind telling me what you're doing?"

"Getting dressed. What does it look like I'm doing?" She turned away from him and reached for her bra. She put it on and fumbled with the hook, then reached for her jeans and her yellow tee shirt.

"I can see that you're getting dressed." He was now behind the curtain with her. He yanked the yellow tee shirt out of her hand and picked up the gown, which Marina had crumbled and thrown on the floor. "Put this back on." He tossed it at her.

They stood looking at each other, neither moving, neither conceding, neither willing to budge. A knock on the door broke the impasse. John stepped outside the curtain, closing it behind him as he opened the exam room door.

Marina took her time and emerged from the changing area fully dressed, her hair – previously piled high on her head as to not be in the way during the procedure – was brushed, falling in sheets well beyond her shoulders, held away from her face by an unobtrusive plain, black headband. John was leaning against the wall and the man in the white coat stood awkwardly in the middle of the room, familiar with patient doubts.

"I'm not so sure about this," she said. "I just want to go home and think about it." Everything had happened so fast.

"Have you lost your mind?" John's face reddened. "Please, let's just get this over with." His ruffled, almost crazed demeanor lost any semblance of the collectedness he is known for.

"Excuse me," the man in the white coat extended his arm in front of John as if halting traffic, "Mrs. Butterfield, you don't have much time." He moved closer to her. "I don't know your circumstances, nor is any of that important to me." He paused for a long moment, looking calmly into her eyes. "It's ultimately your choice, but if you decide you want to abort, at almost sixteen weeks," he looked at her chart, "you have days. Just days."

"I'm just going to go home and think about this," she said firmly, turning to walk out of the room. She didn't close the door behind her and heard John tell the man in the white coat that she had been raped. She didn't need to see the look on the man's face to guess at his response.

***

They drove home in silence. On the ride to the women's health center, they had been cautiously upbeat. On Marina's end it had been forced, but it at least it took some of the edge off. Now John pulled around to the back of the house but didn't put the car in the garage. He got out and went into the house alone. The hot afternoon air swallowed up the sound of the screen door he let slam behind him. Marina sat in the car, expecting Dale to come running out of the house.

She imaged John heading straight for the basement, saying nothing as he blew by whoever might happen to be sitting in the kitchen, then storming down the stairs, taking great care to make a lot of noise as he went. He has not yelled, not yet. It's coming though; she could feel it. He is naturally soft spoken, which goes against the stereotypical loud mouth cop. Most people, when meeting him for the first time, are surprised when he tells them his chosen profession. Rarely does John raise his voice. But when he does, people know he means business. Normally, his tone and way of speaking suggest nothing but a big, kind, pussycat. When he is angry or unhappy the first thing that happens is he gets quiet. The yelling would come later. How much later, in this case, she was unsure.

The door slammed again, and Marina looked up to see John walking past the car on his way deep into the yard. She got out and leaned against the hood, listening to him rumble around in the shed. He emerged with several bags of birdseed and made his way to the feeders. It had been a few days since they were last filled and were completely empty. He had filled them, when? The day Dale arrived, the day before she passed out at the coffee shop. How many days since then? She'd had lost track.

Marina walked over to the edge of the patio and removed two of the smaller feeders from one of four shepherd's crooks. Opening the lid, she held them out to John, one in each hand. He carefully poured the choice songbird mix into the feeders. As she replaced the lids and hung them back up, John moved onto the other six feeders, filling them with different mixes – sunflower, thistle, and for the bluebird, a special pre-husked no-waste blend.

"John, we need to talk." She followed him onto the patio.

"No, we don't need to talk," his tone was cold in reply, as he put the bags of birdseed onto the flagstones. "You need to talk." He looked at her – eyeball to eyeball, not blinking. "You need to tell me what this is all about."

"I don't understand your reaction, John. Why are you so angry at me?"

"I'm not supposed to be angry? This could have been over by now. We'd be celebrating."

"I just need time to think." Celebrating? Not in a million years.

"Think about what?" Now his voice grew louder. "You were raped, Marina. This should be a no brainer. I don't even understand why this happened. I thought they took care of this when you were in the hospital."

Marina shook her head. "I guess with the surgery for my hand and my age, it got overlooked."

John's hand shook as he filled one of the feeders. "Is this some sort of leftover guilt that you have? I know you told Rosen you feel responsible, but we have been through that already."

Marina sat down wearily on a patio chair. "I know we have been over it, but John, this man was once your partner. He was our friend. And I killed him!"

John grabbed her by the shoulders, almost hurting her. "That was not Phil. You killed the man that raped you but that was not the man I knew. The man I knew would never have raped my wife." This last came out in almost a whisper as John hung his head. "I wish I could have killed him for you."

"No John, I don't wish that," she gasped, closing her eyes at the thought.

"I am sorry," John released her shoulders, letting his arms fall. "I just don't understand why you didn't fix this problem, today, as soon as possible."

"Please, it's hard to explain," she said, reaching for his hands. He let her take them. "I'm not saying I won't have the abortion. I just need a minute to catch my breath and think about everything."

"That's just it," he said, twisting his arms so that her hands loosened and fell away from his. "There shouldn't be anything to think about." He stood up. "You never needed a minute to catch your breath and wave off the idea of having kids with me."

"That's not fair."

"No? You tell me. What's not fair about it? It's true. You brushed off my desire for a family every foot of the way." He stared at her for a long moment. Then he picked up the birdseed and walked stiffly back to the shed.

Behind her, Marina heard the back door open and turned to see Dale opening the door with a tray balanced on one hand. She came out and set the tray on the patio table.

"I thought we would have a toast," Dale said, pointing to an ice bucket with a bottle of bubbly sticking out. Next to it were five flutes. John walked right past her without looking up, shaking his head and disappearing silently into the house. Marina slumped down in her chair while Dale looked wonderingly between the darkened back door and her sister's despairing face.

"I didn't do it. I didn't have the abortion."

"What?" Dale inched closer to Marina, as though she wasn't sure of what she was hearing.

"Dale, I don't know. I was undressed, on the table. I'd had the sonogram, which I refused to look at, and signed all the forms. I was pretty much ready to go." She lifted the bottle out of the ice bucket and looked at it, considering. It didn't matter; she planned on having the abortion, just not today. She may as well have some champagne. She twisted the thin metal wire that formed a cage over the cork. She removed the cage and very slowly, very deliberately worked the cork back and forth until it was almost out. She rocked the cork back and forth, waiting for the moment when she knew the pop and spew of foam was imminent. Here it is. She tilted the bottle away from her and gave the cork a gentle nudge. Here it is. The cork launched and landed somewhere in a pile of overgrown flora and Marina caught the bubbly effusion in the two ready glasses. She raised her glass.

"Um, I'm not sure anymore what we're toasting," Dale said as she raised her own glass and lightly touched it to the side of Marina's.

"I'm not sure either. To recovery, I guess." She smiled.

"Now I think you're in denial."

"Maybe I am. I know I need to do this thing," she waved her arm around her belly. "It's just, well, it was awful, sitting in the waiting room and seeing all those kids, some of them reminded me of us when we were in college. Younger even." Marina remembered sitting there thinking that she could have been any one of those girls' mother. And then they were all led to a room – a holding pen, of sorts, and they all just sat there. Waiting. No one talked. No one looked at anyone else. Their names were called, one by one.

Dale watched her, quietly, obviously unsure what to say next.

"Mar, about John's mother," Dale began as she took the chair across from Marina, tucking her bare, freshly pedicured feet beneath herself as she sat down.

"I haven't had time to process that." Marina looked at her own sandal-clad feet, her horrible toenails, her dry, cracked heels.

"But I'm glad you're here," she took a deep breath, "and I'm glad John's mother found someone to make her happy."

"I'm glad I'm here too," Dale said, smiling just a little. "I'm staying for a few weeks, by the way."

"What about work?"

"The earth will keep turning."

"What about your guy, this guitar man you told us about?"

"I've been single most of my adult life. What's a few more weeks? Plus, it will make for a nice reunion." She took a long, slow sip of her champagne. "What's with John?"

"He's beyond upset that I walked out of there." She held her glass up to the sun and watched the bubbles shoot up toward the top of the glass. "He doesn't understand why there should be any thought, any discussion at all." She put her lips to the glass, took a tiny sip, and set it down.

"Marina, I'm your sister. I promise not to judge you. But I must admit that I'm a little surprised you're sitting here with that asshole's embryo inside of you."

"When you put it like that, it sounds awful."

"It is awful!" Dale gulped the rest of her champagne and poured herself another glass. "I mean, not that you walked out of there. The whole thing is awful. The whole, damned thing!"

"I just wish I hadn't killed him, Dale," Marina replied, her voice quiet.

Dale paused, visibly struggling to calm down. "Last year I defended a guy who accidentally backed his car out of the driveway into a young woman on a bicycle. She died. Totally destroyed him. It was an accident and she was a stranger, but he was still devastated. And I know you didn't intend to kill him but let's keep it in perspective. You were fighting for your life."

Marina was frustrated now, always having to explain. "You don't understand. That's not the part that bugs me, Dale. I looked at him after he went down and he was still alive. Then I ran out of there. I ran out! I could have at least dialed 911."

"You were in fight or flight mode. You weren't thinking clearly. Plus, if I understand it correctly, within minutes of you running to John this place was swarming with police and paramedics."

"They needed to be called sooner, even if only seconds sooner." She closed her eyes and tilted her head back, letting the warm sun hold her like a baby. She snapped back, wide eyed. "You know, I'm getting tired of everyone telling me that I wasn't thinking clearly! Dale, at that point, I was thinking very clearly. You should have seen him lying there. He was looking at me for God's sake. Pleading with his eyes. Like a panic-stricken child!"

"Wait." Dale said slowly, her lawyer's mind beginning to focus. "For the sake of argument, let's say you were thinking clearly. Are you saying that in the moment you saw him lying there, you made the decision not to call 911? You made the decision to walk away from your rapist, a man who had used a gun, threatened your life, and violated you?"

Marina sat silently, staring into the yard.

"Is it because you knew him? Is that what makes it harder?"

"No! Even a stranger doesn't deserve to die that way."

Dale went white around her mouth, her lips pressing tighter. Then she leaned toward Marina, leaving very little space between them. "What about you? Stranger or not, he didn't care about the panic-stricken look in your eyes when he pinned you down at gunpoint."

Marina clenched her teeth and leaned back in her chair, widening the chasm. "You weren't there. Plus, if anyone should have even an inkling of what I might be feeling, it's you."

"No, I wasn't there Marina. But your remorse for your rapist is very confusing." Her eyes were red around the edges, her cheeks flushed. "You are now pregnant by the bastard and you aren't immediately having an abortion? Are you insane?" She shook her head. "You know, a moment ago I wanted to understand you. But now, I am not sure I do." Her eyes glistening with tears, Dale rose from her chair. She picked up the empty bottle and got up. She turned toward the house without a backward glance.

"Hey! Why all these glasses?" Marina was willing to latch onto anything to get her sister to return and she knew that asking her outright, at a moment like this, would have the opposite effect. She was not the least bit surprised that Dale ignored the rest of what she said. She wished she hadn't said it and with any luck, Dale would forget she said it and they'd move on.

"Shit. I invited Leslie and Mel to have a toast with us." She held up the empty bottle. "You got anything else in the house?"

"Yeah, there's a bottle of scotch on top of the fridge. *The Famous Grouse*. Bring that out."

A few birds begin to arrive, exploring the refilled feeders as the afternoon waned into twilight. Marina watched them argue and shuffle for position, feathers ruffling and trills echoing across the lawn. She watched them for a long time. Long after she, Leslie, Mel, and Dale emptied *The Famous Grouse*. John never came out to join them.

CHAPTER 2

Hawk

I AM A TINKERER. I'm handy with just about everything and in my quiet moments, I love nothing more than shaping a piece of wood, fitting things together, fixing things. I am particularly proud of what I have done with our old house – from remodeling the kitchen, to building Marina a sunroom for her orchids and winter bird watching.

I am a tinkerer, even when it comes to my wife. Broken isn't the right word for what she is right now, but in some ways, it's spot on. And I can't help but tinker. She told our attorney, Janet Rosen that she feels guilty for killing Riley, a completely illogical response to the events as they occurred. This is outrageous. Once she applied that perfect elbow strike, he was done. It was a thing of beauty, really.

But all my tinkering seems to have missed the mark. She still got up and walked out of that abortion clinic. Who in their right mind does that kind of thing? My wife, that's who. My wife, a bleeding heart who is feeling guilty over a guy's death – a guy who deserved to die. Every time she mentions her guilt, I imagine her naked bleeding body, bending over Phil on the floor of our bedroom, giving him CPR, trying to save him. Is that what she wished had happened?

I can't seem to fix this. And it's frustrating me beyond belief. I've been spending more and more time at the damn boatyard. I hadn't planned on spending so much time here but I keep thinking that if I get it repaired quick enough I could launch it and sail off into the sunset. Leave these feelings behind. Never mind that I hate boats, that I essentially hate the water, and that I don't know the first thing about sailing. I just want this horrific nightmare to be over.

I want things to be back to normal. I know that's selfish and I feel bad about it. I feel bad that I wanted Dale to come, that I look forward to seeing her when I get off work. We've had some fun the past few days. She is so lively, so unlike Marina. I've wanted desperately to have some friends over, maybe throw steaks on the grill, something we used to do all the time. There is something ethereal about standing at the grill on a warm evening, cold beer in hand and the sound of a sizzling steak. Nothing like it in the world. But Marina keeps telling me she's not up to it, maybe later in the summer.

I just can't believe that Marina doesn't want our lives to be back to normal as badly as I do. I can't believe that she left the abortion clinic. She was on the table and casually got up, got dressed and walked out. Like a woman possessed by something unnatural. She was too calm, too collected. How could she do this to us?

*　*　*

I finally had enough of my own petulant behavior last night and went out to the patio to grab Marina for a late dinner. She was watching the birds, what else would she be doing. I don't even want to try and analyze what she might have been thinking. I just went out there, held my breath, and said we'd talk about it later.

She barely touched her food and went up to bed as soon as the meal was over. I like washing dishes and that's what I was doing while Dale companionably cleared the table, rambling on about nothing.

"You wanna sit outside for a bit?"

"Sure," Dale smiled and followed me out, taking the seat next to mine. It was sticky outside, under a hazy sky with a fuzzy halo around the moon, but as the night cooled a breeze replaced the stickiness, a perfect late spring evening. Dale pulled her hair out of her clip, letting the long, dark tresses down to blow in the night air.

"I am glad you came to visit, Dale. I am sorry about all this, you know, drama."

"Me too. It can't be easy to deal with this all on your own. Marina isn't the only one hurting right now. I mean, the guy was your friend, your partner after all. Now you have all this pain, all this betrayal. I don't know how anyone is supposed to deal with that."

I must say I was taken aback at the sudden relief I felt after hearing her thoughts, like maybe I'm not such a jerk to be feeling so raw, so angry all the time. I sat for a long time not saying a thing.

"You just have to give Mar time. I know she's acting oddly, but she's always processed things in her own way, on her own terms." Dale's voice pierced my silence.

"I know. I just want this nightmare to be over. I feel like an ass saying that but it's true."

"You are not an ass. I am sure its normal to feel that way. How is anyone supposed to deal with this and not wish that they didn't have to?"

I went silent again, just glad for once not to feel in the driver's seat of a car with no windows, no way to see the road. I relished this, basked in it, for just a minute. Releasing just a tiny bit of the pain felt indescribable.

In that moment, Dale leaned closer and patted me on the knee, sending a sudden shock wave through my body. I was transfixed. Until she stood up.

"Good night, John."

"Good night, Dale."

CHAPTER 3

May

MARINA AND DALE SAT in silence over their breakfast, Dale drinking her black coffee and nibbling her fruit, Marina sipping her tea over the morning paper, looking at the comics. Avoiding each other's eyes. Avoiding conversation that might lead to more terse words. It was their pattern from childhood, occurring whenever one was frustrated with the other, yet unwilling to leave the room or move onto another topic. As children, the silence lasted two or three minutes, tops, and then one, usually Dale, would display the telltale signs of laughter about to erupt, would try very hard to hold it in, and would spew chortles that echoed and bounced and filled whatever space they happened to be occupying at the time. Soon they would both be laughing. When they finally came up for air, the original impasse would seem less important. But Marina wasn't sure when this impasse would be broken, what could possibly lead them to laughter under these circumstances.

John appeared in his old jeans and t-shirt, pulling a travel mug from the cupboard and pouring himself a cup of coffee. Marina looked up, surprised.

"I am going to the boat," John replied to her unasked question, in a tone that suggested no argument. As if he knew his tone was harsh and wanted to make amends, he went to Marina's chair and kissed the top of her head. She reached up and took his hand lightly, giving it a little squeeze. The little motions of marriage, the messages of reassurance that have helped them navigate choppy waters in the past.

"Don't forget, Leslie and Mel are coming for dinner. You'll be back by then, right?" Dale asked, then continued without waiting for an answer. "We're sitting down at seven so there will be plenty of time before the fireworks." She arched her eyebrow when she mentioned the fireworks, sounding a little like a teenager.

"Aye-aye, mate." Smiling, John saluted and disappeared into the rear garage. Marina never understood John's building a separate garage in the back of their house – the one in front was perfect in size and function. But, it was nice having a separate place to keep birdseed, tools, and John's truck. A moment later Marina heard the gravel of the rear driveway crunching under the truck's tires. He seemed to be in a better mood and wondered what he and Dale may have talked about last night, after she had gone up to bed.

"I still don't get the whole fireworks in May thing, but, hey, whatever. It's New Jersey. Anything goes, right?" Dale said this mostly to herself.

After breakfast, by unspoken consent, they both moved to the sunroom. Dale opened her briefcase and pulled out a fat file of papers and a legal pad, settling in to do whatever it is that lawyers do with fat files of papers and legal pads. Marina moved to her small table by the window and opened her travel watercolor set. In the good morning light, she worked on small, abstract patterns, working her arm, stretching the tendons and exploring the effect on her technique. While she worked, she thought about their silences, how over the years each silence seemed to last longer. Then, when Dale turned eighteen, they began a silence that would last years. One that outlasted Marina's wildest expectations of how long two sisters could try to out stubborn each other.

The morning moved languidly on, and the two women worked in their own domains, until Dale finally sat back and stretched her arms up over her head.

"Wow, I'm tired," she said, yawning, and leaned back into the sofa. She pushed her legal pad to the cushion next to her and yawned again, pulling her feet up under her and lacing her hands behind her head. Her eyelids closed, as though just for a moment, but Marina recognized the faint shadows under the lashes. She counted the breaths; watched the eyelids flutter open and close again. Just like John's, just like when he falls asleep in front of the TV in the basement. The basement.

Marina shook her head, banishing the memory and returned to her watercolors. She tried to concentrate, tried to focus her mind on the brush strokes, but her hand trembled. Maybe she was overdoing it, over-taxing the injury. The colors started to bleed into one another, dark blackbirds swirling slowly into blue sky, spreading dark clouds across the page.

* * *

When Marina and Dale were children, their mother loved to sing, and made up silly songs for almost any weather occasion. She had little songs for spring, boisterous ones for thunderstorms; any sort of season could inspire her. Her favorite was one she had learned from her own mother, a song and dance for the full moon. From the time the girls were very young, Mother would grab them by the hands, run outside, and dance around the yard, singing and laughing, every time there was a full moon. As Marina and Dale grew into their teen years they began to look with disdain on these odd antics. But when Lizzie was old enough to participate, she loved it so much that her joy swept the older girls right back in.

Mother stopped singing the songs after Lizzie died, her eccentricities buried along with her youngest daughter. Three or four years later, when Marina had almost finished college and Dale had just started, and they were both home for the weekend, an October hurricane was headed up the coast, chasing away the few tourists and closing most of the businesses. The authorities had recommended an evacuation, the police even came by, but the wild weather seemed to have invigorated something long dormant in their family, and they decided to stay put.

Even as the winds picked up and the power flickered, there was a warmth in the house for the first time in years. The power went out finally, but in the light of the candles Mother seemed to forget and let her old self shine through. She remembered a hurricane song and insisted everyone join her outside, the night filled with the winds of the storm, still off shore, and they danced and sang, their father looking on in surprised delight.

Back in the house Daddy started a fire and opened a dusty bottle of wine – giving some even to Dale despite her age. In the glow of the flames and warmth of the evening, stories began to flow, safe ones at first. Then Dale, having had more to drink than her eighteen-year-old body could handle, let spill out of her mouth all in one long, softly spoken sentence, that if only she and Marina hadn't told Lizzie that there was a buried treasure in the woods at the camp, explaining in great detail where it could be found – all fiction, of course, but Lizzie was too young and naïve to pick up on the fact that her big sisters were playing a prank, a harmless prank, one that Dale started and Marina encouraged and embellished. It was Marina who made the treasure seem dazzling, something that Lizzie just had to find, had to bring home to the family. If it wasn't for the lure of the buried treasure, Lizzie would never have wandered off in search of it on her last day at camp. She never would have been in the path of that falling tree branch. If Marina could have erased herself from existence in that moment, she would have done it. Their parents' shocked silence swallowed the warmth and the last of their family's songs.

Marina had buried their crime so deep in the magma of their beings, she had falsely thought it might be burned up. Forever gone. But that night she learned that forever is a myth. Things buried can resurface. Or get washed up by violent tides – especially if they are not buried deep enough.

Marina and Dale barely spoke for the next seven or eight years. They communicated as necessary, watching their mother die, then caring for their father until he too passed away. When the silence finally broke, the topic of the storm, buried treasure, the ruined lives, never came up. If they had avoided talking about Lizzie before, after that night it was as if she never lived, as if they never had a sister.

* * *

Blinking back tears, Marina put down her brush and looked out the window. She needed to focus, to right the ship. A brown-headed cowbird was at the feeder, stuffing his crop. When the cowbirds first arrived several years ago, she found them quite annoying, and, in that rare instance when a bird can be ugly, well, she found them ugly. But they have endeared themselves to her. Just a bit larger than a sparrow, they have a black body that merges into a brown head – they almost look like they have hair, rather than feathers, making them look like winged horses. This little bird, five minutes later, was still stuffing his crop. She watched him finally fly off.

Thinking of dinner, Marina got up quietly and went into the kitchen. Dale had promised to whip up her famous pasta and peas dish, but she insisted the recipe only works with fresh peas and Parmigiano-Reggiano cheese. They had talked earlier about going over to the corner market, which was one of the only grocery stores in the area to carry the best cheese. Now that Dale was hard asleep, Marina wasn't sure what she should do. Despite its moniker, the corner market was clear across town and besides, Marina wasn't entirely sure of the recipe. Restless with indecision she prowled through the house, glancing at the mail, flipping through the pages of a magazine. Finally, exasperated with herself, she grabbed the keys, left a note for Dale and headed out of the house.

She decided she would just get some good steaks. Dale could cook another night. John had been wanting to cook out on the grill, and *Fireworks in May* night is the perfect night for steaks. Surprisingly, she wasn't nauseous or dizzy or even particularly tired today. She felt stronger than usual. The market wasn't busy, and she moved breezily through the aisles, picking out the steaks, fresh bread from the bakery, a few tomatoes for the salad. She spotted a beautiful looking fruit tart in the dessert case at the back of the store and decided to buy it, imagining the delight it would inspire when unveiled.

Loading the groceries in the car, satisfied and pleased with her purchases and her plan for the evening, Marina suddenly gained clarity about the abortion. She would do it. Soon. She felt relieved, comfortable in her own skin for the first time in weeks, months really. She would tell John tonight. Her newfound decisiveness inspired her to call her mother-in-law and made a mental note to do that as soon as she got back home.

Once home, she tossed the bags onto the kitchen table and made good on her promise to herself to call John's mother. When the unanswered rings rolled over to the answering machine, Marina started to hang up, then spoke, *Hi Pearl. It's Marina, John's wife. We were thinking of having you up to the house sometime this summer. Call us back.* She hung up wondering if John would be pissed. She didn't care. She peeked around the corner to see if Dale was awake. She was, but only just, rubbing her temples. Marina took the five steaks out of their packaging and placed them in a Pyrex dish for marinating.

"I think I fell asleep in there." Dale appeared in the kitchen, disheveled with *Roseanne Roseannadana* hair. As if aware of this phenomenon, she took an elastic hair band off her wrist and made a ponytail that, to Marina's chagrin, looked chic and elegant, like she'd spent hours at the hands of a master hairstylist. "What time is it?"

"It's too late to go running around town for the ingredients for your dinner. If we leave now, we'll get stuck in commuter traffic on the way back."

"Damn. I'm sorry." She gave and apologetic shrug and looked away.

"It's okay." When Dale looked up, Marina looked at her steadily, ending this episode of silence, her newfound strength spilling out into the kitchen. "Really, it's ok."

Dale quirked an eyebrow at her, then asked, "So what did you decide to make?"

"I got some steaks to grill." She pointed to the slabs of juicy flesh and the note she had scribbled earlier.

"I owe you one."

"No, you don't. Look, you'll make up for it another day while you're here. Perhaps as a post abortion celebration. Minus the champagne, of course."

"So, you are going to do it." Dale leaned forward and steadied herself on the counter with her elbows. "Are you sure?"

"Yes."

Dale stood up straight and walked around to the other side of the counter where Marina was standing and gave her a hug. Marina hesitated for a second and then wrapped her arms around her sister and hugged her back.

"Yes," Marina repeated into her sister's shoulder, "I'm sure.

CHAPTER 4

Hawk

I LIKE TO THINK OF MYSELF as a virtuous man. Not a religious man, by any stretch. I'm basically pleased with how I've lived. Yes, I have been tempted at one time or another, but I have never strayed. I am a man of my word who takes his word, and his handshake very seriously. People trust me. As a cop, trust is essential. I like to think of myself as a loving and devoted husband, loyal friend, dedicated cop.

I know I had been looking forward to Dale's visit, eagerly even. I have always known that anything I ever felt for her was completely one sided, mine alone. Buried after I married her sister. Still, I always looked forward to seeing her, maybe too much, I will admit. Feelings I neither understand nor condone. I have lived my entire adult life, my entire marriage to Marina as straight as an arrow.

I used to think I had a bit of a sixth sense. I had a knack of predicting what people might do before they did it. The other cops call me Hawk. But, I never saw it coming when Dale put her hand on my knee last night, when she looked into my eyes like that. Nope, I never saw it coming. All my feelings for her, suppressed and buried, exploded to the surface.

Ironically, I feel better when I'm working on the boat. I tend to forget, if only for a little while, the trials of daily life – tiptoeing around my house, pretending everything is okay, walking on the proverbial eggs shells, trying to puzzle out what my wife needs. I'm grateful to have the boat as an excuse to be away from Marina. But I still hate the damn boat. I hate it with a passion. I don't know what we're going to do with it once it's fixed.

Marina has made noise in the past about actually using it, sailing it around Long Island Sound. She even suggested taking the boat south, like to DC or Charleston or some other such place by way of the Intercostal Waterway. Maybe when I retire. Which, if I can help it, won't be anytime soon. I need the distraction of work, now more than ever. I just basically smile and nod when she says these things. She is convinced that doing this – fixing the boat, sailing it around the Sound especially, would pay some sort of homage to her parents and little sister.

I know Marina has always viewed herself as responsible for her little sister's death, and in turn, the subsequent deaths of her parents. She can't see it but I suspect her father was the stable one in the bunch. Her mother had been a nut from the beginning, but her father only snapped after the impact of his daughter's death and the implosion of his wife. I fear Marina may have inherited her mother's tendencies. I fear very deeply what this rape and now the pregnancy is going to do to her. The sooner she goes back to that clinic and takes care of things, the better.

Sometimes I wish Marina were more like Dale. I know Dale must carry the same guilt, the same sense of responsibility for Lizzie's death. But she always has been the more realistic of the two. She knows it wasn't specifically her fault. Accidents happen. Plus, Dale is not a mourner. She bounces back. Moves on. Perhaps she has all this stuff buried deep inside her and it will bubble up to the surface when she and the rest of the world least expect it, but honestly, I don't think so. Dale is practical. I can't imagine hidden pain buried deep inside her.

I feel better when I'm at the boat and today was no exception. The gravel and rocks and crushed shells grinding and crackling under my feet as I walked through the boatyard gave me a sort of warm feeling on the inside. Like a premonition that everything will eventually get back to normal and everything will be okay.

I'm not going to harangue Marina about the abortion. I'll give her another couple of days before asking about it and I'll make sure I ask in a very gentle way. Oh, and as far as my feelings for Dale, well, I'm going to put that inside a box and put the box on a high shelf. She'll be gone soon enough anyway.

CHAPTER 5

May

ON THE EVENING OF *Fireworks in May*, Marina, John, Dale, Leslie, and Mel sat around the colorful mosaic table on the patio. A curtain of citronella smoke from the torches that lined the patio perimeter created a festive tableau. The air was humid, and everything Marina touched seemed sticky – her wine glass, the table itself, the food, her skin. She was replete with food. The day left her with a ravenous appetite. It was as if all of her senses had been opened and she tasted her steak with a heightened awareness of its tenderness and could feel every fiber of the animal's flesh. She looked forward to the fruit tart that awaited in the kitchen.

Leaning back in her chair she stretched, listening lazily to the conversation around her and studied the sky. The colors were gloomy, almost damp looking, with a hint of a bright smile, a Cheshire smile, the sun dipping toward the horizon. If Marina were to critique the effect, she would have to say it is the pallet of an inexperienced painter, using watercolors for the first time, not quite sure of the medium's blending properties or even which colors to try and blend. The result: a botched attempt at the beginnings of a lame sunset – blue, red, white, and a little green. Then mixed too much, wiped away, more color added, wiped away again, and finally a dab of water smoothed out with a fingertip.

John got up and started around the table, picking up plates, stacking them one on top of the other, then gathering all the utensils and piling them on the topmost plate. Marina turned away from her artistic reverie and fell into a mild professional discussion with Mel about a botany paper he was considering submitting for a grant. It seemed that every time she talked to Mel, more pieces of the man he was meant to be fell into place. She was in awe of how a veil of depression, even a thin one, robs a person of their true self. How long had Mel been depressed? According to Leslie, forever. Although she didn't realize it when they'd met. Leslie just thought Mel was Mel. And she loved him anyway. The irony is cruel in that it took an impulsive and drastic attempt at ending the pain – jumping in front of a moving train, albeit a slow-moving train, then changing his mind, tripping on a rock, rolling halfway down an embankment, and basically severing the spine in his neck. Had it not been for the pair of joggers who saw the whole thing, Mel likely would not have survived into the next day.

Marina tried to focus on Mel's ideas for his paper, but found it hard – the draw of John's face as he cleared the table had her transfixed, as if she were seeing her husband for the first time. The color of his skin was hard to describe – not quite dark, not quite light, yet nowhere in the middle. When he was happy, the amber specks in his green eyes sparkled like fireflies. Marina stared at him, finding herself studying him as she had studied the sky just a few minutes before. A critique but not a test. His face has changed of course, from when she first met him. His life as a cop changed him over the years, the wearing of the confining mask, the seriousness of his work. She always liked John's face best without the mask – softer, more fluid, just like it is right now.

Breaking off from her reverie and suddenly remembering her guests, Marina announced, "I have a lovely fruit tart in the kitchen. What do you say we go inside and have some?"

"What time do the fireworks start?" asked Dale, turning from her conversation with Leslie.

John looked up at the sky, which was rapidly darkening. "Soon, but we still have time for dessert."

By the time everyone made their way into the kitchen it smelled of freshly ground coffee. John pushed the button on the coffee maker and muttered an apology that the coffee wasn't ready. Marina simply blew him a kiss. He smiled and blew one back. The two of them have been trying on their affectionate selves. When he got home she told him of her decision. He took her hand, but didn't say anything, for once letting her have her space.

As she unwrapped the dessert, John's pager went off. He went into the study to make the call. Marina heard the screen door to the front porch open and a second later, close behind Dale, who had walked out at around the same time John's pager went off. Leslie ogled the fruit tart, as if it was an ancient sculpture on display in a museum.

For the first time this evening, the guarded, superficial nature of the conversation began to irk her. This is how it had been all evening, talking about random nothingness just to fill space. And if enough space is filled with enough nothingness, then the touchy subjects have nowhere to go. Sure, they can try to escape. The pregnancy was on the verge of escaping Marina's mouth but, because of all the nothingness cluttering up the air around the table at that moment, the question of substance had nowhere to go and just stayed right there on Marina's tongue until she got tired of it being there and just swallowed it. Not once did a real topic attempt to come up. Nor did anyone ask how she is doing. Everyone is very careful to not ask that question. She wondered if this – years upon years of avoiding and skirting and hiding and wearing masks and walking quietly as to not disturb the sleeping elephant – is what contributes to a person feeling completely alone and hopeless, even in the midst of a loving family.

She struggled to regain the equilibrium she had felt earlier. Tonight was not a night for rehashed trauma and sad condolence. She had a wonderful husband, a good sister, and thoughtful friends. She made the right decision about the abortion. After the procedure, she will call her therapist and try to reestablish a routine of regularity. She will deal, finally, with what happened to her. But tonight, she was determined to enjoy

her husband and friends. She was determined to enjoy the fireworks.

She cut generous portions of the fruit tart and plated them.
Mel had retired to the family room, wheelchair pushed up to the
TV like some sort of overgrown son home from college. Dale re-
appeared and was now pulling out mugs and hunting for the
sugar.

Turning to Leslie, Marina asked, "How is your mother doing?
I feel horrible that I've paid so little attention to you these past
few weeks."

"No! Please, don't feel bad. Do you have any idea how wonderful it is to see Mel engaged with life? He wants to encourage you.
I know he doesn't explicitly say that, but that's what his visits are
all about."

She was glad she inquired. "I knew that. Still, I've been a shitty
friend to you."

"Nonsense! I love you, you know that." Leslie's voice grew
quiet. "I had one, you know."

Dale brought a tray of steaming coffee to the table, interrupting them.

"I'll take some to John. It looks like he's still on the phone in
the study." Without waiting for a reaction, Dale took one of the
mugs and stepped into John's cave. Marina watched her go, con-
templating her sister's sudden consideration of John.

"You had one what?" Marina turned back to Leslie, who was
putting a little bit of cream in her coffee and instead of stirring
it with a spoon, gently rotated the cup, like one would do just before tasting wine.

"I had an abortion, many years ago, before Mel. I was dating this guy, and, well, I knew we had nothing in common but, well, I was wildly attracted to him."

"Wow. I'm sorry, I think. That must have been difficult."

"Nope." Leslie looked at her feet, then back at Marina. Her eyes were wet. "It wasn't at the time. But I always wonder what it would have been like to have a kid. Mel and I can't, you know that."

"Even before?"

"Yeah, even before."

Marina took both of Leslie's hands and squeezed them. She held them for a long moment before releasing them. She got her wish. Real talk.

The fireworks were audible in the distance. John came out of the study and when Marina looked in, she saw that Dale hadn't been in there with him. Leslie wheeled Mel to the front door, which was wide open so he could see – bugs be damned. John was already on the porch, sitting sideways on the steps, his back against one of the posts.

"Where's Dale?" Marina stood in front of John, raising an eyebrow, as if he had made her sister disappear.

"I have no idea." He shrugged his shoulders.

She sat down on the next lower step, in front of him, and rested her cheek on his knee. The fireworks popped and whistled and moaned. He adjusted his position, moving up from the step onto the porch, leaning against the house. He motioned for her to join him and he opened his legs to let her ease herself between them. She pressed her back to his chest and he wrapped his arms around her. Leslie and Mel emerged from the garage and headed down the driveway toward their house across the street. *He's exhausted*, Leslie called from the driveway, pointing at Mel. Marina and John waved, then sat like that for a long time, not talking, just being. For long, blissful moments everything seemed normal.

***

When Marina woke up, it was still dark but instead of fireworks, she heard the faint cry of an owl. John's arms were still draped across her chest, but looser than they had been. His chest was rising and falling rhythmically, and he was making the familiar puff-puff breathing sound he makes when he just falls asleep. Marina didn't move, her mind still foggy with sleep and disjointed dream images.

One dream had been about poop of all things, baby poop. In the dream, she was looking at some sort of invention to manage baby poop, a device that consisted of nothing more than a grocery store disposable bag and a large plastic jar. She remembered knowing that the jar came in optional colors. In the logic only found in the dream world the mechanics of the poop machine involved merely inserting the lower half of the baby into the bag, which somehow sucked off any level of soiled diaper and dropped it into the jar. Voilà. A poop-free infant. For some reason the dream seemed cast from some sort of infomercial, populated by over-the-top would-be inventors. Marina – in the dream or wherever she was at the time – thought this invention was brilliant. Brilliant!

Now that she thought about it, what were you supposed to do with the jar? Did you keep the poop in it? Treasured samples, kept in optional colors displayed proudly on the mantel piece? Did the babies want to keep the poop? Did the parents? Was this about not letting go of things? Marina shook her head, trying to clear the image.

In another part of her dream, she seemed to be watching a movie. Or maybe she was watching herself. She could see a pregnant woman on a ship, an ocean liner of sorts. The ship was trying to maneuver through a choppy channel, surrounded other large vessels, merchant ships and barges. There was some sort of crash, a brushing up of one ship against another. In the dream, Marina never actually witnessed this crash, although she somehow knew it was going to happen. She could see the pregnant woman vividly – she resembled an actress, but Marina couldn't think of her real-life name.

She was wide-awake now, trying not to dwell on the dream. She gently nudged John awake and said *it's time for bed*. He groggily got up and followed her into the house. She closed the door behind them, her hand on her belly as they made their way up the stairs.

CHAPTER 6

Hawk

ONE OF THE THINGS I hate about falling asleep anywhere other than in my bed is that when I'm finally awake enough to navigate the many stairs in this house without tripping and breaking my neck, the journey leaves me wide awake. No matter how tired I was in the first place I end up lying in bed for hours before gradually descending into a semi-slumber. Unfortunately, I am not the sort that can sleep in, to make up for a sleepless night. Even when I'm on vacation and can sleep until noon if I want, I can't seem to do it. It pisses me off to still be in bed after a certain point in the morning. That point has shifted over the years, a nod to my advancing years, so now it's something like seven-thirty or eight. But no later.

Unless, of course, I'm making love. I'd stay in bed all day for that. All day. But I gave up that fantasy long ago. Marina is the type of woman who is finished when she is finished. Day long marathon sessions are not for her. She might make love in the morning but then she's right back on schedule. She gets crazy in a bad way if her routine gets off kilter. I long ago learned by trial and error to accept this about her. The other thing I've accepted about her is that approaching her for sex once she's asleep is a crime punishable by death. I made that mistake early in our marriage. Still, I can't complain. For most of our life together, she has had a healthy appetite and very rarely refuses my advances. She is a good wife. The best. I can't possibly ask for better.

So why then, am I laying here, wide awake, with a hard on, thinking about not my wife, but her sister? Her strong, intense and beautiful sister. I realize now that asking her to come up from DC was a mistake. Clearly her relationship with Marina is as strained as it ever was. And clearly, I can't shake off my crush like I so gallantly told myself I would. A crush. At my age. Sad.

There was a day moon today. Long ago, Dale and I had argued about a day moon, when Marina and I were first dating. That day, I was at Marina's, on the balcony of her tiny apartment, enjoying the crisp fall air, when Dale came out. I don't even remember why Dale was over there. They kind of hated each other in those days. I think they still do, to a degree. When she came out she leaned against the railing, her curly dark hair a stark contrast to her pale skin, looking at nothing, then turned around and looked at the sky. I ignored her as I pretended to do whatever it was that I was pretending to do. I had a little crush on her in those days, too. I was certain I was falling in love with Marina, but sometimes I wondered if I was chasing the wrong girl.

She made a comment about the blue sky, the way it reminded her of a guy she dated her first year in college. His eyes were that color, she said. Still pretending to be completely focused on what, I don't know, I glanced at her with my peripheral vision and I could see enough of her face to realize she was looking at the sky as if a lover. I felt a surge of jealousy that startled me. I think I would have given my life to have her look at me the way she was looking at the sky. I think if she had, well, I think my life would have been very different.

She stood there for a long time. Marina popped her head out and asked if I was ready to go. I wonder where we were headed that day. I ignored her and cast around for some way to continue standing on the balcony. I pointed to the moon. Look at the moon. A day moon, I said.

With a snap Dale erupted into a sarcastic and condescending diatribe about the fact that there is only one moon, not day or night, just one, giving me a tongue lashing that left me feeling like a skinned cat. She went on and on about lunar orbits and implied that no one would expect a stupid cop to know any better. With my tail between my legs I bid my farewell and went in to find Marina. It was a very, very long time before I looked back.

CHAPTER 7

May

LIGHT POURED INTO THE WINDOW through the closed plantation shutters that never closed quite tight enough. The morning sun sliced through the slats, creating yellow stripes in an otherwise darkish room. Marina looked at the clock on the night table – almost six-thirty. She and John had crawled onto the bed only a couple of hours ago, not bothering to even get undressed. The exhaustion – mainly emotional – of the past few days had taken its toll. She looked at John. He was on his back, mouth agape, snoring gently and rhythmically, unaware and uncaring of the brightening room. One leg hung over the edge of the bed and the other protruded straight in front of him with his foot pointing outward like a duck. His fingers were interlaced and resting on top of his chest. She rolled over onto her side and watched him sleep, wondering what he was dreaming about, wondering if his dreams were as odd and as telling as her own.

She closed her eyes. When she opened them again, the numbers on the clock were different. Somehow, somewhere they had changed, or someone turned them upside down. Just a second ago, it was six-thirty. How in the world did it become nine-thirty? She sat up and realized that John was no longer on the bed. She could hear him in the shower. Her senses began to come alive and now she smelled bacon. She thought about the cartoons she watched as a kid, the ones where the crafty hunter used the luscious, scented, visible steam from a cauldron of stew to lure the rabbit right into the pot with the vegetables and spices. The steam turned into a hand with a crooked finger that summoned the rabbit as he floated on the steam's tendrils right into the boiling water. What boiling trap waited at the source of this morning's tantalizing bacon lure?

She went into the bathroom to brush her teeth and throw some cold water on her face. The quicker she could get downstairs to the bacon, the better. John was in the shower, his head covered with shampoo. His eyes were shut tight as he scrubbed his scalp – a routine that he has performed every morning for as long as they've been married. She was not feeling the least bit amorous, but she was feeling playful. She quickly undressed and snuck into the shower while his eyes were still closed. She scooted her body behind his and wound her arms around his torso. His body tensed as he continued scrubbing. He bent his head forward into the falling water, shampoo running off his head and all over his body and her arms.

"Hi," she said when the water once again ran clear.

"What are you doing?" He peeled her arms from his body and turned to face her.

"Just being affectionate, that's all." She turned him around and massaged his lower back – something that has bothered him off and on since he fell on his tailbone shooting hoops with Nester and Phil about ten years ago. Phil. John steadied himself by placing both palms on the shower wall, giving her easier access to his back, but now unwelcome thoughts of Phil made her recoil. She stepped out of the shower, tucking a towel around her body, ignoring the slight tremble in her hands.

"Where are you going?" He turned his head but was still holding onto the wall. He looked like a criminal about to be frisked. He stood there for a second and then turned off the water.

He grabbed a towel and stepped out of the shower. Marina, who was now standing in front of the mirror brushing her teeth, saw the beginnings of an erection. She left the bathroom without rinsing her mouth.

John followed her, came up behind her and turned her around a little more forcefully than necessary, kissing her hard on the mouth. She resisted and pulled away, not sure that she wanted this now but he was persistent, pushing her back against the dresser, pulling the towel from her body and dropping it on the floor. Without warning she felt her body beginning to respond, even as her mind still fought against the panic. But she kissed him back and now he pushed her down to the floor, making love to her in a hard, urgent way, the way that you make love when the tension builds to the point of explosion, but you didn't even realize there was tension until you lay panting in the aftermath.

***

John didn't move for a long time, having found a comfortable and relaxed position on the carpet. Marina gave him a kiss and rose to follow the smell of the bacon. Dressing in loose slacks and a light pullover, she headed downstairs to find the pan of bacon but no Dale. The strips were getting shinier by the minute, just the way Marina likes them – soft and greasy. She picked up two pieces and shoved them into her mouth. The kitchen smelled faintly of cinnamon and Marina quickly located the source – a stack of cinnamon pancakes warming in the oven. She pulled them out and wondered where her sister had gone.

"Oh, there you are," Marina said as Dale appeared in the kitchen.

"I see you found the goodies," Dale tossed the morning's newspaper onto the kitchen table. She removed the plastic delivery bag and blew it up like a balloon. She tied it in a knot and tossed it up in the air and caught it. She did this several more times, almost mindlessly, as she leaned over the table and flipped through the paper.

"Aren't you having any?" Marina watched Dale hold the makeshift balloon in one hand, and slam the other hand against it, making a loud pop.

"Nah, I'm not hungry." Dale had an edge about her face – an almost angriness that Marina read precisely. She knew that look. Her perfect sister struggling over some flaw, a wrinkle in her conscience. Now she wondered if Dale had heard the sounds of their lovemaking. She had been so caught up in the moment that she'd forgotten that a third person was in the house. She'd forgotten how thin the walls were.

"Something's wrong. What is it?"

"Nothing's wrong."

"Something is. You're doing that thing with your face."

"What thing with my face?"

"I don't know how to describe it." And then, before she was able to stop herself, Marina continued. "It's like the look you had right after you told mom and dad that we lured Lizzie into the woods with stories about a buried treasure." Marina put her hand over her mouth, her stomach dropping. "I'm sorry, I honestly didn't mean to bring that up."

"Actually, you did, you just didn't know you did." Dale replied coolly, the guilty look vanishing.

Marina considered this. "You know, for some reason I was thinking about it yesterday when you fell asleep on the couch. You were drunk that night, the night you let everything hang out."

"I wasn't that drunk. I remember telling them."

Marina didn't argue. She felt her face get hot, felt the blood pooling in her cheeks. She was shocked that they were finally having this conversation.

"I was horrified that you told them. We promised each other we would never tell them, that it would likely kill them, or kill their love for us."

"But Mar, it shouldn't have. We were just kids. But you were right. Oh, they never said as much, but they did blame us." Dale picked up the pieces of the now deflated plastic bag and walked it over to the trash bin under the sink. "After that night, Dad never looked at me the same way again. Literally. He never looked in my eyes. Always at my nose, or my forehead. Never my eyes."

"Same. Mom too. Well, she barely looked at me before Lizzie died. I know I disappointed her some way. I've never been able to quite figure out how or why."

"Don't take it personally," Dale answered brusquely, "You know she was always a little weird with me too. It was her, not us."

"Yeah." Marina pulled the plate of pancakes out of the oven and set them on the counter, near the bacon.

"You know, I think I will eat," Dale said. "It looks good, if I do say so." She was looking over Marina's shoulder, smiling.

Taken aback by this sudden change in Dale's demeanor, Marina whipped her head around and saw John standing in the doorway, freshly shaven, clean, looking guilty. As if what they'd just done on the bedroom floor was somehow wrong. This puzzled and upset her. She's not even sure if she enjoyed the rather boisterous rolling and knocking about. She was confused, to say the least. She walked over to where John was standing and gave him a hug. "Let me make you a plate."

"No, I got it." He topped a pancake with two strips of bacon, poured some syrup over it, and repeated the process two more times until he had an impressive stack. He poured himself a coffee and sat down at the table.

"It was Rosen who paged me last night," he said and Marina felt like he was watching her carefully, gauging her reaction. For Dale's benefit he explained. "Rosen is our lawyer, Marina's criminal defense lawyer."

"What? Why was she calling? And at dinnertime on a Saturday?"

"It seems she's been out of town and was just going through her business mail. It seems that Bridget wants to stop the abortion," he said through the hefty bite of food working its way through his mouth.

"What? You mean, she wants the baby?" Marina sat down hard in her seat as questions exploded in her mind, her eyes going wide.

"Who's Bridget?" Dale said as she took a chair across directly across from John, her interest piqued by a potential legal matter brewing.

"Why would Phil's daughter want any baby, let alone this baby?" Marina ignored Dale's question, her hackles rising to this fresh assault on her sensibility.

John shrugged, still chewing. Dale, suddenly witting, raised a pointed finger, as if she were about to launch into a diatribe.

Marina forestalled her. "So, she wants the baby. She can't have the baby. I'm aborting the baby tomorrow." The baby. She imagines Phil's baby. A boy or a girl. Cute little outfits. Toys. Bridget, bouncing it on her knee. Taking it for walks in a stroller. Feeding it. She looked at John, who seemed strangely calm and unconcerned. "What else did Rosen say?"

She had her elbows on the table and was resting her chin in her hands. Her eyes bored holes into John's, as if she was accusing him of something. He expressed his discomfort by shifting in his chair and then, once settled in his new position, tapped his foot under the table.

"Rosen said Nester went to see Bridget and tried to talk her out of doing this, but she won't budge." He shifted again and started tapping the other foot.

"Talk her out of doing what?" Marina was incredulous that she was only hearing about this now. Why didn't John share this with her last night?

John tilted his head back to get the remaining drops of his coffee out of the cup and into his mouth. He stood up and took his plate over to the sink. He refilled his cup and sat back down at the table. "There's no easy way to say this." He poured some cream into his cup and stirred it with his finger, a habit Marina found terribly indecent.

"Doesn't that hurt?" Dale's eyes were transfixed on John's wet finger as it went directly from the cup into his mouth. "The heat of the coffee, I mean. Doesn't it burn your finger?"

"No."

"Come on guys! Let's focus here." There was a tension and harshness in Marina's voice that she didn't recognize and suddenly regretted. She said more softly, "John, there's no easy way to say what? What's going on?"

He turned toward Marina and put a hand on her forearm and caressed it, something he often does when he is about to tell her something unpleasant. She yanked it away. John's calm demeanor evaporated, and she could see the tension and the anger he was desperately trying to clamp down. He blinked slowly and started to get up, but she grabbed his arm and made a futile attempt to pull him back down to his seat.

"I'm sorry," she said. "Please, don't go away. It's just that you're upsetting me. Please just tell me what's going on."

He sat back down. "Bridget wants to adopt her little bastard half-sibling." The words flew out of his mouth like poisonous darts.

After a moment to absorb Marina retorted, "What? No!"

"It gets worse." He reached for her forearm again, probably out of habit, and this time she let him. His voice was softer now. "She wants to sue you for wrongful death." Marina stared at him blankly.

"Oh, for God's sake." Dale was out of her chair now, standing with her hands firmly on her hips. "What a bunch of bullshit." She paced the small area between the table and kitchen counter, shaking her head, mumbling like a little old man.

"Can she really do that?" Marina asked John.

"She can try, but I don't think she has a leg to stand on."

"No, she can't do that, no attorney would take that case." Dale was back at the table now. She pounded her fist on her forehead. "Wait, she knows that she'll lose." She looked at Marina, then at

John. "So, are you saying that she's going to claim wrongful death, and then use the baby as a bargaining chip?"

"You mean threaten to sue me unless I give her the baby?" Marina asked. "Or something like that?"

"Bingo. You're both right." John said.

"The law doesn't acknowledge the right of a father to stop the abortion of his own child, but rather places that act solely within the decision of the mother." Dale looked at the two of them. "Not to mention that the father is dead. Dead for a damned good reason." She looked directly at Marina now, whose face felt like it was cooking from the inside and would at any moment explode.

Marina almost forgot. Not that she could ever forget, but almost, in the conflict of the abortion clinic, in the business of her little dinner party, in the not-quite-drunk-but-happily-buzzed stupor of the wine, in the harsh reality of her conversation with Leslie last night and another one with Dale this morning, in sweet slumber on the porch in John's arms and the disturbing sex, she almost forgot. In the past twenty-four hours, Marina did not think about the fact that she killed Phil, that she could have done something to help him and chose not to.

"You're right, Dale," John said, "Like I said a minute ago, Bridget doesn't have a leg to stand on. But she can still try."

"What about Nester? Why didn't he call you? Why did you have to hear this from Janet Rosen?" Marina's voice was an octave higher than normal, as if she was about to cry, which she thought she might, and tried desperately to shove the rising lump in her throat back down.

"I don't know." John lowered his head, avoiding her eyes.

She pushed her chair away from the table and picked up Dale's plate of half eaten food and her own full plate, untouched. She carried them to the counter and came back to the table.

"I thought Nester was a good friend." She looked at John. "Brethren." She glared at him. "Isn't that what you guys call each other? Brethren? What kind of brother would let this go on without telling his brother? What kind of friend?"

"Don't beat up on John, Mar." Dale jumped to defend John, who sat silent with his head in his hands.

Marina turned on Dale in surprise. "You. Stay out of this."

"Marina!" John's head snapped upright as if suddenly awakened. The furrow between his brows was deeper than Marina had ever seen it. The vitriol on his face frightened her. "This would all be moot if you didn't walk out of that fucking clinic the other day."

Marina got up and slowly walked toward the front door. "She could have still tried to sue me, couldn't she have?" She didn't wait for an answer. She let the door slam behind her.

**

The dictionary defines a hallucination as false or distorted perception of objects or events with a compelling sense of their reality or a false belief strongly held, despite invalidating evidence. Marina knew this only because the school year before Lizzie died, she'd helped her write a seventh-grade paper on hallucination, and for some reason, this definition lodged itself in her brain. She often wondered what the difference was between a hallucination and the simple consequences of an overactive imagination.

Marina knew she had a vivid imagination. Maybe she even hallucinates sometimes. She thinks everyone does it. Isn't imagination the same thing as controlled hallucination? When we imagine, we see things in our mind's eye, things that don't really exist, like the threat of killer tornados on the mildest of days, or the man behind the deli counter with the ugly scowl turning into a three-headed monster. Imagination is a blessing. Isn't it?

Hallucinations might be fun too, which, Marina supposed, is why so many people risk everything to obtain and experiment with drugs that entice your mind into a hallucinogenic state. She realized that it is a stretch to say that to hallucinate is to imagine. Yeah, it's not the same thing exactly. She knew that when she imagined a three-headed monster, she didn't really see one before her, that it stayed confined within the walls of her mind. She knew that to truly enter a hallucinogenic state, you would not be able to distinguish the real from the imagined.

But she does think there is a fine line between imagination running wild and a full-blown hallucination. Did she imagine the momentary look that passed between Dale and John? A fraction of a second, really. A flash of connection. Where had she seen that look before? Was it her imagination? Was she hallucinating? And if either were true, then why? Why would she imagine or hallucinate an unspoken connection between Dale and John?

If only all of this were a hallucination and not reality. Marina wanted to have imagined the entire conversation about Bridget and the baby and wrongful death and lawsuits. And for that matter, she hoped she imagined the positive pregnancy test and the abortion clinic – another distorted perception of an event with a compelling sense of reality. Oh, and let's not forget Phil. Perhaps she never let him kiss her that one time. Perhaps he never snuck into her house and raped her. Perhaps she didn't kill him. Perhaps that too was only her imagination.

***

The late-morning sun warm on her neck, Marina walked to the bike trail and embraced its welcoming shade. A familiar buzzing sound, almost a purr, broke into her thoughts. She stopped to listen. The purring eased, and Marina stood silent and still, waiting. Then the purring, this time louder, was back: a hummingbird flying in and out of the trees and hovering above Marina's head for long seconds. She was at the foot of the bike trail, marked by a defunct train station, converted to a museum, complete with a red caboose in the grass. Someone had hung a hummingbird feeder on a branch that overhung the park bench in front of the caboose. A male Ruby Throat darted by again. That perfect purring. A trill as eloquent as French or Italian words beginning with the letter *R*. The bird dipped and swooped around her, no more than three feet away. Purring. Trying to tell her something, perhaps. This bird seemed to be expressing some sort of displeasure and wanted Marina to do something about it, but with the endless trilling *R*, he simply couldn't quite get to the point. Marina silently watched, unsure. Frustrated by the lack of response, the bird finally gave up and flew away.

Marina stepped onto the bike trail. She ran, although she is not a runner. She ran for a half-mile or so, an easy trot really, and let her mind drift.

Returning to the house, invigorated from the running and suddenly feeling bad for having verbally attacked John and Dale, she was anxious to apologize to both. But the house was too quiet, too clean. The dishes had been cleared, the counters and tabletop wiped, and the dishwasher turned on. The sun came through the window in one, wide beam, creating a sort of spotlight. Marina's eyes traveled the length of the beam and landed on a small piece of paper sitting on the counter. She picked it up and read it, surprised that she didn't notice it right away. *Went to the boat. Back in time for dinner.* She crumbled it and tossed it into the trash. It landed on a pile of uneaten scrambled eggs, then rolled off to the side, wedging itself between a wet paper towel and a pancake. Although the note didn't explicitly say that John and Dale were out together, she somehow suspected it. She fished the note out of the trash, brushing off a piece of egg that was adhered to it. She smoothed it with her fingers and studied it for clues. Maybe she would find a secret message hidden within the nondescript text, pointing to Dale as John's going-to-the-boat companion. She read the words on the note over and over again, convinced that something telling was woven within this succinct message of John's whereabouts. Why would John and Dale go to the boat together? She checked the answering machine in the momentary hope that John had called, but there were no messages.

"It doesn't mean anything," she said to the empty house. "John makes everyone smile. He's just that kind of guy."

Hawk

WOMEN KNOW ABOUT A MAN in love. They know that he is pliable, like a pipe cleaner or a lump of clay. For a man, sex and love are inextricably intertwined; men need their egos stroked regularly, and given the right set of circumstances a man, any man – I don't care about his stature or religious standing in the community, even priests are not immune – can stumble and fall, all in the so-called name of love. Women may pretend ignorance, but they know these things about love, they know them instinctively.

Marina left the house this morning in a huff. I was in a damned huff too and felt desperate to be anywhere but in my foggy, stormy house. I needed to clear my head and think about the implications of this new development – Bridget and the baby and Nester's silence, in what is now the soap opera of my life. And don't get me started on how frustrated I am that Marina didn't get the abortion the other day. I am so frustrated and angry that I need to put it in a box or else I'm liable to do something I would really regret.

As I was leaving for the boatyard, Dale stopped me and climbed into the truck.

"So, you're coming to the boat with me now?"

"Don't be ridiculous. We need to talk."

"About what?"

"About Marina. I am worried about her." Dale softened her tone, laying her hand on my arm. "We need to talk rationally about what this Bridget person can and cannot do. I will make some calls later but first we need to have our ducks in a row."

I nodded and backed slowly out of the driveway. "Where to?"

"I don't know, coffee I guess. Who is this Bridget person again?"

"The asshole's daughter. Kind of estranged daughter at that."

"That's even better. Better for you and Marina."

I should have turned the truck around and told Dale that I would be more comfortable talking with Marina present, and that in a few hours she would have calmed down enough that we could indeed talk – the three of us. But no. I kept driving.

There were several coffee places town to choose from. Why I chose the farthest shop from the house, the one with the gravel parking lot behind it, is not entirely clear to me. Nor is it clear to me why I bypassed several perfectly fine parking spaces in front of the shop, and instead chose to park in that eerie, deserted back lot. Nor is it clear to me why I lingered in my seat, not opening the door to get out.

Of course, it should have been my unwavering love for my wife that prevented me from lingering those extra seconds. Because those extra seconds are crucial on that high-speed bridge between being faithful and tumbling down the slope of infidelity. And I love my wife. Very much. But I lingered for those crucial seconds and ended up not only on the high-speed bridge but in the very water under it – rushing white water – and now I'm hurtling through rocky, fast moving whitewater, beautiful to look at but lethal. I have no raft to keep me off the rocks, no helmet to protect my head should I get banged around, no floatation device to provide just enough buoyancy for my weary body to stay afloat until help arrives. And I don't even like water. Yet here I am.

Perhaps I wanted it to look like an accident, as if the longer we were in the truck together, the less Dale would be able to resist me by the time we reached our destination.

Dale stared at me as the truck drove itself around to the back of the tiny strip mall. In truth, she didn't protest. Like she knew exactly what was about to happen. Like she wanted it to happen. She never took her eyes off me as the truck pulled itself into a nice spot under a bank of large trees. The truck put itself in park and rolled down the windows. Then, like magic, the key pulled itself out of the ignition. She continued to stare as neither of us got out of the truck. Her hand was perched on the door handle, ready to react, ready to flee, but she just sat there, staring. A breeze blew in one window and out the other, blowing her hair around her face.

And that's when I lost it. I brushed her hair out of her eyes and the next thing I knew we were at each other like a pair of starving animals. Did we make love? No, we didn't, thank God. But we came close. Very close. In the truck. In full daylight. I don't know how long we were at it. I say this with a tinge of sarcasm, but it's a wonder nobody called the cops.

CHAPTER 9

Three Years Earlier

PAM HAD BEEN DOING BETTER. Much better. After her final round of chemo, she was deemed cancer free. In remission. Phil had invited their friends to an end-of-chemo-start-of-remission party at their house.

That's when Phil had apparently decided that it was time Marina knew how he really felt. He kissed her. Right there in his and Pam's home. Marina had gone upstairs into the kitchen to refill her glass and the next thing she knew his arms were around her and he was kissing her, firm and passionate, making her heart pound in her chest. Separated from John, Pam, and the rest of the guests by a floor and a ceiling, his hands roving over her back and up into her hair. Any one of the guests could have popped into the kitchen at any moment but Phil didn't care. And apparently neither did Marina, a fact that shocked and horrified her. When it was over she feigned a headache, said her polite goodbyes, and asked John to take her home. Two days later she donned her lame disguise and found herself in a confessional, pouring her heart out to the young priest who could have been Opie Taylor, right out of Mayberry, in another life.

May

MARINA FOUND HERSELF OBSESSING about what John and Dale might be doing, whether they had arrived at the boatyard yet. A look at her watch told her that they must still be on the road, probably with the windows open, Dale's curly black hair blowing all over, John throwing his head back as he laughs at something witty she might have said.

There had to be a logical explanation for why John and Dale went to the boat together and didn't bother to wait for her. Earlier she hadn't been keen on the idea of driving nearly an hour to the boat, only to sit in the shade with a book or sketchpad while John worked on fiberglass. But she had been thinking of going, if for nothing else because she felt bad for being so terse earlier in the kitchen and for berating him over Nester.

This was not John's fault. If she should be angry with anyone, it should be Nester. And then there's Bridget. The daughter who was mostly absent during all the years that they knew Phil and

Pam. During Pam's cancer, Bridget's name never even came up. According to the police reports after the attack, Bridget described her father as having been struggling in the weeks leading to the rape, but that there had been no explicit warnings he was about to fly back to the East Coast and rape his former partner's wife.

Even though Bridget is a more justifiable target for her present anger, Marina couldn't stop thinking about John and Dale, wondering where they were and what they were doing. She had absolutely no reason to doubt John's faithfulness and loyalty. She's always felt that she would know if John were about to participate in something untoward, well before he took the first step.

When they were first dating, she was apprehensive about introducing him to Dale. And the moment the two looked at each other, her heart was struck dumb. John seemed enraptured with Dale in a way that he had never seemed to be with her. Marina and John had something very physical, but mostly, it was intellectual and deep. Marina knows that she is not unattractive but next to her sister she is plain white daisy next to a perfect red rose.

They had just seen Les Miserables on Broadway and on this day of introductions, Dale looked just like Cossette. John had not started his police training yet and had thick, wavy hair that gently brushed his shoulders, a perfect Marius. She remembered sitting on a chair in the corner of the apartment while John and Dale went on and on about this or that, interspersed with bursts of laughter, their arms around each other as Dale got up to teach him a dance she'd learned.

Eponine. That was who Marina felt like around John and Dale that day so long ago. Yes, John could have been Marius. Dale could have been Cossette. Staring across a flimsy card table, talking softly. Black curls tumbling down, a dark waterfall against lily-white skin, framing Dale's lovely yellow dress. John, lost in blissful wonder, a *heart full of love*, as he briefly twirled her around the room. The mousy friend. Plain and boyish, too awkward to dance. Eponine all the way. *He was never mine to lose*. Marina was certain she had lost John that night and when he left she began to grieve. She retreated into herself, saying nothing to Dale. For a few days Eponine quietly mourned her Marius. But then John called again, and they kept dating as before. He never said anything about her sister and she was thrilled when a few months later he proposed.

Marina had no reason to doubt John's faithfulness and loyalty, hypocrite that she is. She never told him about the time Phil kissed her (and she kissed him back). John is as loyal as they come. And they have talked about jealousies, other women he worked with in the past. Many years ago, there was an incredibly pretty female cop on John's shift. Marina talked to him about it, vulnerably. He laughed when she told him these things, not in an insensitive way, but as reassurance. She still occasionally felt threatened, but vowed then to just acknowledge these things when they come up and let them go. And it worked. While she did fleetingly feel those insecurities over the years, she hadn't let them bother her like this in a very, very, very long time.

But this visit, this moment in time with John and Dale feels different. How could she possibly tell him all of this? All those years ago, when Marius and Cossette danced before her, she never did say anything. She surrendered him to her without protest. Everyone always loved Dale more, as everyone always loved Cossette. Their father had been dazzled with her too, his green-eyed daughter with the dancing black curls. At age two Marina lost her father to her sister and never recovered from it. She would not lose her husband to her. Not now. Not ever.

***

"Hello? Anyone here?"

Marina jumped off the couch and was on her feet, standing at attention, disoriented and dizzy. It was Leslie. Marina liked it that she and Leslie were comfortable enough to walk into each other's houses. Kind of like Lucy and Ethel – something Marina had always wanted in her life – an Ethel Mertz to show up unannounced in the morning for coffee after the husbands have gone off to work, or during an afternoon of house cleaning to borrow a cup of sugar.

"I'm in here," Marina called out, sitting back down. Leslie came in and sat down on the couch beside her.

"I'm sorry if I upset you last night," Leslie said. "You know, when I told you about my abortion" She didn't wait for Marina to respond. "I had no right to thrust my story on you. You didn't ask, and I shouldn't have inserted my history."

Marina raised her hand as if commanding Leslie to stop. "Please, don't. It's okay." She smiled. "I am glad you're being real.

I hate fake. I'm glad you told me." Her face turned serious. "Listen, I'm sorry for any pain you went through. I never would have thought. I'm really sorry."

"It was a long, long, long time ago." Leslie looked around the room and then back at Marina. "Just know that afterward, you know, if you need someone to talk to. Please don't run away like you've been doing."

"I don't know that I'm running away. I think I just need lots of alone time."

"Well, you may think you need lots of alone time after the abortion, but believe me, that's not what you'll need." Leslie opened her arms for a hug.

They embraced for what seemed like a long time, and the tears started flowing. Damn those tears. Marina hated her damned tears.

"Hey now," Leslie said, pulling away. "Just let them come." She found a tissue box on the desk and got up to give one to Marina, who was wiping her eyes on her arm.

"I feel like such a kid sometimes. Look at me." She waved her arm up and down her body, like a fashion model pausing on the runway to bring attention to the displayed ensemble. "Look at me, carrying on like an adolescent." She took a tissue and blew her nose.

"I don't think you're acting childish at all. Why do you say that? Look what you've been through, what you're going through."

Marina weighed her next words carefully. How could she explain to Leslie how sophomoric she feels at her raging insecurity over her sister? What if Dale and John went to the boat? Big deal. She grew more disgusted with herself by the second.

"I guess I'm just hungry and cranky. Dale made a beautiful breakfast and I didn't touch it."

"Hey, let me take you to lunch. We could walk over to that new place on Main."

"That's a great idea, the only problem is that I don't think I can make it that far. I feel I need to have something right now or I'll pass out."

Leslie disappeared and returned a minute later with a full glass of orange juice, which Marina drank in one huge gulp. She knew she would pay for it later with raging heartburn, but for now, it was just the right thing.

***

Marina and Leslie walked the several blocks to the new cafe in silence. The orange juice might as well have been a magical elixir, whipped up by a knowing wizard, for it brought Marina back to life. She had clarity of thought and as they walked, she pondered the craziness of her previous musings. She won't lose John to Dale in the space of a few days. Dale is going back to DC, to her important job, her exciting life, and her young boyfriend. Young boyfriend. Dale has a young boyfriend. From the talk over dinner the other night, Dale seemed smitten with this fellow.

She laughed out loud, threw her head back and did a pirouette, in the middle of a busy, downtown sidewalk.

"What are you doing?" Leslie looked half amused, half concerned.

Marina ignored her and kept twirling. She felt young and old at the same time. She wanted to be this person who is growing less and less concerned with what people think, this person who can twirl in public, break into a song, embrace any form of creativity.

Still laughing, Marina finally stopped and hooked her arm through Leslie's. "Do you think, as we grow older and wiser we sometimes act more childlike and take risks like we did when we were younger?"

"I guess so," Leslie replied, "I know that when we are older we tend to speak our minds more, or at least my mother did, and my grandmother. In fact, my mother speaks her mind all the time now, only it's gibberish and nobody know what she's trying to say. I think I know though. She's mad at the world."

"Well, I'm not ready to be old, but I'm too old to be young. Kind of like adolescence where you're not yet mature enough to be an adult, but you're too old to act like a kid."

"I'd like not to relive adolescence thank you," Leslie's dry humor echoing Marina's own feelings of being a teenager.

But she wondered if mid-life and the proverbial mid-life crisis is kind of like adolescence relived, even if reluctantly. Marina was in her mid-forties but there were times when she sincerely didn't know who or what to be or how to act. There were times when she felt like she acted too youthful. She was caught in the middle between youthful exuberance and age-acquired wisdom.

A block more brought them to the new cafe, called Ian's on Main. The dining room was crowded and noisy, mostly groups of people in business attire, pairs of women with young children, and a sprinkling of couples. They were seated at a table in the corner of the patio, under a large awning. It seemed dark and nicely cool compared with the rest of the world, which seemed blindingly sunny and warm.

Leslie put both elbows on the table and set her small, pointy chin in the cup of her two hands. She looked around the patio then directly at Marina, who was sitting with the back of her head resting on the wall. "Ok, no more fluff. How are you, really?"

Marina sighed. "Why do you ask like that?"

"Come on, Marina," Leslie looked concerned, "I don't think you're dealing with things. Have you talked to anyone? A therapist maybe?"

The dreaded recommendation of therapy again. She wanted to lash out but took a deep breath instead.

"I'm sorry," Leslie said. "Here I go, inserting myself where I don't belong. Again." She stopped talking, but quickly started again. "No. I'm not sorry. I care about you. You were there for me after Mel's accident. Remember? I think you drove me to therapy – you drove me kicking and screaming. Remember? I just wanted to take Mel by the hand and both of us lay on the train tracks. I was so fucking mad at him. I still am. But I know how to deal with it now. The most fascinating thing is that I still love him. For a long time, I didn't think I did. But I do. I still love him."

Marina flipped through her menu then put it down. "I'm doing lousy, if you must know. My moods shift, moment by moment. One second I'm hopeful and elated, the next second I just want to crawl into a hole and stay there until I rot."

Leslie reached across the table and touched her hand. Two iced teas arrived, and with them, a momentary break in the seriousness. Leslie fumbled with a packet of sugar. By the time her friend was situated with her tea, big tears were once again rolling down Marina's face.

"Things are not good between John and me."

Leslie sat still, waiting for more, but it was obvious to Marina that she was being careful not to pry. She blew her nose with the paper napkin that was serving as a coaster for the iced tea.

"We're not talking like we used to. He has an angry aura that was never there before." She took a sip of her tea. "To make matters worse, I think John has a thing for my sister." She tried to breathe deeply through her clogged nose.

"And as if all that isn't enough, I found out this morning that my attacker's estranged daughter wants to take me to court."

Leslie gasped aloud but was saved from having to respond by the arrival of their food. The distraction helped Marina to dry her tears and tell Leslie the details, about Nester and Bridget. She also told Leslie about John and Dale running off to the boat together. These are the true things that were weighing heavily on Marina's heart. She felt naked. She supposed that some things are just better dealt with alone. Yet it felt so good to verbalize these things out loud, to another person. A safe person.

CHAPTER 11

Hawk

I ARRIVED AT THE BOATYARD in record time, dug out my paper suit and slid it up over my shorts and t-shirt. Sweat trickled down my back. I felt a strong desire to punish myself. I put on my mask, poured the resin and hardener into a disposable bucket, and tried to focus. After our little thing in the truck, Dale had me drive her back to the house. I dropped her off a few blocks away because I didn't want to face my wife. Now I'm summarily screwed up in the head. Even more so than before.

I'm really trying to focus. Really, really trying. No such luck. After fifteen minutes of stirring and staring off into space, I realized it was a lost cause. Chucking my suit into the back of the truck, I headed over to Shorty O'Rourke's, the pub just down the street from the boatyard.

I ordered a burger, fries and a beer. Shorty was off today and the dude behind the bar didn't engage me in conversation, thank God. A breeze blew in through the open door. I took off my hat and smoothed my hair and all I could think about was Dale's hair blowing around in my truck.

I still smell her on the neck of my t-shirt. Not perfume, not soap, but a sweet smell that just must be Dale. I sat at the bar looking ridiculous with the top of my shirt pulled over my nose. I sat there with my eyes closed, food and drink forgotten, inhaling the fabric of my shirt. It was no use. I left cash on the counter and walked out of the pub determined to move forward.

May

LESLIE WANTED TO COME IN after lunch. To finish the discussion, to keep Marina talking. *Keep talking. Just keep talking.* There came a point when Marina had talked enough and couldn't utter another word and that is when they finished their lunch, paid the bill, and left. When they reached Marina's house, Leslie followed her up the front walk, up the steps, and onto the porch. *Keep talking, just keep talking.* Marina hugged her friend, thanked her for lunch, and said she was tired and wanted to rest awhile. Leslie hesitated and finally went across the street to her own house.

Standing at the door, Marina fumbled around for her keys, which she couldn't seem to find in the backpack she carried as her purse. Another point against her in the childish column, she thought, as she searched for the keys. There was a fashion article – she couldn't recall where she'd read it – that said women over forty shouldn't use a backpack as a purse. They should carry a smart courier bag instead. Smart. Marina shook her head, wondering who these people were that came up with such nonsense. Her backpack was not a sparkly-little-girl-princess backpack. It was a sleek, high quality suede and leather work of art that she'd paid a lot of money for in a Brooklyn boutique. Her fingers finally found the key that had slipped down into a side pocket.

The key turned loosely, the door obviously not locked. Marina hesitated. She was sure she locked it on her way out earlier. She distinctly remembers inserting the key and looking over her shoulder at Leslie, already on the street waiting for her. What she doesn't remember doing, though, is jiggling the doorknob to make sure it was really locked. She used to always do that and over the years got lazier about it. So technically, it is possible that she didn't lock the door, even though she is almost certain she did.

She pushed the door open and stepped inside, tossing the backpack on the coat rack, then headed directly for the kitchen. She stopped halfway there and stood, unmoving, for what seemed like an eternity. She sensed the presence of something, although she was not sure what. She felt the blood in her face draining and her heart pounding. Swiftly and quietly she turned around and floated toward the door, careful not to make noise as she slipped back outside.

She stood with her back against the door, wondering what to do. She wished she hadn't sent Leslie home. Her hands were shaking and soon she realized that her entire body was shaking. She slid her back down the door until she was crouching on the ground, head hanging between her knees. She took several deep breaths.

Unwillingly, she was back in her bedroom on a rainy December night, standing on the threshold of her bathroom, looking at her attacker, paralyzed, not realizing then that it was the threshold of the rest of her life. She was hyperventilating. Phil was coming after her. She was trapped. She felt the coldness of the gun moving up and down her back. She tried to take a deep breath, but the attempt was futile.

Fight or flight. Her body became a rocket, launched without a conscious thought, across the street, through Leslie's front lawn, up the stairs, onto the porch, pounding on the door as her very existence depended on it being opened.

Leslie opened the door with a bewildered expression and let her in. Marina's entire body was shaking as if wracked by fever. Leslie was silent as she guided Marina to a chair, fishing a fleece blanket out of a basket of warm laundry perched on the counter and draped it around Marina's heaving shoulders. Leslie finally started asking questions, but all Marina could do was shake.

The police arrived – Nester among them – and, after what seemed like forever, calmed Marina to the point where she was able speak in something other than hysterical gibberish. She told them she had been with Leslie, down the street. A few blocks away. They went to lunch. John wasn't home. Where is John? *John is in Jersey City screwing around with my sister.* She wanted to say that, but didn't. She simply said that John was not home, he was at the boatyard in Jersey City working on the boat. Nester nodded when she said this, knowingly, and oh by the way, what the hell is Nester doing here? She almost spat harsh words at him. She must be calming down – she was thinking about these other things again and not the issue on hand. Focus! She told this to herself over and over. Focus!

"There is someone in my house."

Two officers left them there and rushed, but did not run, to Marina's house. Leslie placed two hot mugs of tea on the table and Nester poured a ton of sugar into his. Marina pushed hers away. Where is John, anyway? Why is he always invisible when she needs him? Wouldn't he be proud of her this time? This time, she listened to her intuition.

She imagined the police storming into her house – bobbing and weaving as police on a mission to find a bad guy do – and this time, the bad guy is alive. No matter how bad of a bad guy it is, this time she would not be responsible for his death. The police will catch him unaware – it sounded an awful lot like he was going through her kitchen cabinets, almost like he was putting groceries away. Perhaps it's simply a homeless person filling grocery bags with the food from Marina's kitchen to take home to his hungry family. But why her house? Why not any of the other houses on her street. She thought about this for a moment and decided that if she did indeed forget to lock the door then she simply made her house an easy choice for this person. Why struggle breaking in when you could simply turn the doorknob and walk in?

Nester's radio crackled and the three of them sat up straight in their chairs. Marina was familiar with most of the codes, but she couldn't make this one out. Nester looked over at her and smiled, or was it more of a smirk? Marina couldn't tell.

"Did they get him?" Leslie asked.

"No, but they got her."

Just then the door opened and laughter was all Marina could hear. Female laughter. Familiar laughter? Footsteps. A cop's voice. More laughter.

Laughter. They got her? Her who? The laughing voices got closer. The laughter was very familiar. It sounded like her sister's laughter. The laughter Marina had imagined earlier – Dale and John having a grand old time at the boat together.

Marina felt like she was on the inside, looking out, hearing the action, seeing the figures, but not at all a part of the scene. Here she was sitting in Leslie's kitchen, watching a movie unfold around her, being the center of the action but not knowing why. The laugher was all around her now, and yes, the most dominant chortles belonged to her sister, who was crouched beside her at the table, arm around her shoulder, repeating Marina's name over and over. Marina was silent, unable to make out much else of what she was saying. Nester was now on the other side of her, also crouched down, with a much more commanding voice.

"Marina, it's okay, everything is okay." He said, loudly and in her face. It was like getting splashed with cold water.

She choked a little on the imaginary water and looked at Dale. "Where is John?"

"How should I know?"

"I thought you were with him, at the boat."

"No, I was not with him at the boat."

"Then where were you?"

"I had some errands to run, is all." She looked at Nester – glared at him. "I was in the kitchen unloading groceries when these two cops burst in." She motioned to the two police officers standing in the background. One was handsome, and young enough to be her son. The other was not so handsome, and quite a bit older. Marina did not recognize them, yet they were both familiar in an ugly way, faces from the night of the attack.

"What about the bad guy?" Marina was confused.

"Sweetheart," chimed the older, not so handsome cop, "you're looking at your bad guy." Marina looked around the room, and suddenly realized – with much embarrassment – that there was not a bad guy at all, that it had been Dale whom she heard rummaging around in the kitchen. She was mortified and desperately wished she were watching a movie, watching something happening to someone else, somewhere else, far, far away. She put her head in her hands, certain she was about to cry, but no tears came. For this she was grateful.

Sometime during the commotion, someone must have called John, because when Marina and Dale left Leslie's house, John was running toward them. Could he have gotten back from Jersey City so quickly? Marina looked at her watch. Wow, has it been that long? Yes, he had plenty of time to get back, although not much time working on the boat. Will he be frustrated with her overactive imagination? But the look on his face was one of concern and relief.

She smiled as he got closer. She was relieved that he was here and overjoyed to see him. She felt the hardened crust that had been forming over every inch of her - the tension, the low-grade fighting, the lack of communication – begin to crumble, to break off, catch the wind and fly away as she ran to John. When she got to him so much of it was gone. He grabbed her with two big arms and held her very tightly, pressing his entire being into her as if trying to warm a hypothermic person until help arrives. With the weight of him around her, she felt like a swaddled infant and began to cry. Not the anguished tears that she shed at lunch with Leslie, but instead, tears of great relief. Relief that John rushed home. Relief that it was only Dale in the house. Relief that Dale was in the house and not with John. She was more relieved about that than she would ever admit to anyone.

"False alarm," Nester said, walking toward them. The two other cops followed him out of Leslie's house, waved at the little group gathered on the sidewalk, got in their cruisers and drove away. "There was no boogieman in your house."

Nester moved in closer and John stiffened at the sight of him and loosened his grip on Marina just a little.

"I'm the boogieman," Dale said.

"And I'm confused." John unwrapped himself from Marina but stayed close – his hip touching her hip, a hand on her shoulder.

Marina took a step back and turned to face him. "I came back from my walk, the house was empty, Leslie showed up and we went to lunch." She took a deep breath. "I got home and opened the door, walked in, and heard noise in the kitchen." She shook her head. "I suppose I could have called out or stopped to think that perhaps it was you or Dale."

"Look, you did the right thing by calling us." Nester said, inserting himself into the discussion.

"Are you finished here?" John took a step toward him.

"Hey, calm down dude."

"I really don't want to talk to you right now." John looked at Nester with a fixed gaze.

"Come on man. What is this about?" He paused. "Come on." His face registered recognition. "The Bridget thing? Is that what this is about?"

"You're darn tootin', the Bridget thing." Dale pivoted away from the humor of being mistaken for the boogeyman. Inwardly, Marina chuckled at her sister's choice of phrases. In volatile situations, Dale often used these quips that had been staples of their grandparents' vernacular. Marina would like nothing better than to let her sister rip Nester apart but she didn't think making more enemies would be helpful.

"Dale, stop. Look Nester, we're upset and confused about what Bridget is doing. I don't think I should talk about this with you, or with her for that matter, until we've talked to our lawyer."

"I get it, I really do." Nester turned to John. "But I really would like to talk to you, just for a few minutes. Please."

John nodded and motioned toward the house.

The living room was dark and stuffy. The curtains were drawn, and Marina noticed that the two orchids on an end table were wilting. Almost unconsciously, she stuck her finger in the planting material. It was still quite moist. She opened the curtains and the sunlight that poured in made everyone in the room squint. Dust motes hung in suspension as if waiting for something exciting to happen.

Marina always regarded living rooms as those rooms where you bring people who you want to get rid of quickly. Like the police department wives who streamed in and out with meals in the first few weeks after the rape. Today, she wanted desperately to get rid of at least one of these people quickly. She would hear what Nester had to say, but after that, she wanted him gone.

The four of them sat awkwardly. Before Nester began, Marina found herself playing happy hostess and asked if anyone would like a drink. Dead air was the response. She got up anyway and went into the kitchen to boil some water for tea. The grocery bags that Dale had been unloading earlier were still on the counter. While she waited for the water to boil, Marina pulled items out of the bags – two pounds of shrimp, some green and red peppers, a pound of bacon, onions, a shallot, mushrooms, a yellow zucchini, and a lemon. Stalling for time to collect herself, she put the perishable items in the fridge. She removed the vegetables from their plastic produce bags and arranged them in rows on the counter. She folded up the grocery bags and stuck them in the pantry where she keeps such things, and checked her water which was now at a nice, rolling boil. She made the tea, put four mugs on a tray, and carried it out to the living room, where the characters in this movie have finally broken the silence. She set the tray down on the coffee table and sat on the couch next to John. She picked up her mug and blew on it.

"Did I miss anything important?" She whispered in John's ear. He shook his head no and put his arm around her.

"Look, Marina." Nester scratched his head. He got out of his chair and took a mug from the tray. He stood in front of the coffee table as if suspended like the dust motes. Marina suddenly noticed that he seemed to have aged overnight. Almost as tall as John, but with white hair and a white mustache. He looked a lot like Sam Elliot. Why had she never noticed this resemblance to one of her favorite actors before? When they first met, he had been an undercover narcotics cop. The full facial hair and long dark ponytail all a part of his ruse. There had been a bad boy sort of allure about him then. But today it was long gone.

"Look," he said again. "I wanted you to know that I am sorry about this thing with Bridget. I am the one who told her you were pregnant. I didn't realize what that meant at the time, what she might do with that information. I was just trying to console her, get her through her pain and anger, and I wanted her to see that you were suffering too. And I want you to know that I am trying to talk her out of this. But she is adamant and there's not much I can do to stop her. She's a little off her rocker."

"But nobody has heard from her in forever." Marina said.

"She'd been making amends for the past year or so. She'd moved in with them once Pam entered hospice. I'd been keeping tabs on them. Not enough to have predicted Phil would do what he did. I'm sorry."

"You could start by explaining why you didn't let John in on any of this." Dale said, glaring at him. Nester walked back over the chair and let it swallow him whole.

"It's not that simple." He hugged his tea as if warming his hands. "Bridget reached out. She needed someone to talk to."

"There was no one else in the world she could talk to? She had to talk to you? Specifically?" Dale's sarcasm was barely perceptible. Marina was certain she was the only one to pick up on it. "Well?"

"I'm telling you, it's not that simple. Let's just leave it at that."

Marina sat and listened. She watched. She was careful not to say anything that might dig a deeper hole for her than she was already in. And you could never be too careful in these situations, this much she knew. She chose to do what came naturally for her. She remained silent.

"Why is she doing this Ness?" John said, his tone somewhat softer than before. "Does she want money? She can't possibly want this kid, can she?"

"I have no answers. None of this makes any sense."

"I find all of this hard to believe. She had a shitty relationship with both of her parents. She wants the money, is all." John shook his head in disgust. "Plus, I find it extremely hard to believe she would want the kid knowing how it came to be. And knowing how poorly she treated her parents, for most of her young adulthood."

"Hawk. Listen. She grew close to Pam toward the end. Nobody knows what got into Phil. None of this makes sense."

"What about my sister?" Dale jumped out of her chair and stood in front of the coffee table, as if in a courtroom, defending Marina to the jury. "Why should she carry a baby under these circumstances?" She shot a round of bullets with her eyes. "She was raped. Conception, unfortunately, occurred." Dale reached over the coffee table and touched Marina's arm. "It is Marina's body. If she wants to abort she will abort. No judge in his or her right mind would even bother to hear a case like this." She sat back down.

John pulled Marina a little bit closer. "We're friends, Ness. I expected better from you than this. We could have talked this through before it escalated to this. I would have talked to Bridget. For God's sake, once upon a time they were like family to us." He let go of Marina and stood up.

"Does she have the resources to maintain a long case? If the lawsuit is just a bargaining chip, will she pursue it even if Marina terminates the pregnancy? I cannot envision a judge ruling favorably for her." Dale added, once again playing the lawyer, and playing it well.

"I don't know. That's the truth. I really don't know. I just wanted you to understand my situation. I am very sorry Marina. I was hoping that Bridget would change her mind." Nester got up then and patted John on the back the way guys often do when they are greeting each other or saying good-bye. They walked to the door together and then they both stepped outside.

Marina and Dale were left alone in the living room. Dale opened her mouth, about to say something or other, and Marina raised a hand and said, "Shush." Dale froze and gave Marina a quizzical look and Marina simply said, "I'm glad you're here. Let's just leave it at that."

CHAPTER 13

Three Years Earlier

PHIL HAD KISSED HER in his house. She went to confession two days later, and instead of feeling cleansed and ready to start anew, all she could think about how close she had come to destroying everything that was good in her life. She called Phil. They had a good chat, at least as good as can be expected. He apologized for crossing a line. He promised he wouldn't let it be awkward the next time the four of them were together. She promised the same. She hung up the phone feeling relieved and at peace for the first time in days.

She made herself a cup of tea and took it out to the front porch. The rain that had earlier been stabbing at her had subsided and she was suddenly cold. With every brush of breeze against her skin the goose bumps got bigger and the hair on her arms stood straight up, stiff like the spikes on a cactus. Her tea had gotten cold too. She'd had enough, really, being out here on the porch. Her body was stiff and she felt at least ninety years old as she slowly lifted herself off the step and unfolded from sitting to standing.

She put her tea in the microwave to warm it up and puttered around the kitchen, straightening things that didn't need straightening, wiping things that didn't need wiping. That's when he tapped her on the shoulder and she jumped. The hot tea that she had just taken out of the microwave ended up all over the floor.

"I'm sorry. I had to see you. I let myself in." He came toward her with his arms open, ready to embrace her and more than likely pick up where he left off two nights before.

"What are you doing?" She backed away from him and grabbed a wad of paper towels to sop up the tea that was quickly being gulped by the thirsty wood floor long overdue for refinishing. "I thought we talked about this. I told you I can't do this. You said you understood."

"Marina." He crouched down beside her, grabbed the towels from her and took over the task of wiping the spill. There on the floor he put his hands over hers. "I love you."

"Don't talk like that. You don't love me."

"I love you. I know you feel the same. A kiss doesn't lie."

"The kiss was nothing more than a natural extension of a friendship that had already existed. And the stress of Pammy." She didn't know where these words came from. But they sounded credible, reasonable. Calm, matter of fact. "That's all it was. Nothing more."

But then Phil reached out, put his hands on her shoulders, and pulled her into him. Before she could react, he was kissing her again, but this time she pushed him away, unexpected tears running down her cheeks.

"Please leave. Now." She could barely speak.

He stood up, gathering the damp towels, shoulders slumped as if her presence in his arms had been the only thing giving his body structure.

She escorted him to the front door and after he drove away she stepped back out onto the porch. The rain had turned to snow and now the ground was covered in a thin layer of white. Snow in April. Absurd. She sat on the top step, remembering John's early kiss before he left for work, a moment come and gone for telling him the truth. Looking out on the surprising whiteness, the relief she felt only a few hours before somehow evaporated.

May

MARINA WATCHED DALE PEEL and devein the shrimp she was planning to grill for dinner. Dale's mood was light and airy, a stark contrast to Marina's dark cloud of regret, resentment, and self-flagellation.

"Do you have any regrets in your life?" Marina's expression was expectant. She hoped the response would be that yes, despite appearances, her sister had at least a few regrets. "I mean, other than the obvious ones." Marina's own regrets swamped her mind: regret for a seemingly innocent prank and a sister's death, regret for moments missed with John, conversations she never had with her parents, friendships squandered. Regret that she'd kissed Phil back. Regret that she didn't fight harder or yell louder during the attack, as John often reminded her. Regret that she let Phil die. Regret that she would never know why he did what he did.

Dale dropped a shrimp into the glass bowl where the other crustaceans were lolling in some sort of magical marinade. "Sure, I do." She said without turning away from the sink to look at Marina. "I wish I married Frank."

"Which one was Frank? I'm not so sure you ever told me about a Frank."

"I didn't."

Marina detected a hint of something in her sister's voice, something unusual, something unfamiliar. Could it be that despite the larger than life facade, the younger man, the guitar player, that her sister was lonely? She knew enough about her sister that pushing or even asking a simple question would be the wrong thing to do. Instead, she brought it back around to herself.

"Right now, the thing I regret most of all is that I walked out of that clinic the other day." She put her head down on the table. She listened to the water at the sink, the clinking of a metal fork against a glass bowl, Dale's feet hitting the floor as she flits from the sink to the refrigerator. The door opened and she heard the rustling of plastic, then the thud of a container of some sort hastily thrown on the counter. More flitting, back at the sink, the raspberry sound of a nearly empty Ivory Soap bottle. Footsteps again, closer, a chair being pulled out from the table. Marina looked up and was eye to eye with the glass of white wine Dale just pushed in front of her. She wondered if her sister even heard her last statement.

"I shouldn't be drinking this stuff," she said, waving it away.

"Why not?"

"I'm pregnant, remember? And it's suddenly gone from being a rapist's fertilized embryo to a rapist's daughter's baby."

"Oh, come on." Dale laughed. "Do you really think she can do this? I am telling you, she can't. You cannot be forced to carry a baby. Roe versus Wade. Remember?"

"Dale, she is going to sue me for wrongful death. Unless I give her the baby. You heard John. Unless I give her the baby."

"Honey, she is going to be the laughing stock of the greater tristate area if she tries to do this."

Marina considered this. She hadn't seen Bridget in years. She didn't know what the woman was capable of. "What do you think this is about?"

"Honestly? I think this is about money."

"So, what do I do then?"

"Have the abortion. As soon as possible." Dale pushed the wine at Marina again, who let it sit in front of her, untouched.

"I keep thinking about what would have happened if I went through with it the first time." Marina looked at the wine – very tempting indeed – but decided against it.

"I don't think it would have changed anything. I don't believe for a minute that she wants the kid. She would have slapped you with the wrongful death suit anyway."

"So, I'm doomed no matter what I do. Is that what you're saying?"

"No. Not at all. You're far from doomed." Dale took Marina's hands. "Mar, you did nothing wrong. You killed him in self-defense. You had every right."

John appeared in the doorway and announced that he made an appointment with Janet Rosen for the day after tomorrow. "Nester is pretty upset about this, you know," he said, looking at Marina. "Please don't be too harsh with him."

"I'm not. At least I'm not anymore. But I was. I guess I can understand how it was hard for him to talk to you about this." She attempted a smile. "This is me at my best. I've been so moody lately that I'm kind of feeling bad for him now, but in ten minutes I might shift in the other direction and want to kill him." She cringed at her choice of words and her countenance dropped.

"Does that mean you're finally going to call Zina?" John's voice was hopeful.

"Possibly. But I do think I need to see my own doctor, and soon. I need to know how long I can let this go on." She looked at her belly, then over at the sink where Dale was politely ignoring their conversation.

"I agree."

"I hope you'll forgive me some day for walking out of that clinic. I should have just gone through with it." She tugged at the skin on her neck as tears threaten. "I just should have done it John."

"Hey, it's hard to know what was best. In some ways, the fact that you still have the pregnancy buys us some time with Bridget. If you aborted the other day, well, she may have just decided to sue us."

"You're right." Dale jumped in, not turning around from her task, but providing her thoughts nonetheless. "You need some time to have a lawyer show the court how ridiculous that woman is being."

* * *

The following morning Marina sat awaiting another sonogram. In stark contrast to the morose scene that surrounded her in the abortion clinic's waiting room, the scene in her doctor's waiting room was like a rainbow of color and happiness. The only thing lacking were chirping birds, but that might have been drowned out by the endless chatter among moms to be, some with happy husbands at their sides.

The women in this pleasant setting seemed of average childbearing age, with one older looking woman and one very pregnant teenager. Marina wondered about the story of both outliers, especially the teenager. Why had this young girl, her life stretched out before her like a big, blank canvas, chosen to carry her baby? There was a motherly looking woman with her, though she looked too young to be the mother of a teenager. Perhaps it is an older sister or a trusted aunt. Could be anyone, really.

Marina noticed an unpleasant taste in her mouth. Kind of bitter, with a slight burning around the tip of her tongue. She was aware of the burning moving toward the back of her throat. And, she could feel a thin line of fire making its way down her esophagus in the direction of her gut. Uncharacteristically distracted this morning, she had forgotten to rinse her hydrogen peroxide mouthwash from her mouth. Grabbing a travel mug of tea on her way out the door, she was halfway to the appointment before she realized she was swallowing the remaining mouthwash.

Did I swallow enough to do harm? Most people would laugh at themselves for washing the peroxide down with the tooth-staining tea that created the need for the peroxide in the first place. She too was laughing at herself – a little. The difference is that most people would laugh, and then move on. She, on the other hand, was peppering her laughter with bits and pieces of worry. Did I swallow enough peroxide to do harm? Is it boring holes in my stomach lining? Will it hurt the baby? How much hydrogen peroxide is poisonous?

Marina jumped when her name was called. She looked at the oversized clock on the wall above the check-in window and was astounded that an hour had gone by. She fumbled for her back-pack and stood up slowly – something she has learned to do over the last week or so, lest she need to sit right back down with her head hanging between her knees.

She left the big water bottle that she had been drinking – the other item she grabbed on her way out the door – on the seat be-side her. In her panic over the hydrogen peroxide, Marina feared she didn't drink the number of ounces of water required to push her gut out and make it round enough for the magic wand to glide and dance its way to producing a decipherable sonogram picture. A nondescript woman in pink waited for her with a clip-board, led her to a scale, weighed her, sat her down in a chair and took her blood pressure, then led her to a room, handed her a gown, and told her that Dr. Finston would be there shortly.

Marina undressed and slipped her arms into the paper garb. She slid onto the table, suddenly exhausted. She ran her tongue along her teeth and decided that any residual peroxide was gone, and she would probably live to laugh about it with John later. John. The thought of him made her heart sink. She wanted him to come with her, to talk to the doctor together, to learn her options, to have John near, holding her hand.

But John chose to stay home. He said it was only a consult, that he didn't need to be there. He made some excuse about getting caught up after the chaos of the last few weeks. Bills stacked in the study, yard work, then head to the station for his afternoon shift. And besides, it's just a consultation, that's all it is. Excuses.

Yep, excuses. Marina knew her husband well enough to know when he didn't want to disappoint her or hurt her feelings. He simply did not want to go with her. Would it have felt too much like the past? Would it have been too hard to sit beside her, like the happy expectant fathers-to-be in the waiting room, but as an un-expectant, un-happy husband? She wondered what this might have been like years ago, had she agreed to have kids with John. For the first time, she felt the slightest tinge of regret for what might have been.

So many things racing through her mind at once. She felt on the verge of a panic attack again. Deep breaths. Inhale. Hold. Exhale. Okay, that's somewhat better. She closed her eyes and was suddenly aware that she had to pee. Badly. Okay, so she did indeed drink enough water. Where the hell was the doctor?

***

After the sonogram, Marina sat in the car and wondered how Dr. Finston, a woman in her mid-sixties – managed to work nonstop as a doctor, the hospital rounds, delivering babies, and all that. She had looked vibrant when she entered the examining room – her short hair sophisticated but not stiff – playful even – producing a young, vivacious appearance. Yet professional and no-nonsense at the same time. For the first time in many years, Marina wondered if her own longer hair drags her down, making her appear older than she is. Or, worse yet, like an older woman trying too hard to look young. Or even worse – like a crazy cat lady. She pulled down the visor and opened the mirror, smoothing her hair and examining her face. The envelope containing the sonogram photo sat on the passenger seat beside her. She started the car and began to back out of the parking spot, then pulled back in, opened all the windows, and turned off the engine.

A warm breeze blew through the car – a pleasant breeze, the kind of breeze that blows off the ocean in the late afternoon. Of course, this breeze was not tinged with brine, but the way it brushed against her face reminded her of Long Island and the long walks she used to take whenever she needed to get away from her mother's depression, the constant reminder of her own transgression. She would grab the family dog, a German shepherd named Moe, and walk and walk and walk. Most of the time it was at dusk, after her mother had put down almost a whole bottle of white zinfandel, when the beach goers were going home, and the only people left were serious readers unwilling to put their books down long enough to pack up and leave, couples just arriving with a paper sack of gourmet deli, and small families with one or two little kids digging with plastic shovels.

One time she found Dale on the beach, sitting on the sand looking at the water as if willing it to share something with her. Marina sat down beside her, the dog nudged her with his chin, and they sat silent for a long time. When Marina got up to leave, so did Dale, and instead of going home they walked until well after dark. When they finally went home their mother was already in bed and their father was, as he often was, on a ladder in front of the boat, a miner's light strapped to his head, scraping barnacles off the hull by its flickering glow. Working on one more endless task needed to restore the boat.

Sitting in the warming car, Marina unbuckled her seatbelt. She tilted her head against the headrest and closed her eyes. The breeze felt so soothing, so very soothing. A car pulled into the spot next to hers, blocking the delicious flow of air. She glared at the driver, who was unaware of Marina as he got out of his car and hurried into the building. The air in the car was rapidly getting oppressive in the absence of the breeze.

Turning the key in the ignition she surrendered to the cold blast of the air conditioning as she rolled up the window. The radio came to life, and Marina beeped her way through the programmed repertoire of stations, hoping for a sad song, something to suit her mood, but instead getting traffic reports and news. She glanced at the clock on the dashboard – the top of the hour, she should have known better – and silenced the chatter.

The manila envelope sitting on the passenger seat teased her. It was almost smirking, daring her to open it. She had turned her head during the sonogram, refusing to look at the screen. Dr. Finston knew better than to push her, but instead gently encouraged her to look.

Dr. Finston confirmed that the baby is just under sixteen weeks' gestation. Given the situation, she said it would be okay to wait another two or three days, but no more than that. She scribbled a date onto the back of her business card and told Marina she needed to have the abortion by that date. Marina could swear that she saw moisture in the doctor's eyes, but of course, it could have been just the exhaustion of a long day manifesting itself this way. John sometimes came home after his shifts with watery eyes. But in Dr. Finston's eyes, there was a sadness too, not just moisture, and for a fleeting moment, Marina wanted her to take off her doctor hat and just tell her what to do, tell her that it is simply too late to have an abortion.

The moment came and went, and Marina never asked. The doctor kept her opinions to herself. They shook hands and she gently closed the door behind her, leaving Marina alone in the room to get dressed. She was slipping into her shoes when there was a strong, single knock on the door and before Marina could respond to it, Dr. Finston was back in the room. She removed her glasses and looked at the floor. After what seemed like a long time she looked at Marina and simply said, "There are other options if you decide this is too much for you. Call me if you need to." Marina nodded, and the doctor was gone.

Hawk

"I CAN'T LEAVE HER." I couldn't believe I said that. What's even harder for me to comprehend is that I even entertained the thought of leaving her. Dale seemed to be ignoring me, so I moved closer to her. "I can't leave her, Dale."

Dale turned from washing the breakfast dishes to stare at me, the smell of her shampoo welcome and tantalizing. She turned off the water and it quickly became eerily quiet. She dried her hands on the towel hanging from the oven door and turned to face me.

"What are you talking about John?"

I was so fucking embarrassed that I wanted to bolt for the door. My legs had other ideas as my feet stayed planted, right where they were. I babbled and stammered about this thing, this feeling between us. "You know. What happened in the truck. It can't ever happen again. I love my wife."

"I love your wife too, which is why you don't have to say any of this stuff. As far as I'm concerned, it never happened." Her eyes were softer than they had been a minute ago. A little sad even.

"It was a wild-eyed dream, right?" I laughed a little and took both her hands. "It was just a dream, right? Crazy that we might have had the same exact dream, but that's all it was. A wild-eyed dream. It never happened, right?" My eyes searched hers for something, anything. I'm not sure for what, an ethereal thing, but I'd know it in an instant.

She pulled her hands out from my gentle grip and let them fall to her sides. She crossed her arms. "And what do you mean you can't leave her? Who ever said anything about leaving her?"

"Well, it's just that I can't do two lives. I can't love two women. I can't be two people. If I were to kiss you again, I'd have to leave her. Period. I don't do things casually."

When she laughed, and laughed and laughed, my heart fell about three or four inches into my gut.

"You are taking this way too seriously." Her eyes narrowed mockingly. "How do you go from kissing in the truck to living two lives or being two people?"

My neck got hot. I was afraid of what my face must have looked like. It couldn't have been good looking.

"John, I don't know what came over me. I did not get in your truck with impure intentions. I just wanted to discuss Marina's situation. I saw an opportunity for some privacy and now I wish I'd just stayed behind."

"I know, I know." I moved back a step and drew an imaginary line on the floor. I would not cross that line. Not even a toe. "I've had a crush on you for years. I've kept it under wraps forever. I think the stress of the situation, and then your hair blowing around in the car. I couldn't help myself." I inched a tiny bit closer to the line. Just a tiny bit closer.

"Nothing happened John. Emotions have just been running high lately. For all of us. We just need to clear our heads." Dale smiled. Or was it more of a smirk? "Oh, and I always knew. You did a lousy job of keeping it under wraps." It was a smile! Not a smirk. Because her eyes were smiling then. I think everything will be okay. Yes, everything will be okay. I felt like a boy on Christmas morning. A kid who did well all year, slipped up once, was convinced that Santa would bypass his chimney, and yet awoke to a sea of the best presents a boy could ask for.

May

THE HOUSE WAS QUIET. She heard the shower running up-stairs in the guest bathroom. The lawn had been mowed and looked great. She looked at her watch – John was probably out running. He didn't have to be at work until three. She figured she had a little bit of time to pour through the literature she had picked up on her way home. Without fully understanding her actions, she had found herself at a crisis pregnancy center, mumbling something about needing some information for a friend. She walked out with a stack of pamphlets and other such documents.

Setting herself down in the study she made room for her mug on the table, pushing a neat stack of addressed and stamped envelopes to the side. The bills. John made good use of his time, she supposed.

She opened the first packet in her stack. It was a compilation of comments from women – girls mostly – that have had abortions. She quickly scanned the little blurbs. The names and ages of the women were listed, and she looked for comments from someone even remotely close to her own age. There weren't any. She closed her eyes and flipped through the pages, but not seeing where her finger landed, in a somewhat skewed rendition a boardwalk carnival wheel. She opened her eyes to see where the wheel landed. She didn't read the page from the beginning but jumped in somewhere toward the end.

Nora, 27: They let me go about two hours later. I had to bring my own napkins, because they didn't provide any. I got an infection and had to go see my doctor afterwards. Luckily, I recovered physically enough to have a baby three years later.

Marina closed her eyes again and imagined the boardwalk at Coney Island, where they used to go when she and Dale were very young, before Lizzie was born. Barely able to reach the counter, her father held her up so she had a full view of her choices. She put her quarter on a red dot. The man behind the counter spun the wheel with all his strength and power. A blur of sound – ticktickticktickticktick – then slower – tick tick tick tick tick – and slower still. Tick. Tick. Tick. The blue dot, not the red. Marina didn't win. She never won. But her father always gave her a quarter and held her up to see the spinning wheel.

Caroline, 19: When I woke up I was in recovery, I just felt empty. One minute I had a life living inside me and the next minute it was gone. I started crying so hysterically. The nurse came up to me and told me to be quiet because I would worry the other girls.

Marina paused on this one, then read it again. She didn't think she would feel like this. Or would she? Had she gone through with it the other day would she have walked out of there feeling empty? She wondered.

Haley, 23: I cried for a week as I made my decision. I didn't want to have an abortion but there seemed to be no way out.

Was there really no way out for this young woman? Is abortion the only way out? Marina was not so sure anymore. She hated how indecisive she felt. Why was it so hard to just take a stand on something and live according to that stand?

Pilar, 16: I got dressed and walked out into the waiting room and started screaming and crying. My mom was crying too, asking me why I did it. I had to be carried into the car. I cried all the way home.

Well, that made no sense. Pilar's mother was asking Pilar why she did it? If Pilar's mother was in the waiting room, surely, she knew what her daughter was doing. Had probably driven her there herself.

What if it had been her? At sixteen. Or Dale. Marina closed her eyes and tried very hard to picture this. Dale young, confused, upset. Tears on her face, red and puffy with crying. Marina saw their mother assuming an illness, a romantic crush going sour, and the little dramas of high school. Then Dale confessing, I'm not sick, Mother. I'm pregnant. How would Mother have reacted? She could only imagine that it wouldn't have been pretty.

Irene, 31: I had been there a few minutes when my husband appeared, looking white like a ghost. He sat down next to me and gave me a tight hug – this was a decision we made together. I woke up the next morning, had only a little discomfort, only a slight amount of bleeding, and emotionally I felt fine. Today I feel so empowered and blessed that I made the decision not to bring a child into the world.

Marina paused here. Empowered. Is this how she would feel? Free of the baby? Free of Phil? Free of confusion? Free to return to painting, trips to the boat with John, normal life.

A small fire was beginning to burn in her gut. She could feel it radiating behind her naval. She imagined the orange glow, lighting her internal organs in that region, even lighting up the baby. Her body had never sheltered a baby. She didn't want to think of the growth inside of her as a baby. But her body kept betraying her. She thought about the manila envelope that was still sitting in her car. She never opened it. The fire was spreading. It was all throughout her torso now. She took a deep breath. When she exhaled she thought she saw smoke.

She turned away from the packet of literature and reached for the paper bag sitting on the floor beside the desk. She pulled out a navy-blue candle, a large one, etched with stars and moons – constellations and the different lunar phases – and placed it on the desk. She reached in again and pulled out a yellow ceramic plate for the candle to sit on.

After sitting in Dr. Finston's parking lot for nearly an hour after her appointment, she drove out of her way to the crisis pregnancy center that recently opened in a worn-out strip mall. When Marina first noticed it, she wondered why anyone would open such a place here, amid a coin laundry, a pet groomer, a pawnshop, and a dollar store. Working up the courage to go in, she found herself browsing the isles of the dollar store and saw the candle. She wasn't particularly into celestial scenes but felt drawn to this candle because it reminded her of her grandmother. She stared at it for long moments and lost herself in the extragalactic nebula, seeing her grandmother's face floating above a table covered in tarot cards, her little hobby, golden in the candlelight. She didn't need to buy a candle – she had lots of candles all around the house. She bought it anyway, convinced her long-deceased grandmother was trying to tell her something.

She pulled a book of matches from the desk drawer and lit the candle. The screen saver on her computer kicked in and startled her. A bright photo of John, herself and the two dogs they'd had fifteen years ago. They were all standing in the middle of a pumpkin patch. She and John were happy then. Could her grandmother have predicted any of this? If she were alive today, would she have seen this in her cards? Would her grandmother have looked away and reshuffled the cards as she sometimes did when she saw something unpleasant? Ignore it and it will go away. Turn your eyes away from bad things and the bad things won't happen. Gather up the cards and reshuffle the deck. Why didn't they ever get another dog? Maybe they should. She would suggest it to John once this chapter of their life was closed.

The pile of literature on the table beckoned for another look. She read through more stories, more names, more ages, most of them young, none past thirty, none, except Irene. *Irene, 31*, the married woman who decided with her husband to not bring a child into the world.

Her belly began to burn again. She knew several married women who have chosen, with their husbands, to not have children. Herself included, although it was her decision alone – John would have loved to have kids. But would any of these women have had an abortion if they'd found themselves with an unplanned pregnancy? What if they were over forty, approaching fifty, and became pregnant?

It's funny how one's perspective changes. Today, many women were just beginning to grow and blossom in their thirties and forties. They were just beginning to ripen as women. She often wondered if she would have been a good mother. John eventually, reluctantly agreed to a vasectomy because Marina hadn't wanted to face the more invasive tubal ligation surgery or side effects of birth control pills. And there had been no accidents. But what if she had gotten pregnant before the vasectomy? Or even after the vasectomy, particularly in the beginning stage of resuming their sex life? What if the doctor had left a tiny hole – just room enough for some rogue sperm to squeeze through? Would she have considered an abortion? No, it would not have entered her mind. At least she didn't think so.

She touched her belly, barely a visible bump, but rounder than it had been just a few weeks ago. If this had been an unplanned pregnancy – even at her age – with John, abortion would not have entered her mind. Even with her having never wanted children. Even then, there would be no question whether or not to keep it. She sighed, wishing for the first time that she'd faced the invasiveness of the tubal, protected herself from this fate, the indecision, with a single act so many years ago.

Her reading became more frantic as she desperately searched the packages to find another story that was positive – someone else who had an abortion and had no regrets. She wondered if today Irene still feels like she made the right decision. Or if she has since had a baby or two. Or if she and her husband are still together. She put the package down and pulled out another folder of paper. More stories, most of them horrible, most of the women scarred for life.

She powered up the computer and opened Netscape Navigator. She felt silly for not having thought of this before. She typed the words *abortion after rape* and was presented with a list of hundreds of links. She felt suddenly hopeful – surely, she would find an entire community of cyber-friends out there.

She clicked on each link and spent a second or two on each and if she didn't find what she was looking for, jumped to the next. She noticed the cowbirds in the yard again, swooping to the feeders just out of sight of the office windows. Ah, there it is. Finally. Exactly what she had hoped to find.

Alee, 38: To this day I can't close my eyes without reliving what I went through. That is a pain I would never wish upon anyone. Nobody deserves to be raped. When I found out I was carrying the monster's bastard child, there was no question what I would do. That devil inside me had to come out.

She read it several more times. It made sense. This was what she felt like, or imagined she should feel like. Although she had never really thought of the baby as a devil. It's just a fetus, innocent – it had no input or voter's rights or veto power about when and where and how it was going to come to be. Still, she had been raped. Brutally. Phil would probably have killed her. Maybe once he had been a good man, but that night he was the monster of any woman's nightmare. Abortion was the only answer. This was not a hard one to figure out. Or at least it shouldn't be. But what about Bridget?

Damn. She had forgotten about Bridget. She should just go ahead and have the abortion anyway, then just deal with the lawsuit. That's what John wanted her to do. He made an appointment to see Janet Rosen. Dale promised last night to attend the session with them. They could talk about it then. There was always the chance that Bridget's case would get thrown out of court, or, if it didn't, that she wouldn't win. There was no guarantee that she would win. Yes, she should have the abortion. Soon. She didn't want to wait the three or four days.

Hawk

THE BIKE TRAIL WAS SPARSELY POPULATED. As I ran, Dale occupied my entire brain. I shudder every time I think that someone might have seen us in that parking lot. We were so engrossed that someone could have been standing right at the open window and I wouldn't have noticed. Or cared at that point. And that scared me.

I made a deal with myself. I would put all of this in a box for now and would allow myself to ponder and ruminate later. Dale said she needs time to clear her head, which I get. I completely get that. I need to clear my head too, but not just yet, not until I replay our time together with enough repetition to satisfy my longing, and I haven't even come close to that yet.

Late last night, lying in bed with Marina asleep beside me, I let my foot rest on her foot. Then I let my thigh touch her thigh. Over the years, through good times and bad, this is what we've done. We don't go to sleep without at least some sort of physical connection. Always. Even just a foot on a foot. Even now.

God, what have I done?

I keep trying to decipher what I saw in Dale's eyes a little while ago in the kitchen. I dread going home; dread having to pretend everything is okay. Damn my wife. Damn her for not getting that abortion. I am so fucking angry with her it's not even funny. If she only fought Phil sooner. None of this would be happening. Because if she fought sooner there would have been no rape, and if there had been no rape, there would be no pregnancy.

Ness told me to go easy on her. Man, he's another one. I can't believe he knew about Bridget's scheme and then talked to her without so much as a word to me about it. I am sure his excuse made sense to him, but Bridget is the daughter of my wife's fucking rapist.

I wish a giant boot would come out of the sky and kick me in the face. Hard. So hard that it punts me all the way to the moon. Because on the moon, I won't have to worry about anything except breathing and keeping my feet planted on an inert dusty rock.

I need to go home. I need to go home to my wife and pretend that whatever happened with Dale never happened. The box idea seems to be working, finally. I know I won't be able to escape my own accusations, my list of failings for long, so I need to embrace it while it lasts. And my list of failings now includes making out with my wife's sister.

CHAPTER 18

May

MARINA HEARD THE STAIRS creaking a bit. She turned from the computer screen and saw Dale descending them with extreme care and delicacy. Her shoes were in one hand and with the other she was carrying her rolling suitcase. There was a thin sweater draped over her shoulders and a small backpack dangling from one arm. When she reached the bottom stair, they made eye contact and Marina motioned for Dale to come into the study. She hesitated for a minute before putting down her things and stepping through the door. Marina wondered if she had missed something, some important bit of information from dinner last night. There had been no talk of her leaving today. They'd had a pleasant dinner. At least she thought they did.

"There's a case starting and one of the partners, Trudy, needs me in DC to go over it before the arraignment. I'm really sorry, but I have to leave."

"Oh. Does John know you're leaving?"

"No, but you'll give him my love?"

Marina nodded, and her eyes welled up. This embarrassed her a little. She reached for a tissue and blew her nose. "You know, I was getting used to having you around here. I'm going to miss you."

Dale reached into her backpack and pulled out a legal pad. She tore off the first two pages and handed them to Marina. "Here. I jotted down some points and things to keep in mind when you and John talk to that lawyer."

Marina nodded and put the paper on the desk beside the computer.

"Well." Dale looked at her watch. "I really need to hit it."

Marina felt like Dale was falling away from her, escaping somehow. Stalling for time, she asked, "How about some coffee for the road? Tea?"

Dale waved her hand in negative gesture and said something about meeting Guitar Man for dinner, which would give her a little over four hours to get back to DC, make a high-speed stop at her apartment to change clothes, and dash, panting, to the restaurant.

Marina stood up to hug her sister, still stunned by the suddenness and confused by Dale's hesitating manner. As she pulled away Dale peered over her shoulder at the computer screen.

"I'm not even going to ask what you're doing," her sister's sarcasm felt reassuringly normal.

"Research. Just some research." She glared at Dale. "Were you planning to sneak out of here without even leaving a note?"

Dale reached into her back pocket and pulled out another sheet of legal paper, this one folded, and handed it to Marina. "No, I was not going to sneak out without a note."

Marina smiled, big sister to little sister. She walked over to the couch and grabbed the suitcase by the handle and rolled it toward the front door. Dale followed. Silently they stepped into the afternoon heat, down the steps and out to the street. Dale opened the trunk of her BMW and Marina lifted the suitcase in. The backpack followed. The trunk slamming shut startled Marina, its sound echoing down the humid street, abandoned for air conditioning and ice water. Marina shivered.

"Thank you for everything." Marina said as she hugged her sister one more time.

"Of course. Keep me posted and let me know how you are doing, after, you know."

Getting into the car, Dale turned the key and lowered the window. "Tell John that I am sorry I have to bolt, ok?"

"He'll understand. DC calls. All that." She smiled and stepped back from the car. "Next time you will have to bring that Mr. Guitar down for a visit."

Dale seemed to pale a little, but smiled and waved. Pulling out, she drove away, leaving Marina watching, even after the street was empty, trying to shake the feeling of being left behind.

**

Marina was reluctant to go back into the now empty house. Despite the heat, she sat down on the front step. The front flowerbeds showed their neglect. John mentioned something about yardwork but he certainly didn't get around to the weeds choking out the tiger lilies. Reaching for the nearest interlopers, Marina found herself pulling and pulling and pulling, bare hands becoming streaked with green and brown.

A few weeds turned into a few more weeds. Since she's out here she might as well pull the wild onions growing along the edge of the porch steps. And the weeds among the daisies. She was suddenly astounded by all the weeds, unable to believe that she had let the front of her house come to this. She was sweating through her shirt, puddles of moisture along her chest and armpits. Finally, she stood up and admired her satisfyingly large pile of enemy greenery. She went back up the steps and into the cool of the house. A glass of water was what she needed now. And maybe a shower.

She walked past the study and practically fell over a red duffle bag sitting in the middle of the hall. She didn't remember Dale carrying a red duffle bag. She bent down to get a closer look then saw something in her peripheral vision, certain that she was not really seeing what she thought she is seeing. She turned back and stood in the open doorway of the study. She was not hallucinating. It was Bridget – a female Phil, uncanny in the family resemblance – sitting at the computer, scrolling through the list of abortion web sites.

As if sensing Marina's presence, she turned around. All at once her eyes told everything yet said nothing. The wet face, the red nose, and of course, the puffy eyes that glared at her. "Marina." Back to the computer. "How did you know?" Bridget's face was filled with anguish and accusation.

"Get out of my house." Marina was paralyzed, the words seeming nonsense. How is Bridget here? What is it with that family, coming and going into people's houses at will. What could have brought her here now? After everything. Oh, my God, what could have brought her now? She gasped for breath, bracing herself.

"What did Nester tell you?" Bridget yelled.

"Get out of my house or I'll call the police." Marina yelled too.

"Bullshit. What did Nester tell you?"

"My husband will be home any minute!" She couldn't keep the hysteria and the rising anger out of her voice. "Get out!" Marina only now saw what she should have noticed right away. Saw the rounded belly under the t-shirt, the full breasts. She was built like her father, small boned and slightly hunched. Except for the belly and breasts, this was a female version of Phil. Pam was nowhere on her daughter. Marina groped for the edge of the chair in the corner, certain that if she didn't she would end up on the floor – involuntarily. Pregnant. Rape victim and rapist's daughter. Pregnant together. Not as nature intended.

She looked at the candle, still burning in the corner, bright flame against the dark blue and swirling stars. Could her grandmother have predicted any of this with her cards? Did she know Lizzie was going to die? Was this why the card readings abruptly stopped? Marina closed her eyes and willed herself to wake up from this nightmare. Ignore it and it will go away. Turn your eyes away from bad things and the bad things won't happen. Gather up the cards and reshuffle the deck.

***

Marina and Bridget were sitting at the kitchen table when John came in from his run. She was clenching her mug of tea with both hands. John sat next to her, post-run sweat still rising on his skin, water glass neglected as he stared at nothing, absorbing her words.

"Pregnant." John looked straight at Bridget.

"Yes." Marina answered for the younger woman.

"And the baby's father?"

"My father." The sobs came uncontrollably. "My father raped me."

"Fuck!" John said. "If I could, I'd kill him all over again. Bastard."

Marina had managed to get a nominal amount of information out of Bridget before John got home. Her stunned reaction and faint collapse in the study somehow opened the floodgates and Bridget told her everything. Phil had violated her on and off during her entire childhood. She never confronted him, never told her mother. That certainly explained the estrangement. Out of a sense of duty she moved back home when Pam's cancer metastasized. Phil had been drinking, a lot, Bridget said, during the worst of Pam's illness. Pam had been lucid up until the last few days. One day, shortly after they'd moved Pam into hospice, Bridget came home and her father was crazed. He attacked her. She was powerless. She didn't want her mother to know. She didn't want her mother's last weeks of life to be tainted with such horrific knowledge. And then Pam died. And Phil was a mess. And Bridget moved out. And now this.

"That's enough for now. We'll deal with this later." Marina led Bridget to the newly available guest room and suggested a bath and a nap before they talked again.

"I can't believe this." John interrupted her thoughts, shock wearing off, anger rising. Marina flinched as if in pain. He walked across the kitchen to the sink, opening a cabinet, for what, Marina didn't know. The cabinet flung with such force that it hit the wall behind it and bounced back shut.

"I guess we never really knew him."

"That's an understatement." She joined him at the kitchen sink to pour out her now cold tea. "Nester knew the whole story."

"I figured as much. She's really screwed up in the head, isn't she?"

"Another understatement. John, this is surreal." Her voice trembled a little and the tears came.

John looked at her, sighed and put his arms around her. Despite his sweat Marina was grateful. They stood there like that, Marina leaning against the counter, John leaning against Marina, neither of them moving. How ironic, she thought. Two women harmed at the hands of the same man – a man they both had, at one time or another, trusted. A hauntingly similar place, the magnitude of which neither can possibly know right now.

Releasing her after a tight squeeze, John stepped back. "I better take a shower. Don't worry about dinner. Maybe we should just order in for the four of us."

"Oh, I almost forgot. Dale's gone."

"What do you mean she's gone?"

"She left. I was working in the study and I heard her coming down the stairs." She paused. "Sneaking down the stairs is a better word. It was obvious she was trying to not be seen."

"I'm confused." John's brow was wrinkled; his eyes looked lost.

"Well, she said something came up at work. Some important case or something like that. Had to head south right away. Or something like that."

"So, she was just going to leave? No goodbye or anything?"

"I asked her that very question." Marina felt her eyes welling yet again and willed the tears to stay back. "Apparently, she was going to leave a note."

John grew quiet. After a beat he continued, "It must have been something extremely important for her to leave like that. I could picture her telling her partners to go jump off a cliff if it wasn't."

Marina laughed a little, the tears safely back in their pockets. But new thoughts started to blossom in her mind.

"But what if there was no meeting John. Do you think she left because she knew something about Bridget? Knew she was on her way here?" Now the tears start rolling, apparently very determined to have their way.

"How would Dale have known this? Maybe she's be talking to Ness?"

She shrugged.

John reached again for her, rubbing her arms as she cried, his lips pressed into a straight line. She wiped her eyes and in a soft voice, "I guess that's the real reason she left. She knew what was coming. Never gave us any warning."

"I can't believe she would have known something. She couldn't have." She thought about this for a second. "But you know Dale. Nothing she does surprises me anymore."

John winced. "Do you want me to call her?"

"No. I don't want you to call her. Not now. Not like this. We're both too upset. And if anyone calls her," her voice hardened with anger, "it's going to be me."

***

Marina wished she could rewind the clock to last night, during Dale's delicious shrimp dinner, and search for clues. An expression. A sentence spoken in a higher or faster pitch than normal. Incongruent twitches. That thing Dale does with her face when she is hiding something. She feels completely and utterly stupid for not paying attention. There must have been some hint. Something that would have tipped her off. Something that might have indicated that Dale was packing up and leaving – right on cue, as if staged well in advance.

No, it couldn't have been staged, at least not that far in advance. Bridget surely made an impulsive decision – a desperate decision – to show up here today. Had Dale known in advance she would have simply scheduled to leave today. Or perhaps Dale planned it this way to make the farce seem more realistic. No, that's not Dale. Why would Nester have shared the details with Dale. He'd never even met Dale before the other day. Doesn't know her from a hole in the wall. Dale was relaxed and comfortable last night. The three of them had some good discussions about the impending lawsuit, demand for the baby, and Dale even gave them some things to think about – some courses of action to explore with Janet Rosen. Case law and legal tips. With this new insight from Bridget, her wanting Phil's other baby made even less sense. You simply couldn't make this stuff up. Crazy.

She longed for the future, when she would be far beyond this moment. She longed for the crisp cool days of fall. She longed for a night of dreamless sleep. Hibernation. Just one, long, cool, crispy night. Snuggled up in a blanket. John wrapped around her. The world spinning and orbiting the sun, pushing the present farther and farther into the past, to a blip no bigger than a dot on the retreating horizon.

But that future night won't save anyone. That future night would never come. Marina knew this. She knew that her nights forever more would be peppered with fitful sleep and the kind of dreams where black poison seeps in and leaves inky stains on her sheets in the morning to remind her that her life would never be the same.

CHAPTER 19

Hawk

I MUST CALL HER. I need to tell her how hurt I am that she left without saying goodbye. I could just picture myself at age ninety, sitting alone in my wheelchair in an old age home, telling anyone who will listen, this is how my heart was broken. How could I be reacting like this? I feel like I've been kicked in the nuts. I wanted it to be over, which is ridiculous because it never really started. Or, it did start but never finished. That's it. It never really finished. I figured there would be more discussions, deeper ones about how we'd ended up in each other's arms. And this doesn't even begin to address what just happened in my house. Phil's daughter. How much did Dale know about this? The thought of her having deep discussions with Nester makes me crazy. She should have been talking to ME about these things. I want to die right about now. Could this be the sort of thing that makes a man want to throw himself in front of a moving train? Was my neighbor Mel as crazed then as I feel now?

I'm wondering if I what I really wanted was for things to progress with Dale. I was serious when I told her that it had to end. I meant every word of it. At the time. Never again was I going to touch her, kiss her, nothing like that ever again. But I saw something in her eyes in the kitchen, and it gave me hope. A giddy kind of hope that yes, she felt the same way about me as I feel about her, and yes, we would always carry that little secret between us, and maybe even have fun with it sometimes, but always keep the tension – sexual and otherwise – out of reach.

I felt energized around her, alive. I was glad she would be around a few more weeks, a few more stolen moments. I am committed to my wife, I know that. But it felt good to be around Dale.

I can't believe she left without saying goodbye. I can't believe it. I feel like a lost treasure has been ripped away from me. I don't know if she left because of what happened between us or because of this Bridget thing. Shit. The Bridget thing. I can't deal with both issues at the same time. Holy Shit. What am I going to do? I can't believe she didn't at least say something to me about the Bridget situation, if she even knew anything beyond what we all knew, or thought we knew.

I must call her. Alone in my bedroom, the bedroom I share with my wife, I started pressing buttons. I panicked before the first ring and hung up. What could I possibly say? The shattered pieces of my heart are coming undone. I crouched on the floor, an emotional wreck, my mind filling with the vision of Dale meeting up with her boyfriend tonight. Bile rose in my throat and I crawled to the bathroom, dry heaving. The feeling of imminent spewing subsided, and I splashed cold water on my face. I dabbed it dry with the towel hanging over the shower.

But I must call Dale. I need to see her. Maybe she doesn't really care about me. Perhaps this is all just an illusion that I created to make up for the longing that I kept locked up in a box all these years. I wish my head would stop spinning.

CHAPTER 20

May

LIKE A BAD CASE OF DÉJÀ VU, Marina and John sat in Janet Rosen's waiting room, all its crayon glory bright in the early morning sun. John took a seat on the couch beneath the wall of amusement park rides. Marina was captivated by one photo from the 1920s, wooden rails and small open cars. Women with bobbed hair, men in button shirts too formal for a carnival ride. One man's face reminded her of Phil and she looked away.

She moved her eyes from picture to picture, then down the wall to the top of John's head, his neck, the top of the couch that his head was resting on, the stucco ceiling that he was intently studying, back down the wall, finally landing on his shirt. Anything to distract herself. Her breathing was becoming rapid and her mind was racing. She stood up and walked a few steps around the coffee table then back again. She sat down. John was oblivious.

"I can't do this."

"What are you talking about?"

"Right now. I can't do this right now." She put her head in her hands, and then opened them just wide enough so she could see John through the crack.

"Sit down, would you?" He was sitting upright now, ready to spring into action at any moment.

"No." She walked toward the door and was about to open it when she felt the presence of a third person in the room.

"Leaving so soon?" A familiar, yet unwelcome voice broke the spell. "Sorry to keep you waiting so long." She looked at Marina's belly. "Nice to see you again."

As if she were a teenager caught sneaking out of the house, Marina let her hand fall off the doorknob and followed Janet Rosen and John out of the waiting room and down the hall.

"I have reviewed the situation," Rosen began, opening the same file from the last meeting. "I have even consulted with a colleague of mine, just to be sure, and he concurs. The plaintiff in this case has no grounds to force you to carry this fetus to term. Even if she were to achieve the highly unlikely wrongful death conviction, she does not have a claim to the fertility rights of her deceased father."

"Even with the latest development?" Marina was afraid to hear the answer.

"She checked herself into a psychiatric hospital. She needs help. She suffered tremendously at the hands of her father. As did you."

"God." Marina felt her heart breaking for the young woman, who, in a moment went from being the enemy to being a victim, perhaps even traumatized in worse ways than she was. She wondered if there was a way she could help her in some form or another, down the road.

John interrupted her thoughts, "So, that means?"

"Go ahead and have your abortion." The lawyer smiled confidently, the bearer of good tidings, her words chiming through Marina's head.

Go ahead and have your abortion. Smiling words, catchy pop song lyrics, ringing through her skull like a chorus.

As her words sunk in, John smiled, made a fist, and slammed it down on the desk in front of him. "Yes! Dammit! Yes!"

Marina tried to feel relief. Isn't this what she wanted? Someone to tell her what to do?

**

John put on a pot of coffee.

"Make it strong," Marina called from the study. She quickly gathered up the abortion literature that was strewn about. This was the last thing that John needed to see. She shoved everything under a pile of her art supply catalogs – things she knew he wouldn't touch. She was about to help him in the kitchen when she remembered the computer. She closed the Netscape Navigator window and shut the whole thing down. Janet Rosen's words were still echoing through her mind. Go ahead and have your abortion.

"Do you think we should check in on Bridget?" John asked.

"Wow, you read my mind. I think we should. She looked so young and broken. I just don't understand how her own father could have done those things to her. It's bad enough that he did them to me."

John sighed. "I know, I know."

"I think we should give it some time though." She looked up at the calendar on the side of the fridge. "Maybe in a week or so. After I have the abortion."

John didn't respond, his back turned toward the coffee pot.

What kind of bruise will Bridget be left with after the acute pain of all that has happened to her is in the past? Will it be a simple bruise, light brown and fairly contained? Or will it be one of those blood bruises – big and ugly and purple – covering her heart. Marina considered her own bruises and imagined them expanding and merging together like a hundred Venn diagrams, soon to cover her entire being, circles overlapping and creating new pain in the middle. She really should talk to her therapist, or someone. Talking to Leslie or Mel or Dale or even John didn't count. It bled off the pain a little, the pressure escaping just enough to prevent a rupture. Spill a little; cope a little.

But that would only get her so far. For the bruises to go away one by one, or two by two, or even entire planes of them at a time, she would need professional help. Logically she knew this. But she was paralyzed when she thought about the overlapping bruises – each representing one aspect of the attack and the aftermath and the things it has stirred up and brought to the surface. Not to mention the little package sitting inside her. She still had a day or two before her deadline to have the abortion.

John finished his coffee and stepped outside to get the mail. Moments later he bounded back into the kitchen, warm with the sunshine, seemingly invigorated by Janet Rosen's declaration.

"I think we should find a way to talk to Bridget. See how she's doing." Marina said.

"One problem at a time Marina. We'll make your appointment, get you back on track, and then deal with Bridget, ok?" He kissed the top of her head.

Marina tried to keep a happy look on her face, but it just refused to stay. She tried and tried but couldn't seem to connect with the optimism that was making John so giddy. She gets it. She really does. To John, an abortion represents a path back to normalcy. Without the pregnancy complicating things, all she would have to do is deal with the rape, get over the rape, and move forward. Get back to the place they were when she walked into the house, wet from rain, on a December evening. Get back to the night when John went to the basement to fix a vacuum, never expecting to end up with a broken wife. Yes, she gets it. But it just isn't that simple.

She thought about calling Dale. Her anger at her sister bubbled back to the surface and she decided to leave it alone. There would be plenty of time to think about that later. To find out what Dale knew, if anything.

***

Marina didn't hear John go back outside. She found him sitting on the front porch thumbing through a West Marine catalog. She looked at him and realized that while his hands were flipping through the catalog, his forest-colored eyes were looking past the pages, past her, as if searching the horizon for something that was apparently not coming into focus. She stared at him, momentarily sucked into the horizon-searching gaze, wondering what he was searching for. Whatever it was he didn't find it. His eyes returned to focus on her own, regaining their position as prominent features. She recognized his demeanor and braced herself for a lecture, the cop dressing down the juvenile caught making bad life choices. The kind that always left her feeling like she'd been whacked with a two-by-four.

"Okay then, I'll schedule the abortion for tomorrow," she said, her voice resigned, a child anticipating the reprimand that was about to come.

"Why not today?" Funny how she knew exactly what he was gearing up to say. "I mean, what is wrong with just getting in the car and going over there today. Abortion clinics accept walk-ins, don't they?"

John continued, "But if it makes you feel better, call them up and tell them you'll be there later this afternoon." He was glaring at her now. "I know how you are about schedules. Just schedule it. But soon, please."

"What difference does it make if it's today or tomorrow or even, at the latest, the day after that?"

"And why do I sense that you're dragging your feet. Like you're still not sure. Like you might consider not having the abortion." His face was red, mouth starting to twitch.

"That's not fair, John." She felt anger rushing up through her body and up into her face like mercury in an outdoor thermometer on a rapidly warming summer day. "What's the matter with you?" The anger was so hot in her face that her tears sizzled away before they once again dampened her cheeks. "Why are you doing this now?" Her voice trailed to a whisper. "You seemed so happy a little while ago."

He grew quiet. Marina was about to continue but John's mouth opened as if to speak, then closed again. Finally, he cried out, "I just want my wife back." He put his head in his hands. "I want our life back and I don't understand why you're hanging onto this."

When he looked up Marina saw that his eyes were wet too. She stood up and opened her arms toward him – a gesture that evolved over the years to mean I'm sorry. Although she was not sure what she was supposed to be sorry for. Yet the sight of her husband with wet eyes melted her heart.

He looked up. But instead of embracing her he stood up and started walking into the house. Stopping abruptly, he said over his shoulder, "I can't stand this, Marina. I can't keep living this nightmare. I've had enough."

She watched in disbelief as he walked through, and then slammed the front door. Leaping up she followed him, panic rising. "Where are you going?"

"I don't know." He grabbed his keys and walked out, this time through the garage door without looking back at her. "Don't wait up for me."

Marina sunk to her knees, mad at herself for following him, mad at herself for a lot of things, although she didn't quite know what they were. Hearing his truck's engine start in the driveway, she sobbed. Abandoned again. Like the night of the rape. Yeah, he was home that night, but he might as well have been on another planet. Abandoned. Always abandoned. His abandoning her now made her feel as raw and as alone as she ever felt in her life. Even more so than the night of the rape.

CHAPTER 21

Hawk

I AM TRYING HARD TO BE NICE. To be understanding. I know I am not being successful. My wife was raped. It wasn't her fault. I know it wasn't. Yet I can't stop blaming her. I can't help but think that she should have reacted differently. She should have gotten directly into her fighting stance. She should have yelled – in a deep and reverberating voice – to stay back. She should have yelled. She should have yelled the word NO!

She says she screamed for me. I know the television was on, I know I was far away, but I still would have heard it. If she yelled loud enough. I can tell you with absolute certainty that I would have heard her if she had yelled properly. Screaming is too high pitched. She knows better. I know she knows better. She should have yelled. Then I would have heard her. And I would have been up those stairs in an instant and I would have killed the bastard. I would have killed him quickly and quietly. He wouldn't have known what hit him.

I am forcing myself to take a deep breath. I had to bite my tongue – hard. I finally removed myself and came out here to vent. I don't want to go back in there. Maybe she will have the abortion. She says she's going to have the abortion. I want to believe her. But I am afraid this guilt she has won't let her.

If only she had yelled properly. If only. Then I would have rescued her. I would have killed Phil. Then the guilt would be on me, not her. Marina always feels so guilty. And now she is going to let her guilt destroy us.

God. Riley. What the fuck happened to you. You're own daughter!

DC. I should just fucking go to DC. I am trying hard to keep what happened between Dale and me out of this for now. I must focus on this thing with Marina. I must get to the bottom of it. There will be time later to sort out things with Dale. I am so worked up right now I could punch things. Throw things. Break things. This is nuts, I know, but the forces surrounding my truck are pointing it in the direction of I-95 South. Pointing it in the direction of DC. Pointing it in the direction of Dale.

May

MARINA AND LESLIE STARED at each other, neither daring to make a move. Horrified at what had just happened with John, she couldn't even begin to process the fact that her friend was witness to it. What did she hear? What does she know?

Marina's knees ached. How long had she been kneeling on the floor like this? How long had Leslie been standing in the foyer? She adjusted her position so that she was sitting on the floor. The grandfather clock by the door chimed, startling her, and she winced with every strike. Fifteen minutes have gone by since John left the house.

The door was still open, and the hot, sticky air coming through the screen began to overwhelm her. John was supposed to put the storm door on weeks ago. Why didn't he? She got up to close the door and was momentarily wracked with panic. She stood at the door and looked out at the scene that spoke of normalcy: the two poplar trees regally flanking the front walk. A watering can, trowel, and gloves strewn about the porch. John's running shoes standing against the porch rail.

Marina closed her eyes and prayed that Leslie would just go away. But she could sense her friend's presence so acutely that it was all she could do to suppress the scream that was building deep in her gut. She wanted to be left alone. Feeling like she was on surveillance, she walked out the door, letting it shut behind her. It flew open so quickly, Leslie must have been on her heels.

"Don't do it!" Leslie bounded down the front steps after Marina. "Don't run after him!"

Marina glared at her and went back into the house, this time, straight up the stairs and into her bedroom, slamming the door behind her. She fell face down on her unmade bed and sobbed into the sheets. She simply could not, for the life of her, understand John's reaction. What did she do that caused him to react that way? He thinks she's not going to get an abortion? Is that what this is about?

Sitting up, her heart raced as she rummaged through a pile of papers on her nightstand. She was certain the number for the abortion clinic was among them. She couldn't find it. She looked again. She threw all the papers onto the floor and ran down the stairs, searching frantically through a pile on the table in the sunroom. She finally found it and dialed, making an appointment for the later that day. She could do it. This way, when John came home she would be able to tell him that it was done, and that everything would be back to whatever semblance of normal they had been before John's new rage. She forced a few deep breaths. He just went to clear his head, she told herself.

Wait a minute. Is John really raging? Marina laughed a little out loud. Why was she making such a big deal out of this? Okay, so he never walked out of the house on her like that before. He never told her, in anger, to not wait up for him. That certainly didn't mean the world was about to crumble around her. It already crumbled – on the night of the rape. But that was a different type of crumbling, a type of crumbling that she and John would walk through and work through together.

What happened today was a blip. A simple, tiny blip. A misunderstanding. John has been stressed, just as she has been stressed. He hasn't been dealing with his feelings toward this whole mess, and it just rose to the surface today and erupted. And she knew she hasn't been dealing with things properly either. In fact, that's another thing she will do to surprise John. She would show him that she was finally going to deal with the rape. She picked up the phone and dials Zina's number – a number that she'd memorized a long time ago – and made an appointment for the following week. Marina nodded, pleased with herself and momentarily soothed.

Dinner. She should prepare dinner now so that she could just rest when she returns from getting the abortion. She went into the kitchen and was surprised and a little uncomfortable to see Leslie sitting at the table. Waiting. Opening the fridge, Marina surveyed her options, but she felt numb, unable to think. Leslie got up when the tea pot she had set to boil whistled. She brought the two cups of tea to the table. A peace offering. Marina reached out and took one. Leslie grabbed one of the other chairs and dragged it so that it was next to Marina's chair. They sat in silence, both sipping their tea, the sipping noises cutting through the silence.

"So, you heard John go off on me."

Leslie didn't respond right away. Marina continued: "I really don't want to talk about it." She took a long, slow, sip. "I don't think I want to talk about it at all."

"I know." Leslie's voice was determined. "I sensed something was going on here today and came over to make sure you're okay. The door was open, and you were in your own world. I saw John leave. I didn't mean to startle you. I wasn't eavesdropping. Please know that."

Marina almost choked. She didn't stop to ensure her words are chosen carefully. She just needed to be direct. "I just need to be alone right now. Please." She paused, out of breath, and a little dizzy. "I don't know why, but I think there's something going on between my husband and my sister." She got up and began to walk out of the room, then turned around and faced Leslie. "I love you. I love you for caring. I think I'm a little bit nuts right now. I'm sure it's all in my head. Stay as long as you want."

Leslie didn't follow when Marina walked out of the kitchen. On the way out, Marina steadied herself on the counter. John would more than likely be home any time now. She decided to go out on the porch and wait for him. She would watch for the truck, which would probably pass right by the house and go halfway around the block to the back alley and pull into the rear driveway.

He would walk in through the back door and when he didn't find her in all the usual places, he would come out to the porch and they would hug and they would talk and she would tell him of the appointments she made and maybe, just maybe he would even go with her. And this day of anger and hateful words would be over.

The air outside was stifling. It was approaching three o'clock and the sun had painted almost the entire floor. There was a time when she had the sun and porch down to a science: In summer, it was deliciously shady in the morning and early afternoon. Then, at around two o'clock the sun was positioned just so, and would shine through the columns to begin painting the floor with light. It would start with a little patch in the far-left corner by the little table and wind chimes. Then it would work its way to the front and right, until it reached the other side, where the porch swing hung. Usually by three-thirty or four o'clock it would be too sunny, too hot, too bright, too humid to sit there. She looked at the swing – the floor was considerably darker around it than the rest of the porch. Good. She could sit for a few minutes before she absolutely had to start making her way to the abortion clinic. She plopped onto the swing and pushed it back and forth with her feet. She quickly became slightly nauseous and dizzy. She stopped and moved her feet up and around, leaning her back and head against the armrest. It was too sunny to even consider watching the street for John, so she closed her eyes.

The screen door squeaked open and slammed shut. She squinted and shaded her eyes from the sun, but it was Leslie standing before her and not John.

"Remember when I said I wasn't eavesdropping? Well, I really wasn't. But, I did hear John talking to someone on the phone before he stormed out of here. For what it's worth, I think he might be on his way to DC." Leslie paused long enough to give Marina a hug and hurried across the street to her own, house, her own issues, her own problems, not waiting to hear Marina's response.

**

The merge onto Baker Street was jammed with cars. Marina glanced at the clock on the dashboard and wondered what was going on. It was not quite the afternoon rush. Not even close. Yet there were at least ten cars ahead of her at the yield sign – something highly unusual. She didn't see any flashing emergency lights or anything unusual in the road ahead. No orange cones or men in hard hats.

She sighed. Her mind returned to Leslie's comments about John going to DC. She laughed out loud. Ridiculous! There was even less of a logical reason for John going to DC than there seemed to be for the traffic. Despite her illogical suspicions, there was no way John could possibly be on his way to DC.

The cars ahead of her edged forward, bit by bit, and when the wave finally reached Marina she lightly tapped the gas pedal. She moved a few feet and soon there were only seven cars ahead of her. She quickly calculated how long she had been sitting like this. And how much time she thought would go by until she was at the front of the line. Luckily the abortion clinic was only two blocks up Baker, and once she merged she would be there within a couple of minutes or so. She should make it on time, but not by much. One false move by someone in front of her, one out-of-synch traffic light, one celestial misalignment, and her whole plan would crumble.

The cars were moving again, this time with more flourish than before. She was third in line now. She would most certainly make it to her appointment on time. No problem. She relaxed a little.

A piercing symphony startled her back to the present moment. Horns blaring and finally, a less-than-amused male voice yelling at her to move. She'd missed her opportunity to merge and punched the gas. She was now the first in line to merge with a procession of angry drivers behind her. Shaking, she looked over her shoulder, paying close attention to her chance to get out into the traffic and disappear forever from the view and consciousness of those behind her. After what seemed like an eternity, a small hole opened between two cars. She merged between them, barely avoiding getting herself pressed like a piece of cheese in a grilled cheese sandwich, and just as she had hoped she would, disappeared into a sea of cars.

The parking lot at the abortion clinic was practically empty. She found a spot at the far end of the lot, shaded by a cluster of bushy trees. She was surprised to look at the clock and see that she had a full fifteen minutes before she absolutely had to go in. She turned the car off and rested her head against the seat. She closed her eyes and took several deep breaths. She felt her belly and tried to recall just how far along she really was. She slid her hand under her shirt, opened her jeans and felt. Was she any bulgier than she had been a few days ago?

The manila envelope on the passenger seat filled her peripheral vision. It had not been touched since Dr. Finston handed it to her. She picked it up and started to open it slowly, the way you might open the kind of envelope that contains the very direction of your future. Like a letter from a college either accepting or rejecting your application. Or a letter from your long-distance boyfriend telling you he wants to see other people. Or the letter from your kid's high school, officially letting you know the terms and conditions of his expulsion.

Marina pulled enough of the celluloid out of the envelope to see the heading – *Butterfield, Marina*. She pulled it out a few inches more. She saw the black background – the Milky Way of swirls and comets. No. She couldn't look. She shoved it back into the envelope and slapped the whole thing back down on the passenger seat. She grabbed her bag and got out of the car. She walked halfway across the parking lot before turning around and running back for the envelope.

There were only two other women in the waiting room. Marina wrote her name on the clipboard and sat down in the back corner of the room. She would be brave and open the envelope. She wasn't even sure why she was so afraid. She wasn't afraid of changing her mind. Her mind was made up. She simply had to do this.

Suddenly the sonogram picture was out of the envelope. For one frozen moment, Marina forgot the way in which this baby came to be. She forgot the trauma and what walking out of this clinic would mean for herself and for her marriage. Her head felt like it could explode at any moment. She stood up and started pacing. Nobody looked at her or seemed concerned with anything other than what was happening in their own heads, their own bodies. She found herself standing once again at the reception desk. She retrieved a pen and drew a thick, black line through her name. The woman behind the desk never even looked up.

CHAPTER 23

Hawk

I WISH I COULD SAY I'm halfway to DC, but I'm not. I figured if I could get as far as the Jersey Turnpike there'd be no turning back. That's how it was when I was a kid and my parents took me down to Philadelphia to visit my grandmother. The trip seemed insurmountable from our house. Ah, but the Jersey Turnpike. The first great signpost marking the journey.

So, here I am, about to cross the point of no return. Marina has no idea where I am. And I never called Dale to tell her that I'm really coming. The frantic call earlier did not go well. She begged me not to come. She promised me we would talk later. But I need to see her. I need to talk to her in person.

Damn. I really should stop somewhere and call Marina. I know she is a wreck. The problem is I don't really care. I can't face talking to her right now. I'm seething and can't think straight. At least I recognize the fact that I'm seething and can't think straight! That says I'm in tune with my emotions, right? Marina.

Fuck. I can't do this. I need to go home. She doesn't deserve to be talked to the way I talked to her. The way I have been talking to her. Maybe I'm just looking for an excuse. Any excuse to be mad at her, pick a fight, and run into her sister's waiting arms. I'm a mess. A fucking mess.

The Jersey Turnpike sign beckons. It sucks me in like a small matchbox car through my mother's vacuum hose. What am I doing here? What am I doing on this road? I really should stop somewhere and call Marina. No. I won't call her. I think she needs to stew a bit and feel the pain of my walking out of the house. I guarantee she will be a new woman when I get home. For all I know she will have even gone in for the abortion or at least scheduled it. This is cruel, I know, but it's for the best. I know my wife well and I know how she operates. Soon I'll be home and she'll be so happy and relieved to see me she won't even remember any of the bad stuff.

May

JOHN WAS STANDING at the kitchen window when Marina returned home. Relief overwhelmed her and she fell into his arms like a rag doll, drained and without a skeletal structure to stand on her own. He held her like a lost thing, found again and feared to lose again. The sonogram envelope was in her hand but it fell to the floor as she wrapped her arms around him. Noticing, he pulled away and looked down.

"What's in the envelope?"

"Stuff from Dr. Finston."

"You went to Finston today?"

"No, it was in the car from a few days ago."

Seemingly satisfied with her response, he hugged her again. Then he gently pulled away and looked at her – his eyes travelled from her eyes, down to her belly where they paused, then back up to her eyes again.

"I'm sorry I wasn't here for you today," he said. "I acted like an ass. I should have stuck around to go with you." He gestured toward the note on the kitchen counter.

Marina knew she needed to tell him that she was still pregnant. She knew she needed to tell him this now. She knew that if she waited even a second longer she would likely lose him again, this time for good. But she was soberly aware that he was likely to walk out the door in an angry fit again, no matter when she told him.

She stalled. "How long have you been home?"

"Not long." He touched her hair and then caressed her cheek. "Now that this is over, after you settle down a little we're going to need to talk. I mean really talk." He rested his head on Marina's shoulder. "Right now, though, I don't want to think about anything. I just want to hold you."

"John, Leslie said something today." Marina rubbed the back of his head, getting the tips of her fingers under his hair and making circles on his scalp. "She said you were on your way to DC." Marina continued massaging his head, but she could feel him tense.

"That's crazy," he said into her shirt. "How would she know where I was? I went to the boat."

Marina remembered when he left the house; she'll never forget that. She calculated the time for the trip to the boat, the time spent returning.

"Actually, I turned around before I even got there. Never actually made it to the boat."

It was like he'd read her mind. He had been nothing but honest in their marriage, and yet, this time she knew he was lying. And not because Leslie said what she said. Marina just knew he was hiding something from her. There was no point trying to get it out of him now. No point.

"John," she said softly as she continued rubbing his head.

He pulled away from her. "Stay right here. I'll be right back."

"But."

"No, no, just stay there. I'll be back in a second, two at the most." He kissed her nose and disappeared.

The sound of his footsteps going down the basement stairs filled her with dread. She heard the faint sounds of bottles and glassware and then footsteps coming back up. She braced herself for what she knew would be her flash point – the point of no return – the point at which there would be no rewinding the scene. It would be finished. John rounded the corner into the kitchen, just as she'd feared, balancing two champagne flutes filled to the brim. He handed her one and raised his. Instead of crystal touching crystal, she set hers down on the counter.

"John. I didn't do it."

"Didn't do what?" He squinted and shook his head, as if trying to understand a difficult concept.

"I didn't have the abortion today."

"Excuse me?" His eyes widened but he shook his head again, denying the words she'd spoken. "Wait, why? Was it crowded? You're going back tomorrow, right?"

"John I'm not doing it. I can't do it." The tears flowed freely.

"Ever?"

"Ever."

"What are you saying? That you want to keep that fucking bastard's baby?" His voice got louder with every word. "Is that what you're telling me?"

"No John, that's not what I'm saying."

"Then what. Tell me. I desperately want to know." He put the champagne glass down with a trembling hand.

"I don't know what. Adoption? Maybe?" She wiped her forehead with the back of her hand, her skin clammy. "I haven't really thought about it."

"The hell you haven't." He was yelling now. "The first time you walked out of that clinic. You knew you wouldn't abort. Didn't you?" He came toward her with pursed lips, then lifted his arms in surrender and let them fall heavily against the sides of his thighs. "I don't understand you. Why would you want to have that thing still inside you? I feel sick every time I think of it. I don't understand why you feel the way you do about this. Do you have any idea how frustrated and angry I am right now?"

"John. Please. It's complicated. I can't even really articulate everything going on with me. I don't necessarily even understand it all." Marina's dry tone belied her trembling hands.

John recoiled. "There's nothing complicated about this. You want to have another man's baby. I pleaded with you to have a baby with me. For years!"

"That was different. I wasn't pregnant then, it wasn't a question of ending something."

"I get that, Marina. I get that. But that doesn't give you the right to decide, unilaterally what you get to do. To us."

"Look, I made an appointment with Zina for next week. We could both go. We could talk this through with her."

"What's there to talk about? That my former best friend, my fellow officer, raped my wife, held a gun to her head, broke her wrist, filled her with his disgusting fluid, left her pregnant, and now she wants to carry his child? That she blames me for not stopping it? That she is angry with me but feels guilty over him?"

His words echoed through the room. Marina could think of nothing to say in this maelstrom, this tidal wave of anger.

John turned away from her, grabbing his keys off the counter.

"Now where are you going?" She followed him to the back door.

"I don't know. I need to get away from here. I need to think."

"John, please don't do this. Let's talk this through."

"Talk this through?" He was yelling again. "What happened to talking it through before you made this decision?" His tone was softer, emphasizing the word before.

"I tried. I tried. I really tried to talk to you. In my own way, I tried." She hung her head.

He opened the door without responding.

"When will you be back?" It was all she could think to say.

"Honestly, I don't know. I need to wrap my head around all this."

Marina stood in the doorway and called after him, "This is only until the baby is born. This is only a short period of time.

Please remember that. I'm not planning to keep it. By September this will all be over."

He got in his truck for the second time that day and drove away.

PART THREE

July

ACCEPTABLE LOSSES. Marina turned this phrase over and over in her mind. Would losing John over this be an acceptable loss? It wasn't as if she were asking him to raise this baby. She just didn't feel she could abort. Giving this baby a safe haven until it was born, assuaged her guilt over letting Phil die. At least it did a little. Surely, she could endure being pregnant for the next couple of months. Why couldn't John? She was the one who was raped. She was the one who was suffering. But if John couldn't support her through this, perhaps losing him over it would be acceptable.

She had worked hard, very hard, on her own and with her therapist to try to see John's point. According to Zina, John was a victim of the rape too. And the hurt he felt that she'd never wanted to have kids.

It was too late, obviously, to reverse her choice. She found herself thinking a lot about Mel, and his choice to lay down on the train tracks, then his choice to panic and run at the last minute. Like her, once that choice was made, the consequences – both intended and unintended – were like toothpaste haphazardly squeezed out of a tube. No matter how frantically you try to scoop it up and put it back in, it is never the same as what you had before – an intact and functional tube of toothpaste. Mel had tripped and broken his neck running away from the track that only a moment before he had been lying on, in wait. Marina had made her choice about the baby and was losing her marriage in the process. Not at all what she expected. What else could she have expected?

John reluctantly attended a few therapy sessions with her. He asked her point blank if she'd ever had feelings for Phil. She gave the best answer that she could: that he had been their friend and that she saw him differently after his wife had become ill. She didn't tell him about the night that they talked under the stars, or running into him in the bookstore. She didn't tell him about the kiss. She just couldn't. But did she ever have feelings for Phil? No, she could honestly say that she did not. Not in the way that John meant. And she told him so.

In a moment of boldness, since John had started this line of questioning, she asked him something similar: did he ever have feelings for Dale. He grew quiet. He didn't answer. And then the moment was gone. She would be sure to never ask again.

John continued to harangue her about the night of the rape. How she reacted. The timbre of her yells. The timing of the fight. That if only she had not been startled into a paralysis that night, perhaps the outcome would have been very different. He blamed her for the pregnancy. Not the assault necessarily. Had she fought properly, there likely would have been no penetration, and had there been no penetration, there would be no pregnancy. She agreed with him on that point. Sort of. The problem was, no matter how much you trained for the possibility of something like this, no matter how spot on your techniques might be, well, there would likely be a period of paralysis before muscle-memory kicked in. As a cop, John should know this.

Face the truth. They both needed to face the truth. But what was the truth? The truth was Marina couldn't bring herself to kill another human being. She just couldn't. John didn't get that. A lot of people didn't. Here's her truth: if she hadn't played a prank on her baby sister – sending her on a wild goose chase to find a non-existent buried treasure, Lizzie would more than likely be alive today, a beautiful, vibrant, woman. Their family wouldn't have imploded. Her relationship with Dale might be better. And her parents might very well still be alive.

If she hadn't lingered with Phil under the stars, if she hadn't lingered with him in a bookstore, if she hadn't kissed him back. If only she hadn't kissed him back. If none of that had happened, then probably none of this would have happened either. He would be alive too. And John wouldn't be gone. None of these losses were acceptable. And none of them were reversible.

***

Marina looked visibly pregnant now. She had been forcing herself to paint daily. With the possibility of divorce looming, she needed the income that she knew her craft could bring. She was in her studio, working her paintbrush over her canvas, her hand stronger, healing slowly, even if her heart didn't seem to be. The sunlight was warm through the windows, illuminating her dark birds as they squawked into being.

A week after he left, John returned to pack a proper bag. They sat at the kitchen table, rigid with ceremony, and laid out the ground rules. It had taken an hour to chart this new course, for him to leave her in this abyss. There would be no phone calls unless it was an emergency, the definition of an emergency having mostly to do with the house or money. No mention of Marina or John's own health. If a car broke down, well, each was on his or her own to deal with it. Same with minor house repairs. And, since it was John who had walked away from Marina, he was the only person able to declare the abyss period officially over. And it could only be over when one of two things happened: either he decides that living apart is too painful and he really does indeed love her, or living apart makes him realize that he doesn't love her. John made it abundantly clear that he did not want to be contacted for any reason regarding the 'monster-bastard' she was carrying. He did, however reluctantly, agree to see Zina with her, at least for a few sessions. She doubted any good would come of those, since he mostly still blamed her for everything. She hasn't even begun to unpack her own feelings of abandonment – that he had been in his own world that night. The betrayal she felt from that alone was too much for her to deal with right now.

For a moment, remembering their last conversation in the house, she began to feel the familiar panic. But she thwarted it, pushing it back down, reminding herself that it was her husband who walked away. Her husband who had left her in this abyss to fend for herself.

Her reverie was broken by the sound of footsteps, John's mother, Pearl, coming up to the studio. Marina was surprised. Her mother-in-law had remained silent since she showed up a little over a month ago, expecting to find her son, and instead found nothing but bitter words from Marina. She was apparently no longer engaged and was moving to Florida and needed a place to stay for a few months. Marina agreed more out of an inability to fight than any desire to help. However, she was unwilling to talk to her beyond the daily necessities. Apparently, Pearl knew more than she initially let on, and fed it to Marina, spoonful by painful spoonful.

Pearl sat down as Marina watched her, uncertain of her mother-in-law's intent.

"I was furious at my son when he left you, but now I kind of feel sorry for him. My heart breaks for him." Marina didn't respond to this opening gambit, suddenly wary. "I just can't believe you. You're going to have a baby. At your age." Pearl leaned in a little closer and Marina recoiled. Pearl was tall and had a commanding presence. And a perfectly coiffed, unmoving silver bob. And too much hairspray. Today especially. Way too much hairspray. "What is this, Marina? Some sort of self-righteous statement?"

Marina closed her eyes and bit her tongue to keep from saying something she might regret. She decided there would be a time and place for more bitter words. For now, Marina simply did not have the gumption. Pearl continued: "How narcissistic can you possibly be? How utterly self-absorbed? How can you make John live with this? You're ruining your marriage." The venom in Pearl's voice startled Marina. "You've never warmed up to me, and now, when I need family you're destroying yours, you're destroying my family."

"What are you talking about, me ruining your family?" Marina's gumption suddenly appeared. "Where have you been all these years? You never warmed up to me. You were quite vocal about who you thought John should have married. Go live on the damn boat with John. If anyone is ruining anything, it's him. Your son. I've had enough of this. Please leave. I beg you." Marina was incredulous. She felt somewhat light headed and stopped talking long enough to take several deep breaths. She put her hands together steeple fashion in front of her face, touching her two index fingers to her forehead and peeking at Pearl through the opening. As soon as she did this she stopped herself – this was something John did when he was frustrated and trying to make a point. Right now, Marina wanted nothing to remind her of John. She let her hands fall to her lap. Pearl sat, unmoving.

"For God's sake Pearl, you confided in my sister about your engagement, the subsequent end of your engagement, and the fact that you were moving to Florida. You said nothing to John or me." She shook her head in disbelief. "You know, John would have been grateful for your support early on. After the attack. I could have used the support. It was a nightmare for a little while. It was like you didn't even care that your son – you can even take me out of the equation – your son needed you. And you were not there."

Pearl spat back: "How could I talk to you? I don't get you! I never have. Even now. How could you live with yourself, carrying that man's conceptuous?" Pearl stopped yelling and now her voice was barely a whisper. "Makes me sick to even think about it."

"Conceptuous?" Marina was momentarily speechless. Her eyes scanned over the worktable scattered with magazine cut-outs, photos, sketches, newspaper articles, anything she found artistically interesting. Especially photos. She kept the envelope from Dr. Finston's office here too, on the corner of her desk.

"Ah. There it is." Marina stood, leaning over the table, and picked it up, wondering if conceptuous is even a word. No matter if it is or isn't – she knew exactly what Pearl meant by it. She opened the envelope and handed the contents to her mother-in-law.

Pearl looked at it. Stared at it intently, then quickly handed it back to her Marina.

"I get that. I do. I've seen plenty of those from my friends who were lucky enough to get grandkids from their kids." She placed it back in the envelope and set it down on the desk.

Marina glared at her, regretting the moment she agreed to let Pearl stay. "You know what? I really think it might be best if you packed up your things and left. I'll give you a few days to get yourself sorted out, but you need to go. Okay?"

Pearl tried to say something but instead squeaked and a series of sobs escaped. She buried her head in her hands, her shoulders silently, rhythmically bobbing up and down. Marina considered sitting down beside her and pulling her close. But she couldn't bring herself to do it. Instead she stood in front of her easel and stared at the broken, older woman before her.

Acceptable losses. Would destroying yet another life be an acceptable loss? Marina knew that if she didn't get up and wrap her arms around Pearl, she would probably regret it. It was a moment likely to not present itself ever again. And quite frankly, she didn't care. But John would care. In his own way, he would care. He hadn't said so, but Marina knew he was pleased that she took his mother in. Even if the only reason for his being pleased was the fact that his mother was not on the boat with him. In the end, Marina concluded that sending her mother-in-law away would not be an acceptable loss. She was angry, confused, baffled by Pearl's vitriol over the past few months, years really, decades. But still, she knew there would be time to work through those things. Marina had barely a crumb of emotional strength left, but she figured she must do the next right thing, which was to get up and hug her mother-in-law, and the rest would somehow work itself out. Of this, she was certain.

Hawk

IT'S FUCKING HOT on this stupid boat. I've been living on it since I left Marina, and living on it meant I had to quickly finish the fiberglass work and have the thing splashed. So here I am. Living on a boat. And I hate boats. The only good thing here is that I can see the twin towers across the Hudson. Very majestic. Standing erect and watching over the river.

There's something wrong with the innards of the boat and I don't yet have my own climate control worked out. So, I basically fry most nights. Lately though there's been a nice breeze and I've been sleeping on the foredeck. It's a pain in the ass commuting back to Maplewood for my shifts most days. But, at least I'm going against traffic. That's something, right?

I can't stop ruminating over the big choices in my life: wondering why I chose the way I chose and wondering, did I choose the path or did the path choose me? I'm scaring myself, thinking this deeply. Cops are not sentimental fools, right? Nor are they particularly deep thinkers. I've always relied on my intuition while on the job. My raw, animal instinct. Hawk, like they call me. But it's different now. It's somehow different.

I'm living on a fucking boat. A boat with no air conditioning. In July! Well, at least it's a place to stay. And it's free. A free, fucking boat that I was supposed to be fixing for my wife, who had this ridiculous idea that if I fixed this boat it would bring her some type of closure with her dead father and help her make peace with her dead baby sister, but all hope of peace and closure evaporated the night Marina was raped.

I never did go to DC that day. Never even called Dale to explain. Never called her again. Haven't talked to her since she tried to sneak out of my house. I wonder what would have happened if I did go. Probably nothing more than me ending up looking foolish. So, I'm sitting here in the heat on this stupid boat, thinking I want to run home to Marina. But then I ask myself if my heart is sincere. Most of the time I think it is. So, I'm thinking about going home, breaking my rules of the abyss. The stupid rules that I put in place. And then there's my mother. I wonder how Marina is dealing with that. I'm actually surprised she's dealing with that. These are the things that keep me up all night. I miss my wife. I miss her.

So, what about those paths? The ones taken and not. Why did I fall in love with Marina? It certainly wasn't love at first sight. When I walked into that bakery and saw her she was just some ordinary girl. With red hair and freckles. A dime a dozen. But the next thing I knew she was staring at me. As if she'd never seen a guy eat a few pastries and chug a gallon or so of coffee. It was damned good coffee, too. Funny that I remember the coffee and I don't even remember what she was wearing.

What if I had never walked into that bakery? I've wondered about this a lot lately. Sometimes I wonder if the reason, the fateful reason I met Marina was to ultimately meet Dale. But when that chance meeting came I was already deeply entangled with Marina. Ah, but when I met Dale – bing, bang, boom. Was that love at first sight? I felt a connection. I am sure she felt it too.

I sometimes wonder if Marina could tell. I'd be surprised if she couldn't. Yet she never said anything. She was very graceful that way. Always so graceful. And I loved that about her. I still do. But Dale is so different. Different to the core. She has a fire in her – something Marina lacks. Dale is lit from within. Marina is so passive – something I always resented about her. So why didn't I confess my confusion early on? Entangled we were, yes. But we weren't married. Hell, we weren't even engaged when I met Dale. Sure, there would have been pain and hurt feelings. But Marina would have gotten over it. She would have met someone more suited to her personality. Marina didn't need an arrogant cop.

But no matter what I tell myself, neither did Dale. When I stared at her, she didn't stare back. When I tried to penetrate her with my eyes, she was impervious. The irrational side of my brain is convinced that had Marina not been in the picture and I had simply met Dale, my life would have been different. I convince myself, revise events, and imagine that Dale would have jumped at the chance to be with me. That we would have jumped at and on each other. Barely coming up for air. Long stretches of time without seeing sunlight. Each day I convince myself this would have happened, each day I wrestle with the past. But, the thing that gnaws at me is this – if it's so much work to convince myself, can it really be true?

How did my life become such a fucking three-ring circus? Now that sounds like a good name for a boat. Three-Ring Circus. I think that's the perfect name for this boat. I wonder what Marina would think of me changing the name from *Lizzie* to Three-Ring Circus? She'd be pissed. Reason enough for me to do it.

August

MOST NIGHTS, MARINA WAKES up in the darkness. Not as regularly as before, but unexpectedly, without warning she finds herself incapable of sleep, isolated in the wee hours of the morning with nothing but her thoughts. Her regrets. The last time it happened, Marina had gone to bed late on a Saturday night with the television as her companion and woke to someone singing something, something that intertwined with whatever she had been dreaming about. She woke up hard, sat straight up in bed, and continued listening to the song – a morbid thing to do, given the feeling. She looked over to where John would have been sleeping, had he been there. He would have been snoring softly beside her, and she would have reached over and held him tight, grateful, oh so grateful for him.

The clock let her know that there were many hours of darkness yet to be endured. She closed her eyes and tried to relax enough to sleep – an impossible feat given the emptiness she felt.

Her days were busy and productive. Her relationship with Pearl was slowly growing tolerable. The harsh words between them had been necessary, she realized a few weeks later. They provided a convenient window into talking about things they had never talked about before. While some topics were still off limits, it didn't take long for mother-in-law and daughter-in-law to fall into a comforting pattern of keeping house, accompanying each other to doctor appointments, having Leslie and Mel over for dinner, spending lazy afternoons in front of the sunroom taking turns reading chapters of books out loud. In this new existence, the acute emptiness of the early abyss days had subsided quickly, which continued to surprise her. Pearl had even gone to see John, to talk to him on Marina's behalf. To no avail, apparently.

Nester came over sometimes too. To check on her. See if she needed anything. He tells her how John is doing. And he tells her about Bridget. He's been keeping tabs on her too. She had a miscarriage. She's in Colorado with a friend. Until she gets sorted out. A happy ending? Not really, but, according to Nester, she's doing okay, considering.

Marina was sitting up now, propped against six pillows, her four and John's two, and stared at the clock, remembering those first days after he left. She had felt like a Mylar balloon unfettered and floating up, alone into the vast blue, then beyond the blue into the colorless universe, sucked into a black hole. A black hole from which there was no escape and that drove her into the fetal position for what seemed like hours and hours and hours.

She willed the empty feeling away, but it was stubborn and stayed put, right in the middle of her soul. Yesterday, she considered breaking the abyss rules and driving over to the station to visit John at work. She wanted to invite him for Thanksgiving, even though the holiday – her favorite – was three months away. She wanted to remind John that by Thanksgiving there would be no more baby. That he could come home, if he wanted to. She wanted to tell him about the couple who were adopting the baby – a boy, she now knew. Yesterday, she had been feeling considerably good about life. Hopeful even. Yes, that was how she felt yesterday, hopeful. She also wanted John to know that she was still working with Zina – twice a week – on everything. The rape, the pregnancy, John's leaving, her guilt over Phil's death, her guilt over Lizzie's death, her guilt over her parents' death, anger at her sister for what feels like years of betrayals, her anger at John for not hearing her frantic cries for help the night of the attack, and her anger at herself for a whole host of failings. But then she remembered her huge belly. A visible reminder. John didn't need to see that. Although she suspected that Nester tells him how big her belly has become.

While she was under no illusions about taking this kaleidoscope and turning it into a Norman Rockwell painting, the regularity of the meetings and the easy way Zina seemed to draw words out of her was helping tremendously. She'd started to call John yesterday to invite him down, then summarily hung up before the last two digits were dialed.

The rules. Her calling to invite him for Thanksgiving would be a strict violation of the rules of the abyss. Marina laughed, wondering how Norman Rockwell might have depicted such a Thanksgiving scene. She laughed even harder, and when the absurd realization of her current reality subsided, she realized that the veil of despair she had awoken with was gone.

***

The bird feeders were empty. Marina stood in the sunroom looking out the window, waiting for the coffee maker's beep to tell her it was ready. Almost immediately upon entering her second trimester Marina found herself craving coffee. Strong coffee. Going on the common knowledge that caffeine and pregnancy don't mix very well, she tried every brand of decaf out there until she found one she could stand. When she mentioned this at one of her prenatal appointments, Dr. Finston laughed and told her it would be fine to have one cup of real coffee every day. Make it good and savor it, she had said, and with that Marina donated four or five nearly full canisters of decaf to Leslie, who laughed hysterically at the prospect of decaf and said she'd give them to Mel for his greenhouse. Apparently, his plants like decaf.

She opened the door to go outside and was greeted by a blast of oven-like air. It was all over the news stations the past few days. A stalled-out Bermuda high. This was only the beginning, they said, of at least another week of well above normal temperatures. It is August, after all.

Marina couldn't stand looking at the empty bird feeders. She braced herself for the heat and slid out the door. She grabbed three feeders at a time, carried them to the shed, filled them, and hung them back on their hooks. She repeated this process two more times until all the feeders were filled. She didn't go back into the house right away, and instead stood on the patio, letting the heat engulf her. It was already sunny. Blinding. A horrible beginning to what promised to be a horrible day, weather wise, but Marina still felt hopeful and excited. She was looking forward to Thanksgiving, three months away, and the feast she and Pearl would create. For Marina, Thanksgiving represented new beginnings. She was due in about four weeks, which would give her two months to deal with postpartum issues. She planned to absolutely break the rules of the abyss the minute the baby was in the arms of his new parents. She felt there was much to be thankful for this year. Yes, there had been tragedy, and yes, she was still dealing with the tragic irony of John leaving her. But for some reason she couldn't quite grasp, she mostly felt hopeful and alive, and the emptiness that she woke up with was an aberration. Truly.

Never too early to plan, she started formulating the guest list in her mind, counting on her fingers just to be sure she had it right: Pearl, Leslie, Mel, John, Nester, and Dale. She had grudgingly reached out to Dale a few weeks ago and they've been talking regularly since. She said she would come up for Thanksgiving, the first time since her hasty departure. She told Dale to bring a guest, if she had one to bring by then (Guitar Man was no longer strumming her chords). Maybe she would invite Bridget. She needed to think about that one. But yeah, maybe. She and Pearl would make the turkey and Marina's world famous caramelized onion gravy and cornbread dressing. She would have several side dishes prepared, with each major color represented: green beans, mashed potatoes, and something orange which she was vacillating over – she couldn't decide between roasted root vegetables and butternut squash puree. She decided to make both. The others would bring whatever they wanted to bring, if anything. All she cared about was having the people she cared about around her. And right now, she felt like she cared about everyone. Everyone in the world. Such a change. The nightmare would finally end. Soon.

Still unaffected by how hot it was outside, she lowered herself down on one of the patio chairs. The baby pounded her hard, right under her ribcage, as if to say, *you're crazy, it's an inferno out here*. She laughed at the thought and returned to the house, to a blast of air-conditioned relief and the smell of fresh coffee. She went directly to the kitchen to pour herself a cup.

"You got any more of that?" Nester walked into the kitchen and helped himself to a mug, as if he'd done it a hundred times before. "Your mother-in-law let me in. She seems to be mellowing."

"Yeah. I guess she is."

They sat down and didn't talk for what seemed like a long time. They never really had much to say to each other, except when he had news about John, or Bridget, or something funny that may have happened on his beat. But for some reason, his presence these past couple of months, his coming and going, was comforting. And she liked him. He was a nice man. She was happy he hadn't abandoned John.

"So. What's the verdict? You like your hair that way?"

"Huh?" She sometimes forgot that she now had short hair. "Oh, this." She ran her fingers through what little hair she had left. She had been looking through a box of old pictures and found one that was taken about a year ago, standing on the beach feeding a seagull. In the picture, the bright sun played tunes on her red hair, which dangled almost like dreadlocks down past the middle of her back. Her head had been tilted slightly toward the camera and the light streaming onto her face didn't do kind things to the lines under and around her eyes. Seeing this picture of herself – a woman she barely knew – startled her. She looked like an old hippie. A Bohemian bird lady, one that wiles away the days on a park bench with a bag of crumbs for the birds. *Feed the birds, tuppence a bag,* no thank you, she would not turn into the bird lady in Mary Poppins. Or, worse yet, she looked like one of those women who refused to accept the fact that the number-line moves forward and not backward. She set the picture aside as a reminder and booked the next available appointment with Leslie's stylist. "Yeah. I like it." She smiled.

"Me too. You remind me of that woman in the movie The American President. What's her name?"

"I have no idea. I've never even heard of that movie."

"Michael Douglas plays a windowed U.S. president who falls in love with a lobbyist."

"Sounds interesting. I'll be sure to rent it."

"Let me know when, and I'll come by and watch it with you."

The coffee was hot and delicious. She sipped it slowly, savoring it, making it last as long as she could, since she was only allowed the one cup and would have to wait until tomorrow to have another. She wondered what John will say when he sees her with short hair. It will be one more thing to signify the demarcation between yesterday and today.

Hawk

"WHAT THE HELL ARE YOU DOING HAWK?"

Here we go again. Ness. The pious one. Suddenly all about family and forgiveness and all that crap. I'm getting tired of him hounding me about my wife.

"What are you doing? She needs you. She's about to pop."

"I don't give a fuck about that. She can pop that bastard out on her own. I want no part of it."

Nester got out of his squad car and stood just a little too close to me. If we were anywhere but here in the station parking lot, I would have shoved him out of my way.

"I'm outta here. You coming over tomorrow? I need to get the air working on the boat. I'm gonna melt if I don't do something soon."

"You can go home to your air-conditioned house."

"Asshole!"

Nester smiled and nodded. I guess I will be seeing him tomorrow.

***

Nester emerged from the cockpit looking like he'd spent three days crawling around in a sewer. But, to his credit, no matter how shitty he looks, he helped me fix the air conditioner. It's been cooling for about a half hour and the difference down below is beyond noticeable. I am so grateful I could hug him.

"Man, you're wasting your life being a cop. You could make a lot more money doing this shit."

"And miss the opportunity to help my fellow citizen, fight crime, and all that." He watched an osprey swoop down to the water and grab a fish. "You know. I hate to bring this up again. I'm not sure what you're doing. I'm really not. You don't know how lucky you are. You have a wife who loves you. Who wants you to come home."

"If you hate to bring this up, then why do you keep doing it?" I'm too hot and dirty to argue with him right now. What I really need is a shower. And a beer. The truth of the matter is that I do think about going home. I think about it all the time. Getting in the car after my shift is hell, because my inner sense of direction, after twelve years in that house, just wants to drive me right there. Getting on the parkway has never been a part of my post-shift life. It's weird. But I started this. And I'm not about to go home and grovel. Because that's what she'll expect. Groveling. A lot of it.

***

"I'm thinking about changing the name." We were at Shorty O'Rourke's, sitting at the bar, finally having that beer. Instead of a shower I just jumped in the water off the stern. Not really allowed, but some people go in the water to clean their boat's hull, I've learned. These die-hard boat racers who are convinced that a barnacle or two will provide enough drag to make the difference between a win and a loss. The one guy who explained all this to me said I should race with him sometime. I could be ballast he said. I wasn't quite sure how to take that.

"The name of what?" Nester was mindlessly eating his burger and focused solely on a pre-season game between the Giants and the Redskins. Redskins. Washington. Dale. I can't help wondering about Dale. Now that I have a couple of months of that little episode in my truck behind me, I'm relieved that's all that ever happened between us. I know it will all come crashing back the next time I see her. But I figure with enough time and distance, well, like we say in my profession: distance buys reaction time. That's something we drill into the students on day-two of the self-defense and crime prevention courses. First put distance between you and the bad guy. Because distance buys reaction time. If there's enough distance, maybe you can escape without having to fight. Maybe you can run to the nearest populated location, if you're outside. Or the nearest phone. Or you can run to the basement where your husband is passed out on the couch.

"I want to change the name of the boat. I want to change the hull color too. Maybe yellow. A happy color. The blue reminds me of my mother's kitchen tiles when I was growing up."

Shorty apparently had one ear on the game and one ear on our conversation. He chimed in: "Hey, my nephew's a painter. A regular painter, you know, and artist. He does boat hulls too. He's painting a mural on the wall in the alley, later, next spring. I'll see if he can do your boat."

"That would be grand. I want to change the name too. Could he do the lettering?"

"Why sure!" Shorty's attention turned to three women who sat down at the opposite end of the bar.

"Have you lost your mind?" Nester was fully engaged now. "This is Marina's boat. You're just living on it. She will be devastated if you change the name. Paint it, okay fine. But please don't change the name."

My hackles were raised and on full alert. "What is this? You're suddenly Marina's advocate? Is there something more here than meets the eye?"

"What are you saying?"

"You know what I'm saying."

"I like her. I like her a lot. She's interesting. And she's very complex, I'll say that." He put down his burger and grabbed me by the shoulders. Not hard. More like brother to brother. "She loves you, Hawk. All she ever wants to talk about is you."

"Yeah, well." I love her too. I'm not about to say that out loud. Ness knows how much I love her. I don't need to say it. "I guess I just can't face her, Ness." Okay, I started it, I may as well finish. "I failed her. Plain and simple. I failed her."

"So, go home. Go make it right."

"It's not that simple."

"Yes, it is. You're the one who's over complicating this."

"You've not lived through it. It really isn't that simple."

"Sure. Whatever you say."

Ness was frustrated with me. I could see that. Nothing I could do about it though. "It is what it is."

"You know. I've always hated that expression." His voice seemed louder than necessary.

"Shut up and eat your damned burger." I was sort of smiling when I said that.

"You're a dick." Ness didn't smile. Not even a hint of a smile.

"I know."

CHAPTER 5

August

MARINA HAD ASKED JANET ROSEN if she would handle the adoption. She seemed to be caught off guard, mumbling about being a criminal lawyer, and then, in the end, smiled and said yes, of course she would handle it. They met formally about a week later and Rosen warned her that although she was within legal rights to change her mind up until a point, even after handing over the baby to the adoptive parents, that it was never a good idea to do it. Too much emotional angst for the couple that already likely has had years of emotional angst. Not to minimize Marina's own emotional angst, Rosen had been quick to add. Her best advice, she said, was for Marina to have her decision chiseled in granite no later than the end of this month. With her due date being toward mid-September, this was a good signpost to shoot for.

Pearl's house in Florida had been ready for the past few weeks, but she decided to stay until after the baby was born, just so there would be someone in the house in case something went wrong. Pearl reminded Marina almost daily that she was kind of old to be having a baby. As if she needed reminding. Marina just let these comments fall to the floor. She didn't get defensive or try to argue. She was reluctantly grateful for the company. For another live body in the house. Just hearing her mother-in-law rummaging through the kitchen in the morning was an odd comfort. They have been softening toward each other. Too bad it has taken all these years. They found an equilibrium and Marina didn't want to do or say anything to upset it. They found a way to exist peacefully and productively under the same roof and have learned how to help each other and how to stay out of each other's business. It was nice and Marina was beginning to cherish it. Someday, she hoped, Pearl would grow comfortable enough to be straight with Marina. To explain why she'd disliked her for so long.

A siren blared in the distance. Marina heard the fire truck and ambulance leaving the station that was at the end of their street. She could tell by the pitch and roar in the sound that the cavalcade was heading down Woodland Road.

"Did John ever tell you that he was deathly afraid of sirens when he was a little boy?" Pearl sat down at the table. Marina shook her head, as she sat down across from Pearl, opening the paper, scanning the headlines. "Yeah, he really was," Pearl continued. "I guess he was about four or five. The sirens were scariest at night when he was in bed."

"Oh, here's the movie section." Marina slid it across the table and Pearl absorbed herself in it, abruptly abandoning the topic of sirens. They had taken to seeing movies together lately. Usually one every Saturday afternoon. They'd seen some great movies and some horrible ones. No matter, they always seemed to enjoy themselves.

Another series of sirens screamed. It sounded bad. Likely other stations were involved.

"The sirens that terrified John weren't these kinds of sirens." Pearl said.

"No?"

"The firehouse by us had a tall, multi-horned structure. It was a call-to-action, a warning thing, tornados, storms, natural disasters, that sort of thing." Pearl slid the paper toward Marina and pointed to a movie. "It was one, long, loud, continuous whistle. It terrified him. So much so that he went through a period where he was afraid to go to bed, in case the siren went off."

"How often did this happen." Marina tried to picture a little John, running into his parents' room, shaking and white as a sheet. He never shared this with her. Why? She wondered.

"Not often at all. I think maybe a handful of times over the years. I just told him if he heard the siren he should just wait it out. The whole thing lasted less than a minute, but for him it seemed like hours."

Just wait it out. Isn't that what she was doing now? Just waiting it out. Waiting out the pregnancy. Waiting it out until John came home. Waiting for this act to end and the next one to begin. Just wait it out.

CHAPTER 6

Hawk

THE HOURS OF COMMUTING back and forth from the station to the boat each week are adding up and I'm tired. Nester's words keep ringing in my head. Tonight, I was in my truck, heading back to the boat, but for some reason couldn't stop thinking about Marina. Not that I don't think about her all the time to begin with. It's just that the things Ness said, well, they cut me to the quick. And yet I still don't know what I should do or how I should feel.

I failed her. Plain and simple. Why, if I'm such a good cop, did I not sense the third party in my house? I'm The Hawk! The alert officer! How could I have missed something as obvious as Riley's obsession with my wife? I'll never be able to un-see Marina's disheveled hair, her swollen face, and her bloody fists banging on my chest that night when she finally escaped.

Distracted and worn out by the familiar anger, I didn't notice my speed. I didn't notice the cop car in the median. It wasn't until I saw the flashing lights in my rearview mirror did I get control, silencing the thoughts that fill every unfocused moment.

I pulled over, well off into the grass. I lowered the window, turned off the ignition, and put my hands on the wheel so the officer could see them.

"Good evening, sir. Do you know how fast you were going?"

"Yes, officer." I tried to keep my voice humble. "I am going to get my license and registration out now. That ok with you?"

The young cop looked strangely at me. "Thanks for letting me know. You must be a cop?" I didn't recognize this kid. But then, I'm not in my jurisdiction.

"Yes, from the other side of the river. Just so you know, my service piece is locked in the glove box."

"Ok," the kid chuckled, "let me go through the motions at least."

I handed over my documents and watched the officer walk back to his vehicle to check everything out. Sitting in the rapidly advancing twilight my mind started to drift again. If only I could have stopped that one night from happening. Then I wouldn't be out here, facing a ticket, headed to Jersey City and a stupid boat. Alone.

The cop came back, gave me back my stuff, but no ticket.

"Hey, not to be nosy, but aren't you the cop whose wife killed that rapist?"

Startled, I nodded.

"You must be awfully proud of her."

"Yes."

The officer walked away. I sat and watched the retreating young cop in my rearview mirror. Then slowly, hesitantly, I started rolling. As soon as he was out of view, I punched it. But in the other direction, toward home.

CHAPTER 7

August

"WELL, IT'S ABOUT TIME." Pearl stood against the kitchen counter. She had already changed into her pajamas – lounging clothes as she liked to call them – and was making herself a mug of chamomile tea. Marina was at the table, stunned at John's sudden and unexpected appearance.

"It's nice to see you too Mother." He stood sheepishly in the middle of the kitchen and inched his way over to hug his mother. She stood stiff but eventually gave into his embrace. Marina was paralyzed, unable to stand, unable to speak, unable to think. He pulled away from his mother and stood looking at Marina. She watched him but didn't acknowledge him. She simply didn't know how to react, how to feel, how to exist in his presence.

"Marina."

"John."

"I'll leave you too. I'm going up. Thanks for gracing us with your presence." Pearl took her tea and practically marched out of the room, leaving John and Marina alone in their impasse.

"How's all that going, buy the way?" He tilted his head toward his mother's invisible footprints.

Marina shrugged. "We're becoming friends, if you can believe it. That's the best way I know to describe it." She reluctantly got up and stood before him, her new hair and belly like elephants in the room.

"You look good." Okay, he slew both elephants with one phrase. Marina was relieved to have that acknowledged right away.

"You look good too, John." She held out her hand as if meeting him for the first time. "Nice to see you again." He took her hand then pulled her in close and hugged her. The baby decided this would be an excellent time to kick. John recoiled.

"Sorry about that. The kid is active." She patted her belly. "It's a boy, by the way."

John took a few steps backward. "I shouldn't have come here." He took a few more steps, shaking his head and mumbling things that she couldn't quite decipher. "You're attached to it already. You're keeping it. Aren't you?"

"John, stop it." She moved toward him and grabbed his arms. "Just stop." She led him to the table and pulled out a chair for him. He sat.

"I can't do this Marina. I love you. I miss you. I want to come home." He put his head down on the table and she could see his shoulders shake. She lost it then and sobbed right along with him.

"I want you to come home. I miss you so much." She said between sobs.

"I can't do this. Seeing you like this. I just can't. I can't. I'm sorry." He caught his breath. "You're keeping that bastard. I just know it. I know you. You're already attached to it."

"John you're killing me. There's a couple adopting it. Janet Rosen is handling all the legalities of it. This will all be over soon."

They sat in silence, the only sound between them were sniffles and sobs. He put his arms around her. They hugged, they kissed. And in the end, he still seemed caught in the illusion of her keeping the baby. She couldn't convince him otherwise. It was as if he were blinded by the sight of her, unable to see anything other than what his mind had formulated. The waiting it out was over. She was losing him. As if on cue and in his softest, humblest, saddest voice: "I want a divorce."

**

She didn't try to stop him this time. Didn't fall into a whimpering heap on the floor. She told him she loved him and let him go. She just let him go. She didn't know what else to do. She didn't want a divorce. She wanted to grow old with this man who knew her like no one else in the world knew her. She couldn't identify the specific thing she was feeling. It scared her a bit that she was as calm as she was. She tried to will the tears back. The sobs between her and John at the table, at least on her part, were sobs of love and relief. She honestly thought he had come home.

Really come home. For good. Now that he was gone, possibly for good, she couldn't cry. She didn't even feel the familiar lump that had been a frequent visitor in her throat over the past few months. No lump. No eyes filling to the brim. No tears. Simply none.

"He isn't coming back, is he?" She didn't hear Pearl come into the kitchen and wondered how long she had been standing there, how much she had heard, how much she had seen.

"No. He isn't."

"I'm sorry. I'm really, really sorry."

"Yeah. Me too." The tears came then.

***

Marina found herself standing in the vestibule at Saint Vincent's. It was the first time she'd been in a church in three years. This time she was not disguised. This time she didn't hesitate at the door; she walked right in. Everything looked the same. Yet everything was oh, so different. She asked to see Father Andy, not even knowing if he was still there. He was. And he seemed pleased to see her.

"Nice to see you again. I was hoping you'd come back."

"You remember me? I look kind of different."

"I remember you. I just wish you came back sooner. I know what happened to you. I've been following your story. I've been praying for you, daily. And not since all this happened. Since that first time you came to see me." He regarded her huge belly. "You're strong and brave." He motioned for her to follow him and this time, instead of the confessional, he led her to his office. She sat down on one of two chairs in front of his desk. He surprised her by taking the chair beside her, forgoing the formality of the desk.

"If you've been praying for me, then why did all of this happen? If you were praying for me, clearly God could have somehow locked the man who raped me out of my house. Or made my husband hear me screaming. Or not allowed me to get pregnant. Everything was right and then suddenly it was wrong. And here I am, almost forty-six years old, carrying a baby that isn't my husband's because I was stupid and didn't fight back soon enough." She hung her head and didn't stop the tears from coming. He handed her a tissue and she saw that his eyes were genuinely sad for her – eyes that were not filled with pity or judgement, just plain, ordinary, raw sadness.

"Listen." He held out his hand to take her crumbled tissue and tossed it in the wastebasket next to his desk. "God never, ever promises anyone an easy life. That's what trips so many people up. They're believers and when the bad starts rolling in they throw up their hands in frustration and say *well, what's the point.* The point is, that God pretty much promises hard. Sometimes very hard. No one is immune. We all will experience hard. Each. And. Every. One. Of. Us. Sometimes it seems like this person or that person has it all together, has been blessed with a happy, pain free life." He grew quiet for a moment before continuing. "You're not seeing the whole picture when you look at people and think they have it better."

Marina understood this. Innately. However, she still wonders what she did wrong to deserve so much pain. So much. Maybe it was kissing Phil. This was somehow her punishment.

"You didn't cause this." How could someone so young be so perceptive? "You're probably thinking that your indiscretion three years ago – the kiss – somehow marked you for this future trial. I'm telling you, with complete faith and absolute certainty that nothing you did or didn't do caused any of this."

How did he remember so much, and in so much detail? "So where is God now?" She truly wanted to know because, even if she really believed in God, she certainly wasn't feeling it.

"God doesn't promise easy. What he does promise is that he will be with us through the hard. Right beside us. That's a guarantee."

"My husband wants a divorce."

"I'm sorry. You know we," he waved his arm around his office, indicating the church in general, "well, we don't encourage divorce. In fact, we do all we can to discourage it." He looked hard at her. "But sometimes a spouse's heart hardens. Only God can soften it. But sometimes, sometimes," he paused, "sometimes a heart is just too hardened."

"What are you saying," she searched his face, "that I should just let him go. Without a fight?"

"I would counsel you to do everything you can to fight it. But in the end, you're the one who needs to decide what's right for you, in your situation. You may need to let him go."

"I keep hoping that once the baby is born and in the arms of the adoptive family. Maybe then. It's hard for him to see me like this. There's history there too. He always wanted kids and I never wanted them." She felt shameful revealing this.

"God will show you a way forward. He always does. You just need to open yourself up to it."

CHAPTER 8

Hawk

I'M BACK IN THE ABYSS, but this time it's void and without form. It's a black hole with no end. A bottomless pit. And there is no turning back. I told her I want a divorce and I meant it. At least I meant it in the moment. But less than a few blocks from the house I panicked and turned back. Pulled up to the curb a few houses down and sat in the truck. Just sat. I inched my way up the street and stopped again, this time right in front of the house. It was dark. The whole damned house was dark. I went in anyway. Found my wife in the kitchen. She didn't even look that upset. I asked her if she was sure about giving up the bastard for adoption. She showed me the papers. Of course, she doesn't get to sign them until seventy-two hours after the birth. Stupid, stupid rule. She wanted me to feel it kick again. I told her no thanks. She asked me to stop calling it a bastard. I saw something in her eyes then. Something imperceptible to anyone but someone who has lived with her for as long as I have. There's no way she's signing those papers. She is attached to this kid. Attached. I would almost bet my life on the fact that she has already named the kid, in her mind. I almost asked, but was afraid to hear the answer. She didn't ask why I came back a second time. And she didn't ask why I was walking out yet again. She didn't need to.

Two weeks later and I'm with Nester now, trying to tell him all this. We're the only people in the bar tonight. I think Shorty would have closed early, but he knows what's going on with me and I think he's taking pity. The cop who's messed up in the head. He's acting like he's not interested in our conversation, but I'm pretty sure he's listening.

"The thing that gets me is that I would have loved to have kids. I know some guys who would stick by her and help her raise it, but I can't. I just can't. It's like a slap in the face. I keep thinking that if I'd accidentally gotten her pregnant she would have aborted it and maybe not even told me."

"Bullshit." Nester looked angry, tired of my crap. I can't say as I blame him. I really am a mess. "You don't know that. She's not that kind of person."

"How do you suddenly know what kind of person she is and what kind of person she isn't?"

"You seem to keep forgetting that I've known the two of you for years." He laughed. "You ass."

"Sorry." I handed him a folder. "So, you'll do it. You'll serve her the papers."

"I think you're making a colossal mistake, brother. Colossal." He shook his head and took a long, slow swig of his beer. "But yeah, I'll do it." He put a twenty on the bar, stuck the folder under his arm, and started to walk out.

"Keep your money, this one's on me." He nodded but kept walking.

***

Where the fucking hell am I? I don't hear myself, not really, but I must have asked the question because I hear Nester's voice, amid a ton of other voices, male, female, unfamiliar.

"You're in the hospital. You left Shorty's and tried to break up a fight. You pulled your badge and the guy pulled a gun. You reached for yours then he tackled you and you hit your head." I'm not really understanding any of this. "Looks like you have a really hard head." Nester squeezed my hand. "Your leg is pretty messed up though."

***

The guy who jumped me did a number on my leg. My right leg. Snapped the tibia and fibula. Like Joe Theismann. Almost exactly. The main difference is that my bone didn't break the skin. Still, I'm in for a hell of a lot of rehab. Looking at anywhere between four and six months. The department isn't saying anything but Ness says I should prepare myself mentally for them to retire me. I'm almost fifty. And now this. Fuck.

Marina told me I could come home. After rehab. I just looked at her with her giant belly and sparkling eyes and told her no. No thanks. Shorty already said I could stay with him. Liberty Landing's gonna pull the boat then, and Shorty's nephew will paint the hull yellow and rename it Three-Ring Circus. I told him he could take creative liberty and do a little logo of sorts. Maybe a crazy looking clown on a unicycle or something. Something creepy, not cute. Of course, I've told none of this to her. I'm not even sharing this more detailed plan with Ness. He seems to stick up for her a lot. Makes me nuts. I hate my fucking life right now.

"I'm still divorcing you, you know." I didn't look at her when I said it.

"I know."

"Where's my mother?"

"She's out in the lounge area. I'll go get her." She bent over and kissed my forehead. "I love you, John. I always will." And with that, she left and didn't come back. And that's the moment I knew that she flipped the switch. Binary. Ones and Zeros. On and off. Hot and cold. That was that. I could beg, I could plead. But she flipped the switch. For Marina, it's over.

・ C H A P T E R   9 ・

September

WHEN NESTER CALLED TO SUGGEST he come over and bring dinner, Marina suspected there was an ulterior motive. It was a chilly, ordinary day in September, neither a holiday nor birthday nor milestone with John's recovery. She was a little less than two weeks away from her due date, so she figured he wanted to pop in and make sure she's okay. She tried to anticipate this when he called, and told him she was fine, then quickly realized there was no talking him out of it. She suggested Chinese food and told him that she wanted egg foo young and fried won tons. She also asked him to pick up a few sets of chopsticks. She hadn't seen Nester much since John's accident. Which was fine. She really didn't need to be fussed over. She told John's mother the same thing. Pearl had seemed conflicted on helping Marina and being there for John. Marina told her to go to her son. That she'd regret it forever if she squandered this opportunity to be there for him. Pearl half-heartedly agreed, but once

the idea took root, she threw herself into searching for a tempo-
rary, furnished rental near the hospital. She saw this as a perfect
way to finally get to know her adult son. He was immobile
enough so that he couldn't run away, but his life was not in danger. A perfect world for a mother wishing to repair a rift. Marina
was sorry to see her go, but relished the long hours to paint and
just be with herself in ways she never would have expected. Leslie
was on call for any labor and delivery emergencies. And Mel still
made regular visits for scotch. So, she was hardly alone.

She wrapped herself in a wool shawl as she sat on the porch
waiting for Nester. A steaming mug of green tea warmed her
hands. It was chilly enough that she could see her breath. He
pulled up to the curb in his squad car, clearly having just finished
his shift. She put the tea down and met him at the car, where she
could see the bags of food through the window. It looked like
enough food to feed the neighborhood. Tucked between the
seats she saw the top of a yellow folder. He pulled it out and
opened his door, tucking the folder under his arm. He walked
around to where she was standing, then opened the passenger
door to get the food. The sweet and savory smells of Asian cuisine
enveloped her – she was suddenly ravenous.

They walked silently into the house. He put the bags of food
on the counter then carefully pulled the folder out from under
his arm and gently placed it on the kitchen table, which Marina
had earlier set for dinner.

"Is this what I think it is?" She picked up the envelope and
started to walk into the sunroom. Nester followed her.

"I'm so sorry Marina. I really didn't want to be the one to have to give you this, but you know, he was pretty determined. Then I thought to myself, well, at least it's me and I'm guessing it's better this way because you know me and it's not some random schmuck standing over you while you consider your entire future."

"That's one way to look at it." She opened the folder and pulled out the legal documents. She tried to read but was unable to focus. Scenes from her long marriage played in her mind like a movie. The tangible remnants were tucked away in every room and every corner of this house. Not literally tucked away in boxes, but tucked away in her memories of before the attack, before the beginning of the end. The intangible remnants would be harder to purge, like the smell of John's soap that seemed to permeate every molecule in the house. The memories of the good times. Each room contained so many memories of love. Not all perfect, but love – the messy bits that make up a life. She willed the movie in her head to stop playing but it wouldn't cooperate. She put the papers down. "So, what do I do with this?"

"You just sign the acknowledgment of service form. I'll do the rest."

The pen she reached for didn't want to come out of the tin can where she kept her writing implements. After several determined tugs, the pen broke free and in the process launched what seemed like hundreds of other pens. She watched the pens shoot straight up and then down, hitting the table and bouncing and rolling in different directions, hitting the floor and again bouncing and rolling until finally, finally they all stopped, completely worn out and panting from their unexpected journey. The original pen was still in her hand. She stared at it.

"That was interesting." Nester broke into the scene and gently pried the pen out from between her thumb and index finger. "How about we do this after dinner. The food will get cold."

She followed him into the kitchen, sneaking glances of the battlefield beneath her feet, being careful to not step on any of the wounded soldiers.

***

After dinner, Marina signed the divorce acknowledgment of service form. She handed it to Nester and started to clear the dishes.

"Let me take care of the dishes. You go sit down. Turn on the TV. I'll be right back." He put the papers back in their folder and started toward the front door. He must have sensed her confusion. He turned back toward her: "I need to get something out of the car."

By the time he returned, she had already cleared off the table, put leftover egg rolls, orange chicken, and a hefty serving of won ton soup into containers and in the fridge. She planned to send all of it home with him. He returned carrying a plain brown paper bag and asked her if she had any tape. She pointed at the junk drawer.

"Now, please, get out of the kitchen. Go put the TV on and I'll meet you in there in a minute or two." He was laughing.

She did as he asked and sat down in the family room but didn't turn on the TV. She wondered what he was doing. She listened to the banging and rustling typical of someone doing something in a hurry. He entered the family room a little bit later with the same plain brown paper bag he had been carrying earlier. Only now the bag had been converted into some makeshift gift wrap. The top of the bag was folded over and secured with several strips of tape. A white bow, which she imagined was recycled from a lifetime's worth of presents, was the single adornment. She'd never been one to wait until Christmas to open something given to her several days before. This wasn't a Christmas gift, per se, as Christmas was three-plus months away. However, the shape and weight of the package confirmed its contents. When the surprise of his gesture subsided, she opened it.

"The American President." She couldn't help smiling, the cover of the VHS tape confirming Nester's comments a few weeks ago about her hair. "Do you have time to watch it, or do you need to go back to the station?"

"I'm off for the next three days. I have time to watch it. That's why I brought it, so we could watch it."

She popped the movie in, touched by his gesture. She looked at his wrapping job, now void of the VHS and sitting flat on the coffee table. A tangible remnant that would remind her of how different her story was becoming from the one she had always envisioned. She would tuck away the brown paper bag because even more than what was inside, it was the bag that really made her smile. That plain brown paper bag, with its scotch tape and tired, white bow reminded her of the intangible joys of childhood. It reminded her of a time when a thought, a gesture, or a smile meant more than something of great monetary value. Someday, maybe, she might fill the bag with something. Perhaps she'll fill it with words. Words she's been saving for a rainy day. Words she wants to say to John. Words that until now, she never knew existed.

***

The rewinding VHS tape hummed and murmured as is went from ending to beginning. Nester had fallen asleep in the recliner about five minutes into the movie. She'd thought about waking him, making him a cup of strong coffee and sending him on his way – it seemed weird hearing him snoring softly in her family room. It almost felt like a betrayal to John in an even more powerful way than it did when she had let Phil kiss her. Yet she left Nester to sleep, undisturbed, as she watched and enjoyed the movie. Now she really didn't know what to do. It was after eleven. She stood up to pop the tape out of the VCR and was surprised that her pants felt damp. How did she not notice this before? During the movie, she'd been curled up on the couch, under a blanket. At one point, she felt wet but figured she was just a bit sweaty from the blanket. She had been too cozy and comfortable to move. But now she knew.

"Nester." She whispered at first, then nudged him a bit and shook him gently by the shoulder. "Ness." He stirred. "Can you drive me to the hospital?" And as if on cue, as if he'd been the expectant father with half of his brain on full alert, he jumped up and was ready to do whatever needed to be done. She pointed to the puddle on the couch. "I need to change."

With no idea what to expect, she dialed Dr. Finston's answering service. And she called and left a message for Janet Rosen. When she came down, Nester was cleaning the couch where Marina had been sitting. He was pressing a towel into the spot and told her that he'd come back later and properly clean it for her.

"This is crazy." She grabbed his arm. "John should be here. I'm so pissed that he isn't."

"I know." He looked a little sad at her remark. "I really did try to talk him out of this madness, you know, the divorce and all."

She sighed, defeated. "I'm so glad you're here." She grabbed her belly, the first contraction apparently. "Oh, God, that hurts."

"We need to go now." He led her out the door and into the squad car. He opened her door and helped her in.

"I enjoyed the movie, by the way." She smiled and felt strangely calm.

Thanksgiving

A NORMAN ROCKWELL THANKSGIVING. A scene when at almost any given house, in almost any given city, in almost any given state, some version of this: a half-eaten turkey carcass cast off in the kitchen, one or two people standing over the sink doing dishes, another person setting the table for dessert or starting a pot of a coffee. People in front of the TV, screaming at a referee for calling some sorry play that had the opposing team's player stumbling into the end zone a touchdown. Other people in front of another TV watching The Sound of Music. Someone – usually an older uncle or a grandfather – sprawled in a reclining chair, head perched at an unexpected angle, mouth wide open, rhythmic snores escaping. At Marina's house, the scene inside is not as cozy or as simple to pin down. Modern Rockwell with a twist.

The dinner had been lovely. Served at three o'clock on the big dining room table, they sat around talking and laughing well into darkness. Marina stared at the remains of the blueberry pie sitting in the middle of the table, flanked by a barely touched pumpkin pie, an amply devoured apple pie, and an empty tin of what had contained a chocolate pudding pie. She relished this moment with good friends around a table talking about real life.

She suddenly missed John. Everyone's voices blended together to form a blur of sound, and missed the rise and fall of his voice, his laughter. She tried to fight the tears as she remembered the last days of their marriage. She was so grateful for Ness and the friendship that was forming between them – they'd left their masks at the door and it had been the first time in Marina's life that she felt truly connected to another person. They've never touched, at least not in any meaningful way. And for that she was grateful, because she wasn't looking for that – probably wouldn't be for a very long time. They spent most days together, and the fascination he took in the baby was endearing. John had been right – she'd bonded with the baby long before she had to decided what she'd do with him. She tearfully backed out of the adoption process. And when he was born and placed in her arms, she felt so strongly about keeping him that her guilt for disappointing the adoptive parents, well, it evaporated quickly. The most remarkable thing, while it was still too soon to tell – much too early – was that he looked like Marina, complete with red hair. He looked nothing like Phil.

Everyone around the table seemed happy and chatty and still hungry. They helped themselves to more dessert and Dale went around topping off wine glasses. When the last drop hit the last glass, she helped herself to the last piece of blueberry pie.

It was at that precise moment that Marina heard the back door open and close. With a mouthful of apple pie, she turned to look. John on crutches. Dirty and unshaven. Dale lifted the baby from the bassinet beside the table and held him close as if protecting her heart with a shield.

"Dale, it's okay," Marina said.

"No, it's not okay." Dale got up with the baby, walking past John without a word.

"I invited him and his mother." She leaned in closer and whispered in Dale's ear. "I didn't think they'd come."

Nester got up and went to John. Hugged him. Just then, Pearl came in, carrying yet another pie.

Leslie got up and started clearing the table. Mel sat with his scotch, looking like he was bracing himself for a scene. John didn't move, his feet glued to the floor, planted like a tree, swaying slightly but unwavering. Marina sat back down in her chair and was just as still, staring at him, unable to speak.

"Come on Mel, I need your help in the kitchen." Leslie called over her shoulder.

"Right. Help from a quad. You lie."

Marina shot him a mock annoyed look. "Go on and help your wife." She winked at him and he wheeled away.

Closing her eyes, she could hear the sink in the kitchen and dishes being washed, but no voices. She squeezed her eyes tighter, but nothing happened. She pressed her fingers into her eyes as hard as she could stand it, trying to see colors and swirls and paisleys. When she was little she liked the paisleys best, especially when she was sent to her room for one offense or the other. After the tears subsided she would rub her eyes real hard, close them real tight, and then sit back and enjoy the show. Colors and swirls and paisleys. She had to rub especially hard to invoke the paisleys and sometimes even that didn't work. She would wait with great anticipation for a big yellow blob to form blue edges, then turn orange and red and sometimes green. And then she would watch as the blob shimmied and divided like a cell and the separate pieces, if she was lucky, turned into paisleys of intricate beauty.

She saw nothing now. Her mind and vision were blank. Resigned, she opened her eyes. John was now sitting in the chair next to her, studying her, looking like he wanted to say something, but had, for some reason been struck mute. She looked away from him and promised herself that she would not look back. Inviting him had been a mistake. She wished now that she hadn't. The candles all around the table that had been burning for hours were little flickering nubs, ready to fizzle out at any moment. She considered blowing them out, getting up, and walking away but couldn't seem to make her body move.

Marina had imagined this scenario many times since John left her. In her imagination, he usually found her in the garden and would have something clever to say and the triteness of his demeanor always sent the most wonderfully rebarbative words out of her mouth. Sometimes she imagined he would walk up to her and she would greet him in a decidedly indifferent manner. In her mind that would set him off into a tirade and she could walk away in her indignation. But the way someone plays things out in their mind rarely ever comes to pass when they are caught off guard with the good news that they have indeed been cast as the stars in their own made-for-TV drama.

Now all she wanted was to be far away from here. On an island in the middle of the ocean. Any island. It didn't really matter. Big, small, hilly, flat. None of that mattered. Small would be decidedly better. Because if it was small, there would be less chance that there would be other people there to bother her. A small island. With a single palm tree. The palm tree would provide coconuts for her to eat, coconut water for her to drink. She would catch fish and eat them raw. She's always liked sushi.

Opening her eyes, she looked askance at John and then looked away. John was now saying something about time, about how it flies, about how by the time you reach a certain age the minutes seem like seconds. She found this incredibly hard to believe. Time goes so slowly. The past several months moved incredibly slowly. Slower than anything has ever moved in her life. Oh, how she wished she were on her small island with the one palm tree where no people and no clocks exist. Just her and the tree and the fish and the water and the coconuts.

John continued muttering about this or that – she was pretty sure he had gone onto a new topic and she was doing her level best to tune him out. Why she just didn't get up out of her chair is beyond her comprehension. She tried at last, but she too was glued.

She was determined to not let him have this effect on her. She was determined to move on with her life. She had nothing more to say to him and berated herself for feeling sorry for him and inviting him home for Thanksgiving. She remembered her mother making a lame attempt to send all of them to family therapy after Lizzie died. Marina had nothing to say to the therapist and spent the three sessions they attended staring at the clock. Her mother had threatened to ground Marina if she didn't start participating, talking. But the therapist must have told her mother to leave her alone. Must have recited some sort of psychobabble, promising that a child can't out-stubborn him and to just hang in there. Her mother was wrong. She did out-stubborn him and in a fit of frustration her mother stopped making them go. Marina often wonders if things would have turned out differently if they'd all just worked a little harder.

She slowly averted her eyes from John to the flickering candles that still seemed to be burning even though they were now nothing more than wicks floating in small puddles of wax. John had stopped talking. She noticed that he was holding a tissue. She watched him twist it and twirl it around between his fingers. She wanted desperately to yank it away from him, but she didn't. She watched his big, familiar fingers working the tissue, and thought about her island. The small one with one tree. And lots of water. If she got too bored, she supposed she could always try to swim back.

Christmas

HO HO HO. Shorty did a special price fixe Christmas dinner menu. Price fixe. Way too fancy sounding for an Irish pub situated just outside of a boatyard in Jersey City. The regulars are not the type of people to embrace price fixe or necessarily even know what that means. Yet they came in droves today. I couldn't believe it. Shorty apparently has been doing this for years. Prime rib, salmon, soup, salad, one glass of complementary wine, chocolate mousse, and strawberry cheesecake. Ho ho ho.

I'm still recovering from my injury. My leg is in its second cast in four months. I'm getting around okay on crutches. Shorty took me in – he has a spare bedroom and full bath on the main level of his house. What luck, right? I hate to say this but I can't wait to get back on the boat. My boat. Marina said I could have it – that she realizes it will never bring her sister or father back. She has made her peace, I guess. Apparently, she and Ness have become tight friends. He took her to Long Island so she could rehash her childhood memories and slay the demons. Why didn't I ever think to do that with her? I'm peeved that Ness is moving in on my wife, only he isn't moving in on her. He's a good guy and is taking it slow. But I know where this is going. It's okay. I'm okay. Nah. Not really. Nevertheless, the day after the Thanksgiving debacle at my, or should I say her house, she said the boat means nothing to her anymore. I could keep it, sell it, live on it, change the color, change the name. Didn't matter. She said it was mine. Ho ho ho.

Ness stopped by this morning to wish me a Merry-Merry and told me I look like shit. After he left I studied myself in the mirror: full beard, crazy hair down below my chin, and a gut I never used to have. But do I look like shit? No, I can't say as I do. A little disheveled, yes. But like shit? Nope. I've been helping Shorty at the bar a few nights a week. I blend in better now than I ever would have before. Plus, I look like a dude who lives on a boat. I kind of like this new me.

Ho ho ho. I'm on a stool behind the bar, fixing drinks for the regulars that somehow escaped the family bedlam – the regulars that just want libations, not price fixe.

What's this? A pregnant redhead? Walking right in, her dashing husband behind her. The irony of this scene makes me laugh out loud. She reminds me of Marina when we were young. This is what she might have looked like pregnant with MY baby. I hope beyond hope that they don't sit at the bar. Shorty jumped up and led them to a booth. Thank God.

"Stop staring." Shorty startled me. I guess I must have been in my own world and didn't see him sneak up behind me. "Look. I know this is hard on you. Why don't you go to the house? Take a break. Come back at around eight-thirty and we'll eat." Shorty was planning to close the place at eight o'clock and promised me the best prime rib I've ever tasted. I doubt that, but I agreed. I'm not that big into Christmas but I've never, in my entire life, spent it alone. I wasn't about to start now.

"I don't need a break."

"Fine, but one peep out of you, one sideways glance at that couple and you're outta here."

"Got it boss." I saluted him, and he whacked me with his Santa hat. It was precisely at that moment when the door opened again. I shivered as a blast of cold air came in with a woman in a heavy parka. "You really need to get a man trap here. Every time the fucking door opens I freeze to death."

"Sure, you want to deal with planning and zoning, be my guest. Oh, and you can fork up the bucks too."

"Asshole." This time I whacked him with my Santa hat. The woman looked around, probably for a coat rack. Shorty jumped up and offered to take her coat. Her back was toward me but I could see Shorty gesturing toward the booths and tables. She shook her head and said something. I couldn't hear her. Shorty turned his head toward the bar and pointed. At me. My hawk-sense is back! Because I knew it was Dale before I even saw her. I was still shivering but it wasn't from the cold. I have no idea why she's here. And at this moment, I really don't care. She's here. Now. Sitting on a bar stool. Smiling at me. Ordering a drink that I can't think of how to make. Telling me I look like shit.

***

ACKNOWLEDGMENTS

First and foremost, I'd like to thank my husband (a.k.a. Sweet Petunia) for his love and unwavering support of my many attempts at writing a novel and my other crazy endeavors. I'm grateful to my friends who gave me brutal and thoughtful feedback on the first, second, third, and forth drafts. Finally, I am indebted to the Fairfax County (Virginia) Police Department officers who took me under their wings and helped me become a volunteer women's self-defense instructor from 2002 through 2005. My hope is that every woman would feel empowered to say *No!* and ***Stay Back!***

ABOUT THE AUTHOR

Lynn Stewart is a retired software developer who is pursuing her dream of writing. She and her husband live on the Delmarva Peninsula. This is her first novel.

CPSIA information can be obtained
at www.ICGtesting.com
Printed in the USA
BVHW031256171219
566937BV00001B/7/P